The Miracle Man

The Miracle Man

Frank L. Packard

ÆGYPAN PRESS

This text from the 1914 Grosset & Dunlap (New York) edition.

The Miracle Man
A publication of
ÆGYPAN PRESS

www.aegypan.com

To
NEARLY
EVERYBODY

I

THE "ROOST"

*H*e was a misshapen thing, bulking a black blotch in the night at the entrance of the dark alleyway — like some lurking creature in its lair. He neither stood, nor kneeled, nor sat — no single word would describe his posture — he combined all three in a sort of repulsive, formless heap.

The Flopper moved. He came out from the alleyway onto the pavement, into the lurid lights of the Bowery, flopping along knee to toe on one leg, dragging the other leg behind him — and the leg he dragged was limp and wobbled from the knee. One hand sought the pavement to balance himself and aid in locomotion; the other arm, the right, was twisted out from his body in the shape of an inverted V, the palm of his hand, with half curled, contorted fingers, almost touching his chin, as his head sagged at a stiff, set angle into his right shoulder. Hair straggled from the brim of a nondescript felt hat into his eyes, and curled, dirty and unshorn, around his ears and the nape of his neck. His face was covered with a stubble of four days' growth, his body with rags — a coat; a shirt, the button long since gone at the neck; and trousers gaping in wide rents at the knees, and torn at the ankles where they flapped around miss-mated socks and shoes.

A hundred, two hundred people passed him in a block, the populace of the Bowery awakening into fullest life at midnight, men, women and children — the dregs of the city's scum — the aristocracy of upper Fifth Avenue, of Riverside Drive, aping Bohemianism, seeking the lure of the Turkey Trot, transported from the Barbary Coast of San Francisco. Rich and poor, squalor and affluence, vice and near-vice surged by him, voicing their different interests with laughter and sobs and soft words and blasphemy, and, in a sort of mocking chorus, the composite effect rose and fell in pitiful, jangling discords.

Few gave him heed — and these few but a cursory, callous glance. The Flopper, on the inside of the sidewalk, in the shadow of the buildings, gave as little as he got, though his eyes were fastened sharply, now ahead, now, screwing around his body to look behind him, on the faces of the pedestrians as they passed; or, rather, he appeared to look through and beyond those in his immediate vicinity to the ones that followed in his rear from further down the street, or approached him from the next corner.

Suddenly the Flopper shrank into a doorway. From amidst the crowd behind, the yellow flare of a gasoline lamp, outhanging from a second-hand shop, glinted on brass buttons. An officer, leisurely accommodating his pace to his own monarchial pleasure, causing his hurrying fellow occupants of the pavement to break and circle around him, sauntered casually by. The Flopper's black eyes contracted with hate and a scowl settled on his face, as he watched the policeman pass; then, as the other was lost again in the crowd ahead, he once more resumed his progress down the block.

The Flopper crossed the intersecting street, his leg trailing a helpless, sinuous path on its not overclean surface, and started along the next block. Halfway down was a garishly lighted establishment. When near this the Flopper began to hurry desperately, as from further along the street again his ear caught the peculiar raucous note of an automobile horn accompanied by the rumbling approach of a heavy motor vehicle. He edged his way now, wriggling, squirming and dodging between the pedestrians, to the outer edge of the sidewalk, and stopped in front of the music hall.

A sight-seeing car, crammed to capacity, reaching its momentary Mecca, drew up at the curb; and the guide's voice rose over the screech of the brakes:

"Now, ladies and gentlemen, we will get out here for a little while. This is Black Ike's famous Auditorium, the scene of last week's sensational triple murder! Please remember that there is no charge for admission to patrons of the company. Just show your coupons, ladies and gentlemen, and walk right ahead."

The passengers began to pour from the long seats to the ground. The Flopper's hat was in his hand.

"Fer God's sake, gents an' ladies, don't pass me by," he cried piteously. "I could work once, but look at me now — I was run over by a fire truck. God bring pity to yer hearts — youse have money fer pleasure, spare something fer me."

The first man down from the seat halted and stared at the twisted, unsightly thing before him, and, with a little gasp, reached into his pocket and dropped a bill into the Flopper's hat.

"God bless you!" stammered the Flopper — and the tears sprang swimming to his eyes.

The first man passed on with a gruff, "Oh, all right," but he had left an example behind him that few of his fellow passengers ignored.

"T'ank you, mum," mumbled the Flopper, as the money dropped into his hat. "God reward you, sir. . . . Ah, miss, may you never know a tear. . . . 'Twas heaven brought you 'ere tonight, lady."

They passed, following the guide. The Flopper scooped the money into a pile in his hat, began to tuck it away in some recess of his shirt — when a hand was thrust suddenly under his nose.

"Come on, now, divvy!" snapped a voice in his ear.

It was the driver of the car, who had dropped from his seat to the ground. A gleam of hate replaced the tears in the Flopper's eyes.

"Go to hell!" he snarled through thin lips — and his hand closed automatically over the cap.

"Come on, now, I ain't got no time to fool!" prompted the man, with a leer. "I'm dead onto your lay, and there's a bull comin' along now — half or him, which?"

The Flopper's eyes caught the brass buttons of the officer returning on his beat, and his face was white with an inhuman passion, as, clutching a portion of what was left in the hat, he lifted his hand from the rest.

"Thanks!" grinned the chauffeur, snatching at the remainder. "'Tain't half, but it'll do" — and he hurried across the sidewalk, and disappeared inside a saloon.

Oaths, voicing a passion that rocked the Flopper to his soul, purled in a torrid stream from his lips, and for a moment made him forget the proximity of the brass buttons. He raised his fist, that still clenched some of the money, and shook it after the other — and his fist, uplifted in midair, was caught in a vicious grip — the harness bull was standing over him.

"Beat it!" rasped the officer roughly, "or I'll — hullo, what you got here? Open your hand!" — he gave a sharp twist as he spoke, the Flopper's fingers uncurled, and the money dropped into the policeman's other hand — held conveniently below the Flopper's.

"It's mine — gimme it back," whined the Flopper.

"Yours! Yours, is it!" growled the officer. "Where'd you get it? Stole it, eh? Go on, now, beat it — or I'll run you in! Beat it!"

With twitching fingers, the Flopper picked up his cap, placed it on his head and sidled away. Ten yards along, in the shadow of the buildings again, he looked back — the officer was still standing there, twirling his stick, one hand just emerging from his pocket. The Flopper's finger nails scratched along the stone pavement and curved into the palm of his hand until the skin under the knuckles was bloodless white, and his lips moved in ugly, whispered words — then, still whispering, he went on again.

Down the Bowery he went like a human toad, keeping in the shadows, keeping his eyes on the ground before him, a glint like a shudder in their depths — on he went with hopping, lurching jerks, with whispering lips. Street after street he passed, and then at a corner he turned and went East — not far, only to the side entrance of the saloon on the corner known, to those who *knew,* as the "Roost."

The door before which he stopped, on a level with the street, might readily have passed for the entrance to one of the adjoining tenements, for it was innocent to all appearances of any connection with the unlovely resort of which it was a part — and it was closed.

The Flopper rang no bell. After a quick glance around him to assure himself that he was not observed, he reached up for the doorknob, turned it, and with surprising agility hopped oven the threshold and closed the door behind him.

A staircase, making one side of a narrow and dimly lighted hall, from down whose length came muffled sounds from the barroom, was before him; and this, without hesitation, the Flopper began to mount, his knee thumping from step to step, his dangling leg echoing the sound in a peculiar; quick double thump. He reached the first landing, went along it, and started up the second flight — but now the thumping sound he made seemed accentuated intentionally, and upon his face there spread a grin of malicious humor.

He halted before the door opposite the head of the second flight of stairs, opened it, wriggled inside and shut it behind him.

"Hullo, Helena!" he snickered. "Pipe me comin'?"

The room was a fairly large one, gaudily appointed with cheap furnishings, one of the Roost's private parlors — a girl on a couch in the corner had raised herself on her elbow, and her dark eyes were fixed uncompromisingly upon the Flopper, but she made no answer.

The Flopper laughed — then a spasm seemed to run through him, a horrible boneless contortion of limbs and body, a slippery, twitching movement, a repulsive though almost inaudible clicking of rehabilitated joints — and the Flopper stood erect.

The girl was on her feet, her eyes flashing.

"Can that stunt!" she cried angrily. "You give me the shivers! Next time you throw your fit, you throw it before you come around me, or I'll make you wish you had — see?"

The Flopper was swinging legs and arms to restore a normal channel of circulation.

"Y'oughter get used to it," said he, with a grin. "Ain't Pale Face Harry come yet, an' where's the Doc?"

"Behind the axe under the table," said the girl tartly — and flung herself back on the couch.

"T'anks," said the Flopper. "Say, Helena, wot's de new lay de Doc has got up his sleeve?"

Helena made no answer.

"Is yer grouch painin' you so's yer tongue's hurt?" inquired the Flopper solicitously.

Still no answer.

"Well, go to the devil!" said the Flopper politely.

He resumed the swinging of his arms and legs, but stopped suddenly a moment later as a step, sounded outside in the hall and he turned expectantly.

A young man, thin, emaciated, with gaunt, hollow face, abnormally bright eyes and sallow skin, entered. He was well, but modestly, dressed; and he coughed a little now, as though the two flights' climb had overtaxed him — it was the man who had headed the subscription list to the Flopper half an hour before in front of Black Ike's Auditorium.

"Hello, Helena!" he greeted, nodding toward the couch. "I shook the rubber-neck bunch at Ike's, Flopper. That was a peach of a haul, eh, old pal — the boobs came to it as though they couldn't get enough."

A sudden and reminiscent scowl clouded the Flopper's face. He stepped to the table, reached his hand into his shirt, and flung down a single one-dollar bill and a few coins.

"Dere's de haul, Harry — help yerself" — his invitation was a snarl.

Pale Face Harry had followed to the table. He looked first at the money, then at the Flopper — and a tinge of red dyed his cheek. He coughed before he spoke.

"Y'ain't going to stall on *me*, Flopper, are you?" he demanded, in an ominous monotone.

"Stall!" — the word came away in a roar too genuine to leave any doubt of the Flopper's sincerity, or the turbulent state of the Flopper's soul. "Stall nothin'! De driver held me up fer some of it, an' de cop pinched de rest."

"And you the king of Floppers!" breathed Pale Face Harry sadly. "D'ye hear that, Helena? Come over here and listen. Go ahead, Flopper, tell us about it."

Helena rose from the couch and came over to the table.

"Poor Flopper!" said she sweetly.

"Shut up!" snapped the Flopper savagely.

"Go on," prompted Pale Face Harry. "Go on, Flopper — tell us about it."

"I told you, ain't I?" growled the Flopper. "De driver called a divvy wid de cop comin', an I had ter shell — an' wot he left de cop pinched. Dat's all" — the Flopper's mouth was working again with the rage that burned within him.

Pale Face Harry, with pointed forefinger, gingerly and facetiously laid the coins out in a row on the table.

"And you the king of Floppers!" he murmured softly. "It's a wonder you didn't let the Salvation Army get the rest away from you on the way along!"

Helena laughed — but the Flopper didn't. He stepped close to Pale Face Harry, and shoved his face within an inch of the other's.

"You close yer jaw," he snarled, "or I'll make yer map look like wot's goin' ter happen ter dat cross-eyed snitch of a guy dat did me — him an' de harness bull, when I —" The Flopper stopped abruptly, and edged away from Pale Face Harry. "Hullo, Doc," he said meekly. "I didn't hear youse comin' in."

A man, fair-haired, broad-shouldered, immaculate in well-tailored tweeds, reliant in poise, leaned nonchalantly against the door — inside the room. He was young, not more than twenty-eight, with clean-shaven, pleasant, open face — a handsome face, marred only to the close observer by the wrinkles beginning to pucker around his eyes, and a slight, scarcely discernible puffiness in his skin — "Doc" Madison, gentleman crook and high-class, polished con-man, who had lifted his profession to an art, was still too young to be indelibly stamped with the hall-marks of dissipation.

His grey eyes traveled from one to another, lingered an instant on Helena, and came back to the Flopper.

"What's the trouble?" he demanded quietly.

It was Pale Face Harry who answered him.

"The Flopper's got it in for a couple of ginks that handed him one — a bull and a chauffeur on a gape-wagon," he grinned, punctuating his words with a cough. "The Flopper's got an idea the corpse-preserver's business is dull, and he's going to help 'em out with two orders and pay for the flowers himself."

Doc Madison shook his head and smiled a little grimly.

"Forget it, Flopper!" he said crisply. "I've something better for you to do. You fade away, disappear and lay low from this minute. I don't care what you do when you're resurrected, but from now on the three of you are dead and buried, and the police go into mourning for at least six months."

"What you got for us, Doc? — something nice?" — Helena pushed

Pale Face Harry and the Flopper unceremoniously out of her line of vision as she spoke.

"Yes — the drinks. Cleggy's bringing them," Madison laughed — and opened the door, as the tinkle of glass and a shuffling footstep sounded without.

A man, big, hulking, thickset and slouching, with shifty, cunning little black eyes and the face of a bruiser, his nose bent over and almost flattened down on one cheek, entered the room, carrying four glasses on a tin tray. He set down the tray, and, as he lifted the glasses from it and placed them on the table, he leered around at the little group.

"Gee!" he said, sucking in his breath. "De Doc, an' Helena, an' Pale Face, an' de Flopper! Gee, dis looks like de real t'ing — dis looks like biz."

"It does — fifty-cents' worth — ten for yourself," said Doc Madison suavely, flipping the coin into the tray. "Now, clear out!"

"Say" — Cleggy put his forefinger significantly to the side of his nose — "say, can't youse let a sport in on —"

"Clear out!" Doc Madison broke in quite as suavely as before — but there was a sudden glint of steel in the grey eyes as they held the bruiser's, and Cleggy, hastily picking up the tray, scuffled from the room.

Madison watched the door close, then he began to pace slowly up and down the room.

"Pull the chairs up to the table so we can take things comfortably," he directed.

"There ain't but two," grinned Pale Face Harry.

"Oh, well, never mind," said Madison.

"Slew the couch around and pull that up — Helena and I will sit on the head of it."

Still pacing up and down the length of the room, his hands in his pockets, Doc Madison watched the others as they carried out his directions; and then, suddenly, as he neared the door, his hand shot out, wrenched the door open, and, quick as a panther in its spring, he was in the hall without.

There was a yell, a scuffle, the rip and crash of rending banisters, an instant's silence, then a heavy thud — and then Cleggy's voice from somewhere below in a choice and fervent flow of profanity.

Doc Madison reentered the room, closed the door, dispassionately arranged a disordered cuff, brushed a few particles of dust from his sleeves and shoulder, and, this done, started toward the table — and stopped.

Helena had swung herself to the table edge, and, glass in hand, dangling her neatly shod little feet, was smoking a cigarette, her brown hair with a glint of amber in it, her dark eyes veiled now by their heavy lashes; on the other side of the table Pale Face Harry coughed, as, with sleeve rolled back, he was intent on the hypodermic needle he was pushing into his arm; while the Flopper, his eyes with a doglike admiration in them fixed on Madison, stood facing the door, a grotesque, unpleasant figure, unkempt, unshaven, furtive-faced, his rags hanging disreputably about him, his trousers with their frayed edges, now that he stood upright, reaching far above his boot tops and flagrantly exposing his wretched substitutes for socks.

Doc Madison reached thoughtfully into his pocket, brought out a silver cigarette case, and carefully selected a cigarette from amongst its fellows.

"Yes; Cleggy was right," he said softly, tapping the end of the cigarette on his thumb nail. "You're the real thing — the real, real thing."

II

A NEW CULT

*D*oc Madison swung Helena lightly down from the table to the head of the couch, sat down beside her, one arm circling her waist, and motioned the Flopper to a chair — then he leaned forward and watched Pale Face Harry critically, as the latter carefully replaced the shining little hypodermic in its case.

"Harry," said he abruptly, jerking his free hand toward the hypodermic, "could you give up that dope-needle?"

"Sure, I could — if I wanted to!" asserted Pale Face Harry defiantly.

"That's good," said Madison cheerfully. "Because you'll have to."

"Eh?" — Pale Face Harry stared at Doc Madison in amazement.

"Because you'll have to — by and by," said Madison coolly. "And how about that cough — can you quit coughing?"

"When I'm dead — which won't be long," sniffed Pale Face Harry. "D'ye think I cough because I like it? How'm I going to quit coughing?"

"I don't know," admitted Doc Madison, frowning seriously. "I only know you'll have to."

Pale Face Harry, with jaw dropped, accentuating the gaunt leanness of his hollow-cheeked, emaciated face, gazed at Doc Madison with a curious mingling of incredulity and affront — and coughed.

"Say," he inquired grimly, "what's the answer?"

Doc Madison took his arm from Helena's waist, pulled a newspaper from his pocket, spread it out on the table — and his manner changed suddenly — enthusiasm was in his eyes, his voice, his face.

"I've steered you three through a few deals," said he impressively, "that have sized up big enough to keep you out of the raw vaudeville turn you, Harry, and you, Flopper, are so fond of, and that would have put Helena here on easy street, if you hadn't blown in all you got about ten minutes after you got your hands on it — but I've got one here that sizes up so big you wouldn't be able to spend the money fast enough to close out your bank account if you did your damnedest! Get that? It's the greatest cinch that ever came down from the gateway of heaven — and that's where it came from — heaven. It couldn't have come from anywhere else — it's too good. And it's new, bran new — it's never had the string cut or the wrapper taken off. It's got anything that was ever run beaten by more laps than there are in the track, and it's got a purse tied on to the end of it that's the biggest ever offered since Adam. But you've got to work for it, and that's what I brought you here for tonight — to learn your little pieces so's you can say 'em nice and cute when you get up on the platform before the audience."

The Flopper's tongue made a greedy circuit of his upper and under lips, and he hitched his chair closer to the table.

A flush spread over Pale Face Harry's cheeks, and his eyes, abnormally bright, grew brighter.

"You're all right, Doc," he assured Doc Madison anxiously. "You're all right."

"U-uu-mm!" cooed Helena excitedly. "Go on, Doc — go on!"

"Listen," said Doc Madison, his voice lowered a little. "I found this tucked away as a filler in a corner of the newspaper this evening. It's headed, 'A New Cult,' with an interrogation mark after it. Now listen, while I read it:"

A NEW CULT?

Needley, Maine, offers no attraction for aspiring young medical men. One who tried it recently, and who pulled down his shingle in disgust after a week, says competition is too strong, as the village is obsessed with the belief that they have a sort of faith-healer in their midst to whom is attributed cures of all descriptions stretching back for a generation or more. The healer, he adds, who rejoices in the name of the Patriarch and lives in solitude a mile or so from the village, is something of an anomaly in himself, being both deaf and dumb. We —

"But that's all that interests us," said Doc Madison, as he stopped reading abruptly and lifted his head to scrutinize his companions quizzically.

Pale Face Harry's eyes had lost their gleam and dulled — he gaped reproachfully at Doc Madison. Helena's small mouth drooped downward in a disappointed *moue*. Only the Flopper evidenced enthusiastic response.

"Sure!" he chortled. "Sure t'ing! I see. De old geezer'll have a pile of shekels hid away, an' he lives by his lonesome a mile from de town. We sneaks down dere, croaks de guy wid de queer monaker, an' beats it wid de shekels — sure!"

Doc Madison turned a sad grey eye on the Flopper.

"Flopper," said he pathetically, "your soul, like your bones, runs to rank realism. No; we don't 'croak de guy' — we cherish him, we nurse him, we fondle him. He's our one best bet, and we fold him to our breasts tenderly, and we protect him from all harm and danger and sudden death."

The Flopper blinked a little helplessly.

"Mabbe," said the Flopper, "I got de wrong dope. Some of dem words you read I ain't hip to. Wot's anymaly mean?"

"Anomaly?" — Doc Madison reached for his glass, tossed off the contents and set it down. "It means, Flopper, in this particular instance," he said gravely, "that there shouldn't be any interrogation point after the heading."

Again the Flopper blinked helplessly — and his fingers picked uncertainly at the stubble on his chin. The other two gazed disconsolately — and Helena a little pityingly as well — at Doc Madison.

Doc Madison flung out his arms suddenly.

"What's the matter with you all?" he demanded sarcastically. "You look as though your faces pained you! What's the matter with you? You're bright enough ordinarily, Helena, and, Harry, you're no dub — what's the matter with you? Can't you see it — can't you see it! Why, it's sticking out a mile — it's *waiting* for us! The whole plant's there and all we've got to do is get steam under the boilers. We'll have 'em coming for the cure from every State in the Union, and begging us to let them throw their diamond tiaras at us for a look-in at the shrine. Don't you see it — can't you get it — can't you *get* it!"

Helena bent suddenly over Doc Madison's shoulder, her eyes opening wide with dawning comprehension.

"The cure?" she breathed.

"Sure — the cure," said Doc Madison earnestly. "The new cult — that's us. Get the people talking, show 'em something, and you'll have to put up fences and 'keep off the grass' signs to stop the lame and the halt and the blind and the neurasthenics from crowding and suffocating to death for want of air. We'll start a shrine down there that'll be a winner, and the railroads will be running excursion-rate pilgrimages inside of two months."

Pale Face Harry's chair creaked, as, like the Flopper, he now crowded it in toward the table.

"I get you!" said he feverishly. "I get you! I've read about them shrines — only you gotter have churches, and a carload of crutches, and that sort of thing laying around."

Doc Madison smiled pleasantly.

"Yes; you've got me, Harry — only we'll do the stage setting a little differently. Mostly what is required is — faith. Get them going on that, and everybody that's sick or near-sick in this great United States, that's got the swellest collection of boobs and millionaires on earth, will swarm thitherward like bees — there won't be anyone left in the sanatoriums throughout the length of this broad land of freedom but the bell boys and the elevator men. Get them going, and all we've got to do is look out we don't let anything get by us in the crush — a snowball rolling down hill will size up like a plugged nickel alongside of a twenty-dollar gold piece when it gets to the bottom, compared with what we start rolling."

"I've got you, too," said Helena. "But I don't see where the faith is coming from, or how you're going to get them coming. You've got to show them — you said so yourself — even the boobs. How are you going to do that?"

"Well," said Doc Madison placidly, "we'll start the show with — a miracle. I haven't thought of anything more effective than that so far."

"A what?" inquired Pale Face Harry, with a grin.

"A miracle," repeated Doc Madison imperturbably. "A miracle — with the Flopper here in the star rôle. The Flopper goes down there all tied up in knots, the high priest, alias the deaf and dumb healer, alias the Patriarch, lays his soothing hands upon him, the Flopper uncoils into something that looks like a human being — and the trumpets blow, the band plays, and the box office opens for receipts."

Helena slid from her seat, and, with hands on the edge of the table, advanced her piquant little face close to Doc Madison's, staring at him, breathing hard.

"Say that again," she gasped. "Say that again — say it just once more."

Pale Face Harry's hand, trembling visibly with emotion, was thrust out across the table.

"Put it there, Doc," he whispered hoarsely.

The Flopper, practical, earnestly so, lifted his right arm, wriggled it a little and began to twist it around, as though it were on a pivot at the elbow, preparatory to drawing it in, a crippled thing, toward his chin.

Doc Madison reached out hurriedly and stopped him.

"Here, that'll do, Flopper," he said quietly. "You don't need any rehearsal to hold your job — you're down for the number and your check's written out."

"Swipe me!" said the Flopper to the universe. "I can smell de pine woods of Maine in me nostrils now. When does I beat it, Doc — tomorrer?"

Doc Madison laughed.

"No, Flopper, not tomorrow — nor for several tomorrows — not till the bill-posters get through, and the stage is dark, and you can hear a pin drop in the house. I don't want you camping out and catching cold and missing any of the luxuries you're accustomed to, so I'll start along ahead in a day or so myself and see what kind of accommodations I can secure."

"Swipe me!" said the Flopper again. "An' to think of me wastin' me talent on rubber-neck fleets!"

A puzzled little frown puckered Helena's forehead.

"I was thinking about the deaf and dumb man," she said slowly. "How about him, when we pull this off — will he stand for it — and what'll he do?"

"Aw!" said Pale Face Harry impatiently. "He don't count! He'll have bats in his belfry anyway, and if he ain't he'll go off his chump for fair getting stuck on himself when he sees the stunt he'll think he's done. He'll be looking for the wings between his shoulder blades, and hunting for the halo around his head."

"Harry is waking up," observed Doc Madison affably. "That's about the idea, Helena. I haven't seen the Patriarch yet, but I don't imagine from his description that it'll be very hard to make him believe in himself. He doesn't stand for anything — we don't deal him any cards — he's just the kitty that circles around with the jackpots while we annex the chips."

Doc Madison reached into his vest pocket, took out a penknife whose handle was gold-chased, opened it, and very carefully cut the article he had read from the paper.

"Flopper," said he, "you've heard of gold bonds, haven't you?"

The Flopper's eyes gleamed an eloquent response.

"Only you've never had any, eh?" supplied Doc Madison.

"Where'd I get 'em?" inquired the Flopper, with some bitterness.

"Right here," smiled Doc Madison, handing him the clipping. "Here's a trainload and a bank vault full of them combined. Put it away, Flopper, and don't lose it. Lose anything you've got first — lose your life. It's worth a private car to you with a buffet full of fizz, and Sambo to wait on you for the rest of your life. Get that? Don't lose it!"

The Flopper tucked the clipping into the mysterious recess of his shirt.

"Say," he said earnestly, "if you say so, Doc, it'll be here when dey plant me."

"All right, Flopper," nodded Doc Madison. "And now let's get down to cases. I've been able to pay my club dues lately, and there's money enough on deck to buy the costumes and put the show on the road. I start for Needley as soon as I can get away. When I'm ready for the support, you three will hear from me — and in the meantime you lay low. Nothing doing — understand? You'll get all the lime-light you want before you're through, and it's just as well not to show up so familiar when they throw the spot on you that even the school kids will know the date of your birth, and the population will start in squabbling over the choice of reserved niches for you in the Hall of Fame. See?"

The Flopper, Pale Face Harry and Helena nodded their heads with one accord.

"Give us the whole lay, Doc," urged Pale Face Harry. "And give it to us quick."

"Me mouth's waterin'," observed the Flopper, licking his lips again.

Helena lighted another cigarette, and swung herself back to her perch on the head of the couch.

Doc Madison surveyed the three with mingled admiration and delight.

"The world is ours!" he murmured softly.

"Oh, hurry up and give us the rest of it," purred Helena. "We know we're an all-star cast, all right."

"Very good," said Doc Madison — and laughed. "Well then, the order of your stage cues will depend on circumstances and what turns up down there, but we'll start with the Flopper now. First of all, Flopper, you've got to have a name. What's your real name — what did they decorate you with at the baptismal font back in the dark ages?"

The Flopper scrubbed at his very dirty chin with a very dirty thumb and forefinger.

"I dunno," said the Flopper anxiously.

"Well, never mind," said Doc Madison reassuringly. "Maybe you are blessed above most people — you can pick one out for yourself. What'll it be?"

The Flopper's thumb and forefinger scratched desperately for a moment, then his face lighted with inspiration.

"Swipe me!" said he excitedly. "I got it — Jimmy de Squirm."

Doc Madison shook his head gravely.

"No, Flopper, I'm afraid not," he said gently. "That's another weak point in your interpretation of the rôle, that I'll come to in a minute. We'll give you an Irish name by way of charity — it'll help to make your classical English sound like brogue. We'll call you Coogan — Michael Coogan — that lets you off with plain Mike in times of stress."

"Swipe me!" said the Flopper, with perfect complacence.

"Glad it pleases you," smiled Doc Madison, "Here's your lay, then. You've got to remember that you were born crooked and —"

Helena giggled.

"I didn't mean it" — Doc Madison's grey eyes twinkled. "You are waking up, too, Helena. I mean, Flopper, you've got to remember that you were born twisted up into the same shape you are in when you hit Needley. You come from — let's see — we'll have to have a big city where the next door neighbors pass each other with a vacant stare. Ever been in Chicago?"

"Naw! Wot fer?" said the Flopper, with withering spontaneity. "Noo Yoik fer mine."

"Well, all right — New York it is, then," agreed Doc Madison. "You're poor, but respectable — and that brings us to the other point. Before you go down there, Helena's going to start a little night-school with a grammar, and teach you to paddle along the fringe of the great American language so's you won't fall in and get wet all over every time you open your mouth."

"My!" exclaimed Helena. "Won't that be nice!"

"I hope so," said Doc Madison dryly. "And don't run away with the idea that I'm joking about this — that goes. I don't expect to make a silver-tongued orator out of you, Flopper, and perhaps not even a purist — but I hope to eradicate a few minor touches of Bad Land vernacular from your vocabulary."

"I've gotcher — swipe me!" grinned the Flopper. "Me at school! Say, wouldn't that put a smile on de maps of de harness bulls, an' de dips, an' de lags doin' spaces up de river!"

"Quite so," admitted Doc Madison pleasantly.

"You won't laugh when I get through with you," remarked Helena, her eyes on the curl of smoke from her cigarette.

"There's just one more thing," went on Doc Madison, "and I'm through with you, Flopper. Don't come down there looking like a skate

— that's too raw. Get new clothes and a shave — and keep shaved. And from the minute you buy your ticket, you keep your bones, or whatever a beneficent nature has given you in place of them, out of joint — see?"

"I'm hip," declared the Flopper — and the doglike admiration for Doc Madison burned in his eyes. "Say, Doc, youse are de —"

"Never mind, Flopper," Madison cut in brightly. "It's getting late. Now, Harry, about you. You've got a name, I believe. Evans, isn't it? Yes — well, that will do. Now, don't kill yourself at it, but the more you work your dope needle overtime before you start, and the harder you cough when you first land there the better. We've got to have variety, you know. You're a physical wreck with the folks back home sending the casket and trimmings after you on the next train in care of the station agent."

"I guess," coughed Pale Face Harry, with a sickly smile, "I look the part."

"You certainly do," said Helena cheerfully, beating a tattoo with her heels on the end of the couch.

Pale Face Harry scowled.

"I ain't no artist with the paint," he sniffed.

"I don't paint," said Helena sweetly. "It's rouge."

"Are you through?" inquired Doc Madison patiently. "Because, if you are, I'll go on. When the train whistles for Needley, Harry, you put the soft pedal on the dope — that ought to help some. And then you begin to taper that cough off and become a cure — that's all."

"I ain't like the Flopper," said Pale Face Harry ruefully. "I told you once I can't stop the hack, and I ask you again how'm I going to?"

"Have faith in the Patriarch," suggested Helena innocently.

"You close your trap!" exclaimed Pale Face Harry savagely; then, to Madison: "Go on, Doc — it's up to you."

"No," said Doc Madison coolly, "it's up to you. You've got to try, and if you can't stop altogether you can make yourself scarce when you feel the fit coming on — you won't have to climb up on the grandstand and cough in people's faces, will you?"

"He might carry a screen around with him and cough behind that," volunteered Helena. "That's enough about the Flopper and Pale Face — what about muh? Where do I get off?"

"You?" said Doc Madison calmly. "Oh, you're a moral neurasthenic."

"And what's that when it's at home?" demanded Helena sharply.

Doc Madison threw out his hands in a comically helpless, impotent gesture.

"It's what we need to keep up the standard of variety," he said. "We're playing to the masses. Don't you like the rôle, Helena — it's the leading woman's."

"What do I do?" countered Helena non-committingly.

"Do?" echoed Doc Madison. "Why, you go down there like a whole parade and a gorgeous pageant rolled into one, in feathers and paint and diamond boulders in your ears — and you come out of it in a gingham apron and coy sunbonnet as sweet sixteen."

"Oh!" said Helena — and her eyes were on the curl of smoke from her cigarette again.

"Say," said Pale Face Harry suddenly, evidently still worried about his cough, "we ain't going to have no easy cinch of this."

"No," said Doc Madison, with a grim smile; "you're not! It's going to be the hardest work any of you have ever done — you've got to lead decent lives for awhile."

"Sure — dat's right," said the loyal Flopper; "but we stands fer anyt'ing dat de Doc says — an' dat goes!"

"It'll come hard on some of us," remarked Pale Face Harry, with a sly glance at Helena, which met with contemptuous silence.

Doc Madison leaned back, felt carefully at his carefully adjusted tie — and smiled engagingly.

"Well?" he asked. "Can you see them coming?"

Pale Face Harry stared at him with a faraway expression in his eyes.

"When we get through with this, if I ain't handed in my checks before," he said dreamily, "it's mine for a brownstone on the Avenue, and one of them life-size landscapes with a shack on it for the season down to Pa'm Beach that they call country cottages. I'll dress the ginks that scrub the horses down in solid gold braid, and put the corpse of chamber ladies in Irish lace — I bust into society, marry a duke's one and only, and swipe her coronet for my manly brow. Did you ask me anything, Doc?"

"Swipe me!" said the Flopper. "Me in me private Pullman in a plush seat an' anudder to put me feet in, an' me thumbs in de armholes of me vest. I wears a high polished lid an' a red tie, an' scatters simoleons outer de window in me travels to the gazeboes on de platforms as I pass — an' den I joins Tammany Hall so's I can stick me fingers to me nose every time I sees a cop."

"Flopper," said Doc Madison in an awed voice, "the honor is all mine."

Helena went off into a peal of rippling, silvery, contagious laughter, and her little heels again beat an exuberant tattoo on the end of the couch.

"Yes?" invited Doc Madison, smiling at her.

"I'm seeing them coming," said Helena — and one heel went through the cretonne upholstery of the couch.

"Good!" said Doc Madison — and from the inside pocket of his coat he pulled out a package of crisp, new, yellow-backed bills. "You understand that down there none of you ever heard of each other or of me before, and you drop the 'doc' — bury it! My name is John G. Madison — G. for Garfield." His fingers passed deftly over the edges of the bills. He pushed a little pile toward the Hopper, another toward Pale Face Harry, and tucked the remainder into his coat pocket again. "That'll do for expenses," he said. "And now, if you understand everything, principally that you're to go to church Sundays till you hear from me, and you're quite satisfied with the lay, we'll adjourn, *sine die*, to Needley."

Helena was holding out a very dainty hand, with pink, wiggling fingers.

"I'll need, oh, ever so much more than they will," she declared, with a bewitching pout. "And, please, I'm waiting very patiently."

Doc Madison laughed.

"By and by, Helena," he said, patting her hand. "Well, Flopper, well, Harry — what do you say?"

The Flopper pushed back his chair and stood up hesitantly like a man unexpectedly called upon for an after-dinner speech. He stood there awkwardly a moment gazing at Doc Madison, his tongue slowly circling his lips; then, with a gulp, as though words to express his feelings were utterly beyond him, he turned and started for the door.

Pale Face Harry, as he rose, shoved out his hand.

"I don't deserve my luck to be in on this," he said modestly. "Only, Doc, push it along on the high gear, will you — I ain't going to be able to sleep thinking about it." He looked at Helena a little undecidedly — and compromised on brevity. "'Night, Helena," he flung out.

"Oh, good-night, Harry," she smiled.

The Flopper turned at the door and came back a few steps into the room.

"Say, Doc," he said, blinking furiously, "youse can wipe yer feet on me anytime youse like — dat's wot!"

"All right, Flopper," said Doc Madison gravely. "When you've joined Tammany Hall — good-night." He followed across the room, and from the doorway watched the two descend the stairs. "Good-night," he said again, then closed the door and came back into the room. "Well, Helena?" he remarked tentatively.

"Well — Garfield?" — Helena clasped her hands around one knee and rocked gently.

"Don't be familiar, Helena," Doc Madison chuckled. "Is that all you've got to say?"

"I'm busy thinking about The Great American Play," she said pertly. "There's one thing you forgot."

"What's that?" he asked, still smiling.

"The curtain on the last act," she said. "The getaway."

Doc Madison shook his head.

"Nothing doing!" he returned. "There's no getaway. It's safe — so safe that there's nothing to it. We don't guarantee anything, and there's no entrance fee to the pavilion — all contributions are strictly voluntary."

"That's all right," said Helena. "But of course we can't really cure them. We can get them going hard enough to make them think they are for awhile, but after they've thrown away their crutches and got back home — what then?"

"Well, what then?" inquired Doc Madison easily.

"They'll yell 'fake!' and swear out warrants," said Helena, her dark eyes studying Doc Madison.

"Not according to statistics," replied Doc Madison, and his lips twitched quizzically at the corners. "According to statistics they'll buy another crutch and come back to buck the tiger again. Say, Helena, tomorrow, you go up to the public library and read up on shrines — they've been running since the ark — and they're running still. You never heard any howl about them, did you? What's the answer to those cures?"

"That's different," said Helena. "That's religion, and they've got relics and things."

"It's faith," said Doc Madison, "and it doesn't matter what the basis of it is. Faith, Helena, *faith* — get that? And we're going to imbue them with a faith that'll set them crazy and send them into hysterics. And talk about relics! Haven't we got one? Look at the Patriarch! Can't you see the whole town yelling 'I told you so!' and swopping testimonials hard enough to crowd the print down so fine, if you tried to get it all into the papers, that you'd have to use a magnifying glass to read it, once we've pulled off the miracle? Don't you worry about the getaway. If there's any sign of anything like that, you and I, Helena, will be taking moonlight rides in the gondolas of Venice long before it breaks."

Helena choked — and began to laugh deliciously.

Doc Madison stared at her for a moment whimsically — then he, too, burst into a laugh.

"Oh, Lord!" he gurgled. "It's rich, isn't it?" And sweeping Helena off the couch and into his arms, he began to dance around and around the table. "Ring-around-a-rosy!" he cried. "We haven't done so bad in the misty past, but here's where we cross to the enchanted shore and play on jeweled harps with golden strings and —"

"Is that all?" gasped Helena, laughing and breathless, as at last she pulled herself away.

"No," panted Doc Madison. "There's a table I've reserved up at the Rivoli that's waiting for us now. We're about to part for days and days, lady mine, that's the tough luck of it, but we'll make a night of it tonight anyway — what?"

"You bet!" said Helena, doing a cake-walk towards the door. "Come on!"

III

· NEEDLEY

"*N*eedley?"

It wasn't wholly an interrogation — it seemed to Madison that there was even sympathy in the parlor-car conductor's voice, as the other took his seat check.

"Health," said Madison meekly. "Perfect rest and quiet — been over-doing it, you know."

"*Needley!*" — the train conductor of the Bar Harbor Express, collecting the transportation, threw the word at Madison as though it were a personal affront.

The tone seemed to demand an apology from Madison — and Madison apologized.

"Health," he said apologetically. "Perfect rest and quiet — been overdoing it, you know."

"We're five minutes late now," grunted the conductor uncompromisingly and, to Madison, quite irrelevantly, as he passed on down the aisle.

Somehow, this inspired Madison to consult his timetable. He drew it from his pocket, ran his eye down the long list of stations — and stopped at "Needley." Needley had an asterisk after it. By consulting a block of small type at the bottom of the page, he found a corresponding asterisk with the words: "Flag station. Stops only on signal, or to discharge eastbound passengers from Portland."

John Garfield Madison went into the smoking compartment of the car for a cigar — several cigars — until Needley was reached some two hours later, when the dusky attendant, as he pocketed Madison's dollar, set down his little rubber-topped footstool with a flourish on a desolate and forbidding-looking platform.

Madison was neither surprised nor dismayed — the parlor-car conductor, the train conductor and the timetable had in no way attempted to deceive him — he was only cold. He turned up his coat collar — and blew on his kid-gloved fingers.

As far as he could see everything was white with a thin layer of snow — he kicked some of it off his toes onto the unshoveled platform. The landscape was disconsolately void of even a vestige of life, there was not a sign of habitation — just woods of bare trees, except the firs, whose green seemed out of place.

"I have arrived," said John Garfield Madison to himself, "at a cemetery."

There was a very small station, and through the window he caught sight of a harassed-faced, red-haired man. There was a thump, another one, a very vicious one — and Madison stirred uneasily — the train, with its five minutes' delinquency hanging over it, was already moving out, as his trunks, from the baggage car ahead, shot unceremoniously to the platform. Madison watched a man, the sole occupant of the platform apart from himself, save the trunks from rolling under the wheels of the train; then his eyes fastened on a rickety, two-seated wagon, drawn by a horse that at first glance appeared to earn all it got.

The train left the platform — and left quite as uninviting a perspective on the other side of the track as had previously greeted Madison's restricted view. But now the man who had salvaged his baggage came down the platform toward him. Madison inspected the approaching figure with interest. The man ambled along without haste, his jaws wagging industriously upon his tobacco, his iron-grey chin whiskers, from the wagging, flapping like a burgee in a breeze. He wore a round fur cap, quite bare of fur at the edges where the pelt showed shiny, and a red woolen tippet was tied round his neck and knotted at the back with the ends dangling down over his coat. The coat itself, a long one of some fuzzy material, with huge side pockets into which the man's hands were plunged, reached to the cavernous tops of jackboots where the nether ends of his trousers were stowed away.

The man halted before Madison, and, reaching a mittened hand under his chin, reflectively lifted his whiskers to an acute angle, while his blue eyes over the rims of steel-bowed spectacles wandered from Madison to Madison's dress-suit case and back to Madison again.

"Be you goin' to git off here?" he inquired.

Madison smiled at him engagingly.

"Well," he said, "I wouldn't care to have it known, but if you can keep a secret —"

"Hee-hee!" tittered the other. "Now that's right smart, that be. Waren't expectin' nobody to meet you, was you? I ain't heerd of none of the folks lookin' for visitors."

"No," said Madison. "But there's a hotel in the town, isn't there?"

"Two of 'em," said the other. "The Waalderf an' the Congress, but the Waalderf ain't done a sight of business since we got pro'bition in the State an' has kinder got run down. I reckon the Congress'll suit you best if you ain't against payin' a mite more, which I reckon you ain't for I see you come down in the parler car."

"And what," asked Madison, "does the Congress charge?"

"Well," said the other, "ordinary, it's a dollar a day or five dollars a week, but this bein' off season an' nobody there, 'twouldn't surprise me if Walt'ud kind of shade the price for you — Waalderf's three an' a half a week. Them your duds up the platform? I'll drive you over for forty cents. What was it you said your name was?"

"Forty cents is a most disinterested offer, and I accept it heartily," said Madison affably. "And my name's Madison — John Garfield Madison, from New York."

"Mine's Higgins," volunteered the other. "Hiram Higgins, an' I'm postmaster an' town constable of Needley. An' now, Mr. Madison, I reckon we'll just get these effects of your'n onto the wagon an' move along — folks'll be gettin' kinder rambunctious for their mail."

Hiram Higgins backed the democrat around, roped the baggage onto the tail-board, picked up the hungry-looking mailbag from where the mail clerk had slung it from the car to the platform, threw it down in front of the dashboard, and got in after it. Madison clambered into the back seat, and they bumped off along the road.

"Had a mite of snow night before last," observed Mr. Higgins, pointing it out with his whip, as he settled himself comfortably. "Kinder reckoned we'd got rid of it for good till next fall till this come along, but you can't never tell. What was it you said brought you down here, Mr. Madison?"

Madison smiled.

"Rest and quiet — complete change," he said. "Nervous breakdown, according to the doctors — that's what they always call it, you know, when they can't find any other name for it. I've been overdoing it, I suppose."

"Be that so!" returned Mr. Higgins sympathetically. "I want to know! Well, now, that's too bad! Lookin' for quiet, be you? Well, I reckon mabbe folks don't scurry around here quite so lively as they do in some of the bigger towns like Noo York, but there's a tolerable lot goin' on most every week, church festivals, an' spellin' bees, an' such. Folks here is right hospitable, but you ain't in no way obliged to join in if you don't feel up to it. I'll explain matters to 'em, an' —" Hiram Higgins stopped, excitedly gathered reins and whip into one hand, and with the other smote his knee a resounding whack. "Well, I swan!" he exclaimed. "An' I never thought of it until this minute! I reckon you've come to just the right place, and just as soon as you get settled you go right out an' see the Patriarch — you won't need no more doctor, an' folks up your way won't know when you go back."

"The Patriarch?" inquired Madison, with a puzzled air. "Who is he?"

"Why," said Mr. Higgins, "he's — he's the Patriarch. Been curin' us folks around here longer'n anyone can remember — just does it by faith, too."

Madison shook his head slowly.

"I might just as well be frank with you, Mr. Higgins," he said. "I've never taken much stock in faith cure and that sort of thing."

"Mabbe," suggested Mr. Higgins deeply, "you ain't had much experience."

"No," confessed Madison reflectively; "I haven't — I haven't had any."

"Well then, you just wait an' see," said Mr. Higgins, waving his mittened hand as though the whole matter were conclusively settled. "You just wait an' see."

"But I'm afraid I don't quite understand," prodded Madison innocently. "What kind of cures does he perform?"

They turned a right-angled bend in the road, disclosing a straggling hamlet in a hollow below, and, farther away in the distance, a sweep of ocean.

"Most any kind," said Mr. Higgins. "There's Needley now. All you've got to do is ask the first person you see about him."

"Yes," said Madison, "but take yourself, for instance. Did this Patriarch ever do anything for you?"

"He did," said Mr. Higgins impressively. "An' 'twasn't but last week. I'm glad you asked me. For two nights I couldn't sleep. Had the earache powerful. Poured hot oil an' laud'num into it, an' kept a hot brick rolled up in flannel against it, but didn't do no good. Then Mrs. Higgins says, 'Hiram, why in the land's sake don't you go out an' see the Patriarch?' An' I hitched right up, an' every step that horse took I could feel it gettin' better, an' I wasn't five minutes with the Patriarch before I was cured, an' I ain't had a twinge since."

"It certainly looks as though there were something in that," admitted Madison cautiously.

Hiram Higgins smiled a world of tolerance.

"'Tain't worth mentionin' alongside some of the things he's done," he said deprecatingly. "You'll hear about 'em fast enough."

"What's the local doctor say about it?" asked Madison.

"There ain't enough pickin's to keep a doctor here, though some of 'em's tried," chuckled Mr. Higgins. "Have to have 'em for *some* things, of course — an' then he drives over from Barton's Mills, seven miles from here."

"And do *all* the people in Needley believe in the Patriarch?" — Madison's voice was full of grave interest.

"Well," said Mr. Higgins, "to be plumb downright honest with you, they don't. Folks as was born here an' are old inhabitants do, but the Holmes, bein' newcomers, is kinder set in their ways. They come down here eight years ago last August with new-fangled notions, which they ain't got rid of yet. You can see the consequences for yourself — got a little boy, twelve year old, walking around lame on a crutch — an' I reckon he always will. Doctor looks at him every time he comes over from Barton's Mills, but it don't do no good. Folks tried to get the Holmes to take him out to the Patriarch's till they got discouraged. 'Pears old man Holmes kinder got around to a common sense view of it, but the women folks say Mrs. Holmes is stubborner than all git-out, an' that old man Holmes' voice ain't loud enough to be heerd when she gets goin'. 'Tain't but fair to mention 'em, as I dunno of anyone else that's an exception." Mr. Higgins pointed ahead with his whip. "See them woods over there beyond the town?"

"Yes," said Madison.

"That's where the Patriarch lives," said Mr. Higgins. "On the other side of 'em, down by the seashore. An' here we be most home. Folks'll be glad to see you, Mr. Madison, and now you're here I hope you'll make a real smart stay — we'll try to make you feel to home."

"Thank you," said Madison cordially. "I haven't any idea, of course, how long I'll be here — it all depends on circumstances."

"No," said Mr. Higgins; "I don't suppose you have. Anyway, I hope you'll take a notion to go out an' see what the Patriarch can do for you. An' now you ain't told me yet which hotel you're goin' to."

"Oh!" said Madison gravely. "Well, since you recommend it, I guess we'd better make it the Congress."

IV

THE PATRIARCH

"*B*et you a cookie," shrilled Hiram Higgins, in what he meant to be a breathless whisper, "that there's where he's goin' now — only he don't want us to know he's give in."

"Shet your fool mouth, Hiram!" cautioned Walt Perkins, the proprietor of the Congress Hotel. "He kin hear you."

"Get out!" retorted Mr. Higgins. "No, he can't neither. He ain't feelin' no ways perky, anyone can see that, an' I'm tickled most to pieces that he's come 'round — I've took up with him consid'rable, I have. Patriarch'll just make a newborn critter outer him — you watch through the window where he goes. Bet you a quarter that's what he's up to!"

John Garfield Madison, outside on the veranda of the Congress Hotel, smiled at the words, as he lighted his cigar and turned up his coat collar. He stepped off the veranda, crossed the little lawn to the village street, and began to saunter nonchalantly and indifferently oceanwards. He did not look around — he had no desire to bring consternation to the massed faces of the leading citizens flattened against the windowpanes — but he chuckled inwardly as he pictured them. There would be Hiram Higgins, postmaster and town constable, Walt Perkins, hotel man and town moderator, Lem Hodges, selectman, assessor and overseer of the poor, Nathan Elmes, likewise selectman, assessor and overseer of the poor, and Cale Rodgers, school committeeman and proprietor of the general store.

Madison sauntered slowly along.

"I have arrived," he said, "not at a cemetery, but at an El Dorado and a land flowing with milk and honey."

There was a humorous pucker around the corners of Madison's eyes, as he reviewed his two days' sojourn in Needley — spent mostly in the "office" of the Congress Hotel beside the stove with his feet up on the wood-box. He had never lacked company — the office stove and the spitbox filled with sawdust was the admitted rendezvous of the chosen spirits who were still gazing after him from the window. Morning, afternoon and evening they congregated there, and he had been promptly admitted to membership in the select circle. At each sitting they had discussed the spring planting and the weather, and then inevitably, led by Hiram Higgins, had resolved themselves into an "experience" meeting on the Patriarch — he, Madison, as a minority leader of one, grudgingly conceding an occasional point. The sessions had invariably ended the same way — Hiram Higgins, with the back of his hand underneath his chin, would stroke earnestly at his chin-whiskers, and remark:

"Well, now, Mr. Madison, 'twon't do you a mite of harm to go out there an' see for yourself. We've kinder got to look on you as one of us, an' there ain't no use in you sufferin' around with what ails you when there ain't no need of it."

Madison's replies had been equally void of versatility — he would shake his head doubtfully, while his cigar-case circulated around the group.

Madison sniffed luxuriously at his thoroughbred Havana. He had passed out of sight of the hotel window now, and he swung into a brisk walk. It was a mile to the Patriarch's by a wagon track through the woods, that led off from the road to the left just across the bridge. He had not needed to ask directions. With magnificent inadvertence Hiram Higgins had mentioned the exact way to reach the Patriarch's a dozen times, if he had once. Also, by now, Madison had learned all that the town knew about the Patriarch — which after all, he reflected with some satisfaction, wasn't much. The Patriarch was over eighty years of age, and he had come, deaf and dumb, to Needley sixty years ago — nobody knew from where, nor his previous history, nor his name. They had called him the Hermit at first, for immediately on his arrival he had gone out to the shore of the ocean, away from the village, and built a crude hut there for himself — which, in the after years, he had made into a more pretentious dwelling. The cures had come "kinder graduallike an' took the folks mabbe forty years to get around to believin' in him real serious," as Hiram Higgins put it; and then, as the Hermit grew old, and the local reverence for him had become more deep-seated, they had changed his name to the Patriarch. That was about all — but it seemed to suit Madison, for his smile broadened.

"I wonder," said he to himself, as he stepped onto the bridge to cross the little river, "if I'm not dreaming — this is like being let loose in the U.S. Treasury with nobody looking!"

"Hullo, mister!" piped a young voice suddenly out of the dusk.

"Hullo!" responded Madison mechanically — and turned to watch a small figure, going in the opposite direction, thump by him on a crutch. Madison stopped and stared after the cripple — and removed his cigar very slowly from his lips. "That's that Holmes boy," he muttered. "I don't know as he'd look well on the platform when the excursion trains get to running. Wonder if I can't get a job for his father somewhere about a thousand miles from here and have the family move!"

The cripple disappeared down the road, and Madison, with a sort of speculative flip to the ash of his cigar, resumed his way. Just across the bridge he found the wagon track, and turned into it. It ran through a thick wood of fir and spruce, and here, apart from now being able to see but little before him — he had elected to "steal" away in the darkness after supper — he found the going far from good.

Half curiously, half whimsically, he tried to visualize the Patriarch from the word pictures that had been painted around the stove in the hotel office. The man would be old — of course. And to have lived alone for sixty years, to have shunned human companionship he must have been either mildly or violently insane to begin with, which would account for his belief in himself as a healer — he would unquestionably, in some form or other, "have bats in his belfry," as Pale Face Harry had put it.

Madison's brows contracted as he went along. A man living by himself under such conditions, with no incentive for the care of his person, not even the pride engendered by the association of others, erudite as the standard might be in his vicinity, was apt to grow very shortly into a somewhat sorry spectacle. Give him sixty years of this and add an unbalanced mind, and — Madison did not like the picture that now rose up suddenly before him — a creature, bent, vapid of face, deaf and dumb, frowsy of dress, and a world removed from the thought of a morning bath. It might be picturesque in a way — but it wasn't a way Madison liked. Somehow, he'd have to jerk the old chap out of his rut and get him rigged up a little more becomingly, before the trusting public, simple as they were, were invited down to see the exhibit. Madison's dramatic instinct, which was developed to a keen sense of what the public craved for, rebelled against any *faux pas* in the scenic effects. He fell to designing a costume that would more appropriately expound the rôle.

"Got to give 'em something for their money," murmured John Garfield Madison. "Some sort of long, flowing robe now, washed every day, sort of Grecian effect with a rope girdle, bare feet and sandals — um-m — dunno about the sandals — don't want to slop over, and besides" — Madison grinned a little to himself — "he might kick!"

Still reflecting, but arrived at no conclusion other than first to size up the Patriarch and see how best to handle him, Madison reached the end of the wagon track — and halted.

It was a little lighter here, now that he had left the woods, and what appeared to be a sweep of snow-covered lawn was before him. Around this, forming a perfect square, was a row of full-grown, magnificent maples — a regal hedge, as it were, bordering the four sides — planted sixty years ago! Madison's imagination fired exhilarantly at the inspiring thought of these in leaf — in another few weeks. He shook hands with himself cordially.

"Behold the amphitheater!" he said. "This is where we stage the greatest act of the century!"

Behind the row of trees, directly across the lawn in front of him, loomed the dark shadow of a long, low, cottagelike building, and from a window a light twinkled out between the tree trunks; while from beyond again came the roll of surf, low, rhythmic, like the soft accompaniment of orchestral music.

"Wonderful!" breathed Madison. "I feel," said he, "as though I had just had a drink!"

He walked across the lawn, passed between the trees, and reached the end of the cottage away from where the light showed in the window.

"The Patriarch being deaf," he remarked, "I might as well explore."

From the row of trees to the cottage was perhaps twenty feet. The door of the cottage, porticoed with trelliswork, was in the center of the cottage itself. Everywhere Madison turned were trelliswork frames for flowers — the walls of the cottage were covered, literally covered, with bare, slumbering shoots of Virginia creeper. In a little while now the place would be a veritable paradise. Madison raised his hat reverently.

"Fancy this on a New York stage!" said he esthetically, invoking the universe. "Could you beat it! I could play the Patriarch myself with this setting, and everybody would fall for it. There's nothing to it, nothing to it, but his make-up — and I'll guarantee to take care of that. And now we'll have a look at Aladdin's lamp and see just what kind of rubbing up will invoke the genii!"

Madison walked along the length of the cottage, past the door, and, as he reached the lighted window, drew well away from the wall — and stared inside. Surprise and incredulity swept across his features, and then his face beamed and his grey eyes lighted with the fire of an artist who sees the elusive imagery of the Great Picture at last transferred to canvas, vivid, actual, transcending his wildest hopes. He was gazing upon the sweetest and most venerable face he had ever seen.

Here and there within upon the floor were strewn old-fashioned, round rag mats that would enrapture a connoisseur, and the floor where it showed between the mats was scrubbed to a glistening white. The furnishings were few and homemade, but full of simple artistry — a chair or two, and a table, upon which burned a lamp. In a fireplace, made of stones cemented together, the natural effect unspoiled by any attempt to hew the stones into uniformity, a log fire glowed, sputtered, and now and then leaped cheerily into flame.

Between the table and the fire, half turned toward Madison, sat the Patriarch. He was reading, his head bent forward, his book held very close to his eyes. Hair, a wealth of it, soft, silky and snow-white, reached just below his coat collar — a silvery beard fell far below his book. But it was the face itself, no single distinguishing feature, neither the blue eyes, the sensitive lips, nor the broad, fine forehead, that held Madison's gaze — it seemed to combine something that he had never seen in a face before, and to look upon it was to be drawn instantly to the man — there was purity of thought and act stamped upon it with a seal ineffaceable, and there was gentleness there, and sympathy, and trust, and a simple, unassuming dignity and self-possession — and, too, there was a shadow there, a little of sadness, a little of weariness, a background, a relief, as it were, a touch such as a genius might conceive to lift the picture with his brush into wondrous, lingering, haunting consonance.

Madison's eyes, slowly, as though loath to leave the Patriarch's face, traveled over the grey homespun suit that clothed the man, the white wristbands of the home-washed shirt, unstarched, but spotlessly clean — and his fancy of flowing, Grecian robes with rope girdles seemed to hold him up to mockery as a crude and paltry bungler before the perfect, unostentatious harmony of reality.

"There's nothing to it!" whispered Madison softly to himself. "Nothing to it! There isn't a thing left to do — not even a chance of making a bluff at earning the money — it's just like *stealing* it. Why, say, it would get *me* if I weren't behind the scenes — honest now, it would!"

Madison drew back from the window and walked toward the door of the cottage.

"It should take me about fifteen minutes to establish myself on the basis of a long-lost son with the Patriarch clinging confidingly around my neck," he observed. "If it takes me any longer than that I'd feel depressed every time I met myself in the looking-glass."

He reached the cottage door, and, lifting the brass knocker that shone dimly in the darkness, knocked once, lifted it to knock again — and his hand fell away as he smiled a little foolishly.

"I forgot the Patriarch was deaf," he muttered. "Wonder what you're supposed to do? Walk right in, or —"

The door swung suddenly wide open, and upon Madison's face, usually so perfectly at its owner's control, came a look of stunned surprise. The Patriarch was standing on the threshold, and, with a gesture of welcome, was motioning him to enter.

V

A STRANGE CONVERSATION

Madison, quite in command of himself again in an instant, stepped, smiling, into the cottage. He took the Patriarch's extended hand in a cordial grip and nodded understandingly as the other, with quick, rapid motions, touched lips and ears to signify that he could neither hear nor speak. But, inwardly puzzled, Madison searched the Patriarch's face — was the other playing a part? Could he *hear,* after all — and perhaps speak as well, if he wanted to! There was certainly no guile in the venerable, gentle face — or was it guile of a very high order?

The Patriarch closed the door, and drawing his own armchair to the table offered it to Madison with a courteous smile.

Madison refused by gently forcing the old man into it himself, pulled another up to face the Patriarch, sat down — and his eyes fixed suddenly on the ceiling above his head. Swaying slowly back and forth was a sort of miniature punkah of waving white canvas. He studied this for a moment, then his eyes shifted to the Patriarch, who was regarding him humorously.

The Patriarch rose from his chair, walked to the door, opened it, moved the knocker up and down — and pointed to the ceiling. The canvas was waving violently now, and Madison traced the cord attachment, on little pulleys, across the ceiling to where it ran through the door and was affixed to the knocker without. It was very simple, even primitive — every time the knocker was lifted the cord was pulled and the canvas waved back and forth. Madison nodded his head and smiled approvingly, as the Patriarch once more closed the door and resumed his seat.

Madison leaned back in his chair and allowed his eyes to stray, not impertinently but with pleased endorsement, around the room, to permit an unhampered opportunity for the scrutiny of the blue eyes which he felt upon him.

"And to think," he mused reproachfully, "that I could have doubted him for a single instant — he certainly hung one on me that time."

The Patriarch reached into the drawer of the table beside him, took out a slate and pencil, scratched a few words on the slate and handed both pencil and slate to Madison.

"Your name is Madison, isn't it?" Madison read. "From New York? Hiram told me about you."

"Hiram," said Madison to himself, "is a man of many parts, and the most useful man I have ever known. Hiram, by reflected glory, will some day become famous." On the slate he replied: "Yes; that is my name — John Madison. It was good of Mr. Higgins to speak of me."

The Patriarch held the slate within a bare inch or two of his face, and moved it back and forth before his eyes to follow the lines. As he lowered it, Madison reached for it politely.

"I am afraid you do not see very well," he scribbled. "Shall I write larger?"

Again the Patriarch deciphered the words laboriously; then he wrote, and handed the slate to Madison.

"I am going blind," he had written. "Please write as large as possible."

"Blind!" — Madison's attitude and expression were eloquent enough not only to be a perfect interpretation of his exclamation, but to convey his shocked and pained surprise as well.

The Patriarch bowed his head affirmatively, smiling a little wistfully.

Madison impetuously drew his chair closer to the other, laid his hand sympathetically upon the Patriarch's sleeve, and, with the slate upon his knee, wrote with the other hand impulsively:

"I am sorry — very, very sorry. Would you care to tell me about it?"

The Patriarch's face lighted up while reading the slate, but he shook his head slowly as he smiled again.

"By *and* by, if you wish," he wrote. "But first about yourself. You are sick — and you have come to me for help?"

The slate now passed from hand to hand quite rapidly.

"Yes," wrote Madison. "Can you cure me?"

"No," replied the Patriarch; "not in your present mental condition."

"What do you mean?" asked Madison.

"Your question itself implies that you are skeptical. While that state of mind exists, I can do nothing — it depends entirely on yourself."

"And if I put skepticism aside?" Madison's pencil demanded. "Can you cure me then?"

"Unquestionably," wrote the Patriarch, "if you really put it aside. Faith is the simplest thing in the world and the most complex — but it is fundamental. Without faith nothing is possible; with faith nothing is impossible."

Madison's grey eyes rested, magnificently thoughtful and troubled, upon the Patriarch.

"I have never thought much about it," he replied upon the slate, after a tactful moment's pause. "But I believe that. There is something here, about the place, about you that inspires confidence — I was prepared to cling to my skepticism when I came in, but I do not feel that way now.

If only I knew you a little better, were with you a little more, I believe I could have the faith you speak of."

"How long do you remain in Needley?" the Patriarch wrote.

Madison got up from his chair, went slowly to the fireplace, and, with his back to the Patriarch, stood watching the crackling logs.

"The old chap's no fool," he informed himself, "even if he is gone a little in one particular. He certainly does believe in himself for fair! Wonder where he got his education — notice the English he writes? And, say — *going blind!* Fancy that! Santa Claus, you overwhelm me, you are too bountiful, you are too generous — you'll have nothing left for the next chimney! Deaf and dumb — and blind. Really, I do not deserve this — I really don't — let me at least tip the hat-boy, or I'll feel mean."

He turned gravely to the Patriarch; resuming his chair with an expression on his face as one arrived at a weighty decision after a mental battle with one's self.

"I will stay here until I am cured. I put myself in your hands. What am I to do?" he wrote quickly — and held out his hand almost anxiously for the other's assent.

The Patriarch smiled seriously as, after peering at the slate, he took the outstretched hand and laid his other one unaffectedly upon Madison's shoulder.

"Be sure then that I can help you," wrote the Patriarch cheerfully. "There is no course of treatment such as you may, perhaps, imagine. My power lies in a perfect faith to help you once you, in turn, have faith yourself — that is all. It is but the practical application of the old dogma that mind is superior to matter. You must come and see me every day, and we will talk together."

"I will come — gladly," Madison replied; and, taking the slate, carefully wiped off the writing — as he had previously wiped it off every time it came into his hands — with a damp rag that the Patriarch had taken from the table drawer when he had produced the slate and pencil.

"This slate racket is the limit," said Madison to himself, as his pencil began to move and screech again; "but I've got to get a little deeper under his vest yet."

He handed the slate to the Patriarch, and on it were the words:

"Won't you tell me something of yourself, how you came to live here alone, and your name, perhaps? I do not mean to presume, but I am deeply interested."

"There is never presumption in kindlincss and sympathy," answered the Patriarch. "But my name and story is buried in the past — perhaps when I am gone those who care to know may know. I have not hurt you by refusing to answer?"

"No, indeed!" said Madison politely to himself. "The element of mystery is one of the best drawing cards I know — it's got Needley going strong. Far, far be it from me to tear the veil asunder. I mentioned it only as a feeler."

But upon the slate he wrote:

"Far from being hurt, I respect your silence. But your eyes — you were to tell me about them."

The Patriarch's face saddened suddenly as he read the words.

"I have made no secret of it," he wrote. "I have been going blind for nearly a year now. The end, I am afraid, is very near — within a few days, perhaps even tomorrow. I think I should not mind it much myself, for I am very old and have not a great while longer to live in any case, but for the time that is left it will mar my usefulness. I have been able to help the people here and they have come to depend upon me — that is my life. I trust I am not boastful if I say my greatest joy has been in helping others."

He had come to the bottom of the slate and held it out for Madison to read; then wiped it off, and went on:

"I have dreamed often of a wider field, of reaching out to help the thousands beyond this little town — but I have realized that it could be no more than a dream. I have been successful here because the people believe in me and have unquestioning faith in me — to go outside amongst strangers would only have been to be received as a charlatan and faker, or as a poor deaf and dumb fool at best."

Madison took the slate.

"But if these thousands of others came to you — what then?"

The Patriarch's face glowed.

"It would be a wondrous joy," he wrote. "Too wondrous to dwell upon — because it could never be. If they came I could help them, for their very coming would be an evidence of faith — and faith alone is necessary. Think of the joy of helping so many others — it is the fullness of life. But let us not dream anymore, friend Madison."

"Of course," communed Madison, studying the illumined face, "he's slightly touched in his upper story on the faith stunt; but he's in dead earnest, and he's got the brotherhood-of-man bug bad. Come to think of it, Hiram did say something about his 'sight failing,' but I didn't think it was anything like this. If he's going to go finally blind in, say, a week, perhaps it would be just as well to postpone the opening night until he does."

Madison took the slate.

"Stranger things than that have happened," he wrote. "I never heard of you before, yet I am one of the thousands beyond this little town and I am here – why not the others?"

The Patriarch shook his head sadly.

"It is but a dream," he wrote.

Madison held the slate in his hands for quite a long time before he wrote again; his attitude one of sympathetic hesitancy as his eyes played over the form and face before him, while the Patriarch smiled at him with gentle, patient resignation. Back in Madison's fertile brain the germ of an inspiration was developing into fuller life.

"What will you do here alone when you are blind?" he asked – and his face was disturbed and solicitous as he passed the Patriarch the slate.

"I need very little," the Patriarch wrote back. "You must not worry about me. My garden supplies nearly all my wants, and there are many in the village, I am sure, who will help me with that when the snow is gone."

"I am quite certain of that," Madison's pencil agreed. "But here in the house you cannot be alone – there are so many things to do, little things that I am sure you have not thought of – someone must cook for you, for instance. You will need a woman's hand here – have you no one, no relative that you can call upon?"

The Patriarch lowered the slate from his eyes, shook his head a little pathetically, and began to write.

"I do not think they would have cared to come, even if they were still alive; but they are all gone many years ago – except perhaps a grand-niece, and I do not know what has become of her."

"Why, that's just the thing," wrote Madison. "Suppose we try to find her?"

Again the Patriarch shook his head.

"I am afraid that would be impossible. I do not even know that she is alive. I know only of her birth, and that is twenty years ago."

"Even that is not hopeless," wrote Madison optimistically, and his face as he looked at the Patriarch was seriously thoughtful. "Where was she born?"

"New York," the Patriarch answered.

"And I never half appreciated the old town nor the fullness thereof until I came to Needley!" said Madison plaintively to the toe of his boot, while his hand scrawled the inquiry: "What is her name?"

"Vail," wrote the Patriarch. "That was her father's name. She is my grand-niece on her mother's side. I do not know what they christened her."

Madison once more, apparently deep in thought, sought refuge at the fireplace, his hands plunged in his pockets, his shoulders drawn a little forward, his back to the Patriarch.

"Fiction," he assured a crack in the cement between two stones, "was never, never like this. It seems to me that I remember the occurrence. It had grown a little dim with the lapse of time, it is true; but now that I recall it, it comes back with remarkable clearness. I am quite sure they christened her — Helena. Helena Vail! Now isn't that a perfectly lovely name for a novel! And she'll be so good to the dear old chap too — washing and ironing and cooking for him — and stealing out into the woodshed for a drag on her cigarette — *not.* No, my dear, not even that — this is serious business."

He turned, came back to his chair, picked up the slate, and wrote:

"I have the fortune, or misfortune perhaps, to be what is commonly called a rich man. Money, they say, will do anything, and if it will I'll find this niece for you."

The Patriarch's eyes grew moist as he read the words, and his hand trembled a little with emotion as he held the pencil.

"I cannot let you do that," he protested. "You are very kind, and it seems almost as though you had been brought to me providentially at the end of long years of loneliness for a purpose, when my hour of helplessness was near; but, indeed, I have no right to allow you to do this."

"They tell me in the village," wrote Madison in reply, "that you have always refused to accept a penny for anything you have ever done for them. I have no doubt you would equally refuse to accept anything from me for what you may do, and I should hesitate to offer it however much I felt indebted, but this is something that you must let me do. It will make me feel more — how shall I say it? — more as though I had a right to the privilege of coming here."

The Patriarch wiped his still moist eyes before he answered.

"What can I say to you? It does not seem right that I should let a stranger do so much, and yet it seems that I should not say no because —"

Madison was bending over the slate, reading as the other wrote, and he took the pencil gently from the Patriarch's hand.

"You must not look on me any longer as a stranger," he wrote. "Let us just consider that it is all arranged — only I would strongly advise making no mention of it until we make sure that she is alive."

"I think nothing should be said," agreed the Patriarch. "For even if you found her she might not care to come — I have little here to offer a young girl — few comforts — the care of a blind man who is deaf and dumb."

"We'll see about that when we find her" — Madison smiled brightly at the Patriarch, as he wrote. "Now that's settled for the time being, isn't it?"

The dumb lips moved and both hands reached out to Madison.

Madison took them in a firm, strong, reassuring clasp, then shook his finger in a sort of playfully emotional embarrassment, excellently well done, at the Patriarch — and picked up the slate again.

"It is getting late," he wrote, "and I must not tire you out. I am afraid you will think I am far more inquisitive than I have any right to be, but there is one more question that I would like to ask — may I?"

The Patriarch nodded his head, and laid his hand on Madison's sleeve in a quaint, almost affectionate way.

"It is about your education. You came here sixty years ago, and you have lived alone. You could have had but few advantages, with your handicap, previous to that, and yet you write and use such perfect English."

"The answer is very simple," replied the Patriarch on the slate. "Until within the last year, I have read largely. Would you care to look at my books? They are there in the nook on the other side of the fireplace."

Madison, promptly and full of interest, rose from his chair, passed around the fireplace, and halted before a row of shelves set in against the wall.

"I pass," Madison admitted to himself after a moment, during which his eyes roved over the well chosen classics. "I've heard of one or two of these before — casually. I've an idea that if the Patriarch's got all this inside his grey matter, it's just as well for the Flopper, for Pale Face Harry, for Helena and yours truly that he's deaf and dumb — and will be blind."

Madison came back to the Patriarch with beaming face, and picked up the slate.

"I read a great deal myself," he wrote. "It is a pleasure to find *real* books here. May I, during my stay in Needley, look upon them in a little way as my own library?"

"You are very welcome indeed," the Patriarch answered.

"Thank you," wrote Madison. "And now, surely, I must go" — he smiled at the Patriarch.

"Come tomorrow," invited the Patriarch. "I would like to show you all around my little place here."

"Indeed, I will," Madison scratched upon the slate, "and do you know that somehow, since I came here tonight, I feel a sense of relief, a sort of guarantee that everything is going to be all right with me in the future."

The Patriarch smiled quietly, almost tolerantly.

"I know that," he wrote. "Keep your mind free of doubt, be optimistic and cheerful as regards yourself, nourish the faith that has already taken root and that I feel responds to mine; keep in the open air and take plenty of exercise."

Slowly, with an apparently abstracted air, Madison read the slate, wiped it carefully, laid it down, and then held out his hand.

"Good-night!" he nodded warmly.

The Patriarch, still with the quiet smile upon his lips, rose from his armchair, and, keeping his clasp on Madison's hand, led Madison to the door, opened it, and with a gesture at once courtly and affectionate bade his guest good-night.

Madison crossed the lawn at a thoughtful pace, turned into the wagon track, and, in the shelter of the woods now, whimsically felt his pulse; then, lighting a cigar, tramped on with a buoyant stride.

"There's only one answer, of course," he mused. "The Patriarch's got a brain kink on faith — it's the natural outcome of living alone for sixty years. Outside of that and his books, he's as simple and innocent and trusting as a babe. I suppose the thing's kind of grown on him — Hiram said it had taken forty years — which isn't sudden unless you say it quick. Hanged if I don't like the old sport though, and if Helena isn't the best ever to him I'll stop her chewing gum allowance." Madison looked up through the arched, leafless branches overhead. "Beautiful night, isn't it?" said he pleasantly.

A little later he reached the main road and paused a moment on the bridge, as though to sum up the thoughts and imaginings that had occupied him on the way along.

"It's a queer world," said John Garfield Madison profoundly to the turbid little stream that flowed beneath his feet. "I wonder why some of us are born with brains — and some are born just plain damned fools!"

He went on again, arrived at the Congress Hotel, and, discovering through the window that the leading citizens of Needley were still in session, negotiated the back entrance. On the way upstairs he stumbled — quite inadvertently — and stopped to listen.

"There he be now," announced Hiram Higgins' voice excitedly. "Goin' up to his room to meditate. Knew he'd come back feelin' like that. I be goin' out there tomorrow to see the Patriarch myself."

Madison smiled, mounted the remaining stairs, entered his room, and lighted his lamp.

"Having got my hand in at writing," he remarked, "I guess I'd better keep it up and write Helena — Vail."

He extracted a pad of writing paper and an envelope from the tray of his trunk, his fountain pen from his pocket, and, drawing his chair to the table and laying down his cigar reluctantly at his elbow, began to write. At the end of fifteen minutes, he tilted back his chair, relighted the stub of his cigar, and critically read over his epistle.

"Dear Kid," it ran.

"Do not be anxious about me — I am feeling better already. Have had my first treatment, and am now eating fried eggs and ham regularly three times a day. A Sunday-school picnic taking to washboilers full of thin coffee and the left-over cakes kindly contributed by Deacon Jones' household, is nothing to the way the boobs will take to the Patriarch — who has kindly consented to go blind to make our thorny paths as smooth as possible for us.

"Do you get that, Helena — he's going blind! In just a few days, my dear, you will be with me, have patience. The meteorological bureau is a little hazy yet on the exact date of the total eclipse, but it's due to happen any minute. Now listen. Your name is Helena Vail. You're the Patriarch's grand-niece, and you're coming to live alone with him and soothe his declining years; but you can't come yet because I've got to find you first, and besides, until he's blind, he'll stick to a nasty habit he's got of asking questions on his little slate. You needn't have any hesitation about coming on the score of propriety, I assure you it is perfectly proper — he is running Methuselah pretty near a dead heat. And, as far as the town is concerned, apart from the fact that you are a grand-niece, or-phaned, you don't have to know anything about yourself, either — that's part of the Patriarch's dark, mysterious past, where the lights go out and the fiddles get rickets.

"That's about all. I'll let you know when to come. Remember me to Mr. Coogan and Harry, and keep my picture under your pillow. Ever thine, J.G.M."

Madison picked up his pen again and added another line:

"P.S. Better buy a cook-book."

He folded the pages, inserted them in the envelope, sealed the envelope and addressed it to Miss Helena Smith — street and number not far from the tenderloin district of New York.

Then Madison yawned pleasantly, tucked the letter in his pocket — and prepared for bed.

VI

OFFICIALLY ENDORSED

*T*en days had passed, bringing with them many changes. The snow was gone, and the warm, balmy airs of springtime had brought the buds upon the trees almost to leaf. It seemed indeed a new land, and one now full of charm and delight — the desolate, straggling hamlet, once so barren, frozen and hopeless looking, was now a quaint, alluring little village nestling picturesquely in its hollow, framed in green fields and majestic woods. Quiet, restful, peaceful it was — like a dream place, untroubled. Upon the farms about men plowed their furrows, calling to each other and to their horses; in the homes the doors and windows were thrown hospitably wide to the sweet, fresh, vernal airs, and the thrifty housewives were busy at their cleaning.

And there had been other changes, too. The ten days had found Madison more and more a constant visitor, and finally a most intimate one, at the Patriarch's cottage — while to the circle in the hotel office his voice no longer rose in even feeble protest, he was one of them. And, perhaps most vital change of all, the Patriarch was nearly blind — so nearly blind that conversation now was limited to but little more than a single word at a time upon the slate.

It was morning, in the Patriarch's sitting room, and Madison was seated in his usual place beside the table facing the other. For upwards of an hour, it had taken him that long, he had been engaged, having decided that the time was ripe, in telling the Patriarch that his grandniece had been found and that now it was only necessary to write and ask her to come to Needley.

The Patriarch's fine old face was aglow with pleasure as he finally understood. Letter writing was beyond him now, a thing of the past, so upon the slate he scrawled:

"You write."

Madison shook his head; and again with gentle patience explained that perhaps it would be better if the letter came from someone holding an official position in the village, rather than from one who, even in an abstract way, would be unknown to her — the postmaster, for instance.

And the Patriarch, patting Madison's sleeve gratefully, agreed.

Out in the garden behind the cottage, where for the first time in sixty seasons the work must be done by other hands, Hiram Higgins, the volunteer for the moment, was busy at his "spell."

Madison stepped to the door and called him in.

"Mr. Higgins," he said, "the Patriarch has just told me that he has a grand-niece living in New York, and he wants you to write to her and ask her to come to him."

"Be that so!" exclaimed Mr. Higgins, gazing earnestly at the Patriarch. "Well, 'tain't no surprise to me — always calc'lated he must have folks somewheres. An' I'm right glad now he needs 'em he's made up his mind to have 'em come. Wants me to write, does he?"

"He can't write anymore himself," said Madison. "He seems to think that you, as the postmaster, as well as the town police official, are the proper person to do it — and I quite agree with him."

"So I be," declared Mr. Higgins importantly. "I'll write it on the town paper, an' comin' from the postmaster there won't be no doubt in her mind that it's any of them bunco games or the lurin' of young women away such as I've read about, for I reckon perhaps she ain't never heerd of him before — never knew *him* to write a letter, an' I calc'late to see most everything that goes out."

Mr. Higgins picked up the slate and wrote the word "grand-niece?" upon it in enormous characters; then, amplifying his interrogation by many gestures of his hands, deft from long practice, he held the slate up to the Patriarch.

The Patriarch nodded, and Hiram Higgins nodded back encouragingly.

"Where be her address?" Mr. Higgins inquired of Madison.

Madison stepped to the bookshelves out of view of the Patriarch around the fireplace, but in full view of Mr. Higgins, and, reaching down the Bible from the topmost shelf, extracted from inside its cover the aged, yellow slip of paper that he had deposited there when he had entered the cottage that morning, and on which was inscribed Helena's name and address in a stiff, old-fashioned, angular hand resembling the Patriarch's — an effect that Madison had stayed up half the night to produce.

"I guess this must be it," he said. "He said it was here — we'll make sure though" — and he handed it to the Patriarch.

Long and painfully the Patriarch studied it, anxiously deciphering the words that he had never seen before, anxious to know all and whatever this might tell him about his niece — then again he nodded his head and expressed his gratitude by, patting Madison's sleeve.

Madison's smile modestly disavowed any thanks, as he passed the slip to Mr. Higgins.

"Reckon that be it," Mr. Higgins agreed. "An' now, I guess I'll go right back to town an' write it — I allow that the sooner we get her down here the better. Folks'll be glad to hear this — the women folks was figurin' on takin' spells an' helpin' out in the house same as the men in the garden — 'pears now there won't be no need of it."

Madison accompanied Mr. Higgins outside and helped him to harness up.

"Look here, Mr. Madison," said Hiram Higgins, as he made ready to go and climbed into the democrat, "would you allow that the Patriarch's goin' blind was goin' to interfere any with his power of curin' folks? It'll be a powerful blow to the town if it does."

"Why, of course not!" said Madison decisively. "Certainly not! Indeed, I wouldn't be surprised if it enhanced his power — it's purely mental, you know. They say that the loss of any one or more of the senses generally tends to make the others only the more acute — it's the — er — law of compensation."

"Glad to hear you say so," said Mr. Higgins, with a sigh of relief, "'cause I got another letter to write 'sides this one for the Patriarch. It come last night, an' I was figurin' on speakin' to you about it." Mr. Higgins dropped the reins on the dashboard, and dove into first one pocket and then another. "Shucks!" said he disgustedly. "Now if I ain't gone an' left it to home after all. But I dunno as it makes much difference. It was from a fellow up your way by the name of Michael Coogan, an' was addressed to the postmaster. 'Pears he read a piece in the papers about the Patriarch which he sent along with the letter. Allows he's been ailin' quite a spell, though he don't say what's the matter with him, an' wants to know if what's in that piece is all gospel truth, 'cause if 'tis he's comin' down. That's why I'm right glad to have heerd you say what you just said. Bein' postmaster an' writin' 'fficially, I got to be conscientious and pretty partic'lar."

"Yes, of course — naturally," said Madison. "And what are you going to say to him?" "Why," returned Mr. Higgins, "there ain't no trouble about it now. Goin' to tell him that if the Patriarch can't help him there ain't nobody on earth can — thought of mentionin' your name, too."

"By all means," assented Madison cordially. "I feel like a new man since I've come here. I only wish more people knew about the Patriarch — it makes your heart ache to think of the suffering and sickness that people endure so hopelessly when there isn't any need of it."

"Yes, so it do," said Mr. Higgins. He picked up the reins. "So it do," he said heartily.

Madison watched the democrat as it started off behind the ambling horse — watched with a sort of fascination at the inebriate, sideways stagger of the wheels, a sort of wonder that the rear ones didn't shut up like a jack-knife under the body of the vehicle and the democrat promptly sit down on its tail-board; then, smiling, he walked back into the cottage. The Patriarch was still sitting in the armchair beside the table. Madison halted before the other.

"Well," said he confidentially to the Patriarch, "that's settled and I don't mind admitting that it's a load off my mind. I hate to think of what we'd have done without Hiram Higgins — in fact, it distresses me to think of it. Let us think of something else. Day after tomorrow Helena'll be along. Helena is the one and only — but you'll find that out for yourself. I don't mind telling you though that she wears a number two shoe, and you can guess the rest without any help from me. Then a day or so later the Flopper and Pale Face Harry'll be along — you'll enjoy them — things aren't going to be a bit slow from now on. I expect the Flopper will bring some friends with him, too, so's to make a nice little house-party — I wrote him about it, and —" Madison stopped abruptly.

The Patriarch, evidently catching a movement of Madison's lips, was gesticulating violently toward his ears, while he smiled half tolerantly, half protestingly.

Madison nodded quickly and smiled deprecatingly in return.

"By Jove!" he said apologetically. "I always keep forgetting that you can't hear. I was suggesting that perhaps you might like to go for a walk — Mr. Higgins says it's a fine day." Madison picked up the slate and in huge letters that sprawled from one end of the slate to the other wrote the word: "WALK?"

The Patriarch rose from his chair with a pleased expression, and Madison helped him solicitously to the door.

They passed out into the sunshine and headed for the beach — the Patriarch, erect and strong, guiding himself with his hand on Madison's arm.

Reaching the beach, the Patriarch paused and turned his face toward the ocean, while he drew in great breaths of the invigorating air — and Madison involuntarily stepped a little aside to look at the other critically, as one might seek a vantage ground from which to view a picture in all its variant lights and shades. Against the crested, breaking surf, the fume-sprayed ledges of rock, the Patriarch stood out a majestic, almost saintly figure — tall, stately, grand with the true grandeur of simplicity, simple in dress, simple in attitude and mien, patience, sweetness and trust illumining his face, his silver-crowned head thrown back.

"I can shut my eyes," said Madison softly, "and see the Flopper being cured right now — and the Flopper couldn't help it if he wanted to!"

VII

THE PATRIARCH'S GRAND-NIECE

*I*t was Hiram Higgins who introduced Helena Vail to Madison, two days later. Madison had led the Patriarch outside the door of the cottage as the sound of wheels announced the expected arrival, and was waiting for her as Mr. Higgins drove up in the democrat. Helena, marvelously garbed, in the extreme of fashion, was demurely surveying her surroundings; while Mr. Higgins was very evidently excited and not a little flustered. A huge trunk and two smaller ones occupied the rear of the democrat, with the dismantled back seat lashed on top of them.

Madison, leaving the Patriarch, hastened forward politely.

"Mr. Madison," said Hiram Higgins importantly, "this be the Patriarch's grand-niece come to stay with him."

From under a picture hat, Helena's eyes smiled down at Madison.

"Oh, I am so glad to meet you, Mr. Madison," she said cordially. "Mr. Higgins has been telling me about you, and how good you have been to my — my grand-uncle."

"You are very kind to say so, Miss Vail," responded Madison modestly. "May I help you down?"

She gave him a daintily gloved hand, exposed a daintily stockinged ankle as she placed her foot a little hesitantly on the wheel, and jumped lightly to the ground.

"That," she said quickly and a little anxiously for Mr. Higgins' ears, indicating the Patriarch, "that is my grand-uncle there, I am sure."

"Yes," said Madison, leading her toward the Patriarch. "And he has been looking forward very anxiously all day to your arrival — it seemed as though the afternoon would never come for him."

"Gee!" said Helena under her breath. "I had the rubes in the village on the run — you ought to have seen them stare as the chariot drove along."

"I don't wonder," said Madison softly. "The sun's rather strong down here, Helena, and if you're not careful you'll scorch your neck with those burning-glasses you've got in your ears."

"Don't I look nice?" demanded Helena, with a pout.

"You bet you do!" said Madison earnestly. "You've got the swellest thing on Broadway beaten from Forty-Second Street to the Battery. Now, here you are" — they had halted before the Patriarch.

The venerable face was turned toward them, as though by instinct the Patriarch knew that they were there — and his hands were held out in greeting.

Helena clasped them firmly, and submitted sweetly as the Patriarch drew her into his arms.

The Patriarch released her after an instant, and his hands, in lieu of eyes, reaching out to search her face, came bewilderingly in contact with the picture hat.

Helena, a little uncertainly, looked at Madison.

"Is he *all* blind?" she whispered.

"Quite blind," said Madison sadly.

Helena's face clouded a little, and into the brown eyes crept a strange, sudden, sympathetic look.

"Doc," she said, "it — it isn't fair. It's a shame — he can't fight back."

"One error to you, Miss Vail," said Madison pleasantly. "Eliminate the 'Doc.' Don't shed tears, you're down here to be sweet to him, aren't you — well, get into the game."

Helena turned from Madison, and, impulsively taking the Patriarch's groping hands, guided them to her cheeks and held them there.

"Lucky dog!" observed Madison; then, raising his voice: "I am sure you would like to be alone together, Miss Vail — perhaps you will take him into the cottage. If you will excuse me, I'll help Mr. Higgins with the trunks."

Madison turned and walked over to where Mr. Higgins, beside the democrat with a handful of chin whiskers, was observing the scene.

"Fine girl!" declared Mr. Higgins, as Helena, with the Patriarch's arm in hers, disappeared inside the cottage. "'Pears she must have money, an' I'm right glad 'count of the Patriarch — said her father an' mother was dead an' she was alone in the world — them jewels she wore must have cost a pile. Reckon she's been used to livin' kinder different from the way folks down here do — hope 'tain't goin' to be so hard on her she won't want to stay."

"I was thinking about that myself," said Madison gravely, knotting his brows as he nodded his head. "There's no doubt it will be a big change for her, but I imagine she had some sort of an idea what to expect — it is certainly greatly to her credit that she would give up her own interests unselfishly and come here to devote her life to the care of a relative whom she had never seen before. I've an idea that the girl who would do that is the kind of a girl who's got grit enough to see it through."

"So she be," said Mr. Higgins heartily. "Ain't everyone 'ud do it — not by a heap!"

"I'll give you a hand with the trunks," said Madison thoughtfully.

They carried the large trunk between them into the cottage and, as Helena called to them, down the little hallway past what Madison knew to be the Patriarch's bedroom, and stopped before the next door, which was open. Madison remembered the room, when nearly two weeks ago now the Patriarch had shown him through the cottage, as a sort of store-room full of odds and ends. Mr. Higgins, too, evidently had known it only in that guise, for he whistled softly and reached for his whiskers.

"Well now, if that ain't right smart of the Patriarch!" he exclaimed. "Real set he must have been on makin' you feel to home, Miss Vail — an' never said a word to no one, neither."

"Yes," said Helena, "isn't it pretty? And did he really fix this up for me all by himself?" — she was looking at Madison, as she stood in the center of the room beside the Patriarch.

"Must have," said Madison, surveying the room.

It wasn't luxurious, the little chamber, nor was there over much of furniture, nor was that even of a high order — there was a bed with a red-checkered crazy-quilt; a washstand with severe, heavy white crockery; a rocking chair, homemade, of hickory; a rag mat, round, many-colored; and white muslin curtains on the windows. It wasn't luxurious, the little chamber — it was fresh and sweet and clean.

Upon the Patriarch's face was a sort of pleased expectancy, and Helena promptly took his arm and pressed it affectionately.

"Isn't it perfectly dear of him!" she said softly. "To think of him going to all this trouble for me when he could scarcely see!"

"Well, 'tain't no more'n you deserve," said Mr. Higgins gallantly, as he slewed the trunk around against the wall. "I'll lug them other trunks in myself, ain't but small ones, they ain't" — and he hurried from the room, as though fearful that Madison might secure a share in the honors.

"I guess you've made a hit with Mr. Higgins, Helena," observed Madison, with a grin.

"Have I?" returned Helena absently; then abruptly: "This is a real nice lay you've steered me into, John Madison."

"Yes; not bad," said Madison complacently. "Bring your uncle into the front room, Helena; and then you can get Hiram to show you the well and the old oaken bucket and where the pantries and cupboards are, he knows more about them than I do — it's pretty near time for you to be thinking about getting supper."

"Are you going to stay for it?" inquired Helena pertly.

"For the first attempt!" ejaculated Madison, with a wry face. "Good Heavens, no! I'm just convalescing from a serious illness."

In the front room Madison settled himself to a study of the Patriarch's beaming, happy face, while Helena under Mr. Higgins' attentive guidance explored the cottage.

"D'ye know, old chap," he said, and leaned across the table to touch the Patriarch's hand, "I feel like a blooming philanthropist. An outsider might think I was playing you pretty low and taking advantage of you, and even Helena's got a budding hunch that way it seems — but just think of the mess you'd have been in if it wasn't for me, just think of the good you're going to do, and just look at yourself and see how pleased and happy you look."

The Patriarch smiled responsively to the touch upon his hand.

"Of course you are," said Madison affably.

Presently there came the sound of an axe busily at work, and a moment later Helena came laughingly into the room.

"He's filling up the wood-box," she explained, and darting across to Madison put her arms around his neck. "Aren't you going to tell me you're glad to see me?" she whispered coyly. "Oh, I've been longing so for you! Kiss me" — she held out tempting little red lips, invitingly pursed up.

"Nix on that!" said Madison, smiling but firm, as he disengaged her arms. "Soft pedal, Helena, my dear."

"But he can't see or hear," pouted Helena.

"I should hope not!" said Madison, with a gasp. "But you never know who else might, or when they might — we begin right, and run no risks — see? People have a charming habit of dropping around informally here — everybody's at home."

"Don't you love me anymore?" inquired Helena, unconvinced, and still pouting.

"Of course, I do!" asserted Madison, laughing at her. "Don't be a goose, Helena. You remember what I told you all in the Roost, don't you? Well, I haven't been living in a Maine village ten days or two weeks for nothing, and what I said then goes now more than ever. Now, don't get sore, kid — there's a big stake up, and if we're going to play the game we've got to play it to the limit. We live perfectly, ultra-proper, decent lives, mentally, morally, physically, till we beat it out of here for keeps."

"Ain't we going to have a nice time!" murmured Helena sarcastically.

"Oh, cheer up!" said Madison. "It may be quiet for a day or two — but not much longer than that. Now tell me about the Flopper and Pale Face before Higgins gets back — have they got things straight? And pat your uncle's hand while you talk, Helena — get the habit."

"I don't have to get the habit," said Helena a little crossly, perching herself on the arm of the Patriarch's chair and taking his hand. "I think he's a perfect dear, and for us to sit here and take advantage of him when he trusts us is —"

"Now cut that out," said Madison cheerfully. "Think of those gondolas in Venice when we get through with this — that'll make you feel
better. Go on about the Flopper and Pale Face — can the Flopper speak
any English yet?"

Helena laughed in spite of herself.

"I've had a dream of a time with him," she said. "He's broken his
neck trying, at any rate; and he's not so bad as he was — quite."

"Good!" said Madison. "And?"

"I read them your last letter saying they were to come together and
work the train on the way down," she continued. "The Flopper got the
postmaster's letter, too."

"How did it size up as a testimonial?" inquired Madison.

Helena's dark eyes flashed with amusement.

"Lovely!"

"Too thick — fishy?" asked Madison.

"Oh, no," said Helena, "not if you have faith — just strong. It's all
right, though; I told him he could use it — it's a drawing card in itself,
for some of them would be curious enough to get off and see the finish.
Everything is all fixed — they'll be here tomorrow."

"Good girl!" said Madison approvingly. "We'll pull it off out there
on the lawn where all the multitude can see — you'll have to lead his
nibs out and guide him to the Flopper while the hush falls and you
look kind of scared — you know the lay. There's no one can touch you
when it comes to playing up to the house. And now, there's just one
thing more — you'll need someone around here to help you and keep
an eye on the offerings when they begin to come in. Well, that's the
Flopper's rôle in the second act — see? Overwhelmed with gratitude at
his cure, he attaches himself to the Patriarch with doglike fidelity —
beautiful thought! — get the idea? And —"

"Hush!" cautioned Helena. "Here's Mr. Higgins coming."

"All right," said Madison, rising and moving to the door. "I'm going
now, then — guess you understand. See you in the morning for the final
touches. Tell Mr. Higgins I'm waiting outside for him to drive me
home." He raised his voice. "Good afternoon, Miss Vail," he said, and
stepped out onto the lawn.

VIII

IN WHICH THE BAIT IS NIBBLED

*T*here was a group around the Flopper on the Portland platform beside the Bar Harbor express; some wore pitying expressions, others smiled a little tolerantly — Pale Face Harry, from the circle, sneered openly.

"Nutty!" he coughed, and touched his forehead. "Nothing doing in the upper story — someone ought to look after him."

The Flopper, a crippled thing on the ground, fixed Pale Face Harry with a pointed forefinger.

"Youse don't look like you had many weeps to spare for anybody but yerself — yer fallin' to pieces," said the Flopper. "I didn't ask you nor any of youse to butt in — I was talkin' to dis lady here" — he motioned toward a young woman in a wheeled, invalid chair, who, between a trained nurse on one side and a gentleman on the other, was regarding him with a startled expression in her eyes.

She turned now and spoke to the gentleman beside her.

"Robert," she said, in a low, anxious tone, "do you think that — that there can be anything in it?"

"Have you lost your head, Naida?" the man laughed. "The age of miracles has passed."

"But he is so *sure*," she whispered.

"Poppycock!" said her companion contemptuously.

The Flopper, in good, if unfashionable and ready-made clothes, fresh linen, and a clean shave, turned a bright, intelligent face on the man at this remark.

"I guess youse are de kind," he said, with a grim smile, "dat ain't had to kill yerself worryin' much about any kind of trouble, an' it ain't nothin' to you to cut de ground of hope out from another guy's feet an' let him slide. Mabbe you think I'm nutty too, because I know I'm goin' to be cured — but it don't hurt you none to have me think so, does it? Mabbe someday you might like to hope a little yerself, an' if —"

"'Board! All aboard!" — the conductor's voice boomed down the platform.

The young woman leaned forward in her chair toward the Flopper.

"I know what it is to hope," she said softly. "Will you come back into our car after awhile? I'd like to have you tell me more about this. Please do."

"Sure," said the Flopper amiably. "Sure, mum, I will, if youse wants me to."

The crowd broke up, hurrying for the train; and the Flopper, dragging a valise along beside him, jerked himself toward the steps.

"Swipe me, if I ain't got a bite already!" said the Flopper to himself. "An' outer a private car, too — wouldn't dat bump you! An' say, wait till you see de Doc t'row up his dukes when he listens to me handin' out me sterilized English!"

The brakeman and a kindly-hearted fellow passenger helped the Flopper into the train — and thereafter for an hour or more, in a first class coach, the Flopper held undisputed sway. The passengers, flocking from the other cars, filled the aisle and seriously interfered with the lordly movements of the train crew, challenging the conductor's authority with passive indifference until that functionary, exasperated beyond endurance, threatened to curtail the ride the Flopper had paid for and put him off at the next station — whereat the passive attitude of the passengers vanished. The American public is always interested in a novelty, and on occasions is not to be gainsaid — the American public, as represented by the patrons of the Bar Harbor express, was interested at the moment in the Flopper, and they passed the conductor from hand to hand — it was the only way he could have got through the car — and deposited him outside in the vestibule to tell his troubles to the buffer-plate.

The Flopper was in deadly, serious earnest; there was no doubt, no possible room for doubt on that score — one had but to look at the flush upon his cheeks and note the ring of conviction in his voice. Even Pale Face Harry's gibes and sneers melted before the unshakable assurance, and he became, with reservations, noticeably impressed.

A metropolitan newspaper man was struck with the idea of a humorous series of articles to pay for his vacation, entitled, "Characters I Have Met In Maine" — and forthwith, perched on the back of the seat behind the Flopper, proceeded to sketch out the first one, with the mental determination to get off at Needley for the local color necessary to its climax.

A soap drummer nudged a fellow drummer whose line was lingerie. "Ever do Needley?" he grinned.

The lingerie exponent had a sense of humor — he grinned back.

"My house is everlastingly rubbing it into me to open up new territory," said the soap salesman.

"Me too," responded the white-goods man.

"Needley," said he of the soap persuasion, "would be virgin soil for any drummer."

"I'd like to see the finish," said the lingerie man — still grinning.

"Well?" inquired the soap man — still grinning. "What do you say?"

"You bet!" said the man with eight trunks full of daintiness in the baggage car ahead. "It's Needley for ours — you're on!"

The Flopper was an artist — and he was in his glory. Where his position was indubitably weak, he side-stepped with the frank admission that he knew no more than they. He knew only one thing, and that was the only thing he cared about, the rest made no odds to him, he was going down to Needley to be cured — and he let them see Mr. Higgins' letter.

A porter from the rear car squirmed and wriggled his way down to the seat occupied by the Flopper.

"Mistah Tho'nton, sah," he announced importantly, "would like to see you in his private car, if you could done make it convenient, sah."

"Sure!" said the Flopper.

The passengers crowded up, standing on the seats and arm-rests, to make room for the Flopper to crawl down the aisle, while the porter preceded him to open the doors.

Through the car in the rear of the one he had occupied, the regular parlor car, the Flopper, a piteous spectacle, made his way — chairs turned, the occupants craned their necks after the deformed and broken creature, while smothered exclamations and little cries of sympathy from the women followed him along. The Flopper's eyes never lifted from the strip of carpet before him, but his lips moved.

"Gee!" he muttered. "Dis has de gape-wagon skun a mile. Wish I could pass de hat — I'd make de killin' of me young life. Pipe de hydrogen hair on de gran'mother wid de sparkler on her thumb an' weeps in her eyes, an' look at de guy wid de yellow gloves rolled back on his wrists to heighten de intelligint look on his face, dat she's kiddin' — I could play dem to a fare-thee-well if I only had de chanst. Oh, gee!" — the Flopper sighed — "an' I got to let it go!"

With regret still poignantly affecting him, the Flopper passed on into the private car, and the porter ushered him into a sort of combination observation and sitting room compartment. The Flopper's eyes lifted and made a quick, comprehensive tour of his surroundings. The young woman who had spoken to him on the platform was reclining on a couch; the nurse sat on the foot of the couch; and the man was tilted back in an armchair against the window.

The young woman raised herself to a sitting posture and held out her hand.

"I am Mrs. Thornton," she said, with a smile. "This is my husband, and this is Miss Harvey, my nurse. It was very good of you to come,

Mr. — ?" she paused invitingly.

"Coogan," supplied the Flopper. "Michael Coogan."

"Let me offer you a chair, Mr. Coogan," said Thornton, a little ironically, pushing one toward the Flopper. "Or would you be more comfortable on the floor?"

The Flopper's eyelids fell — covering a quick, ugly glint.

"T'anks!" he said — and swung himself, by his arms, into the chair.

"I want you to tell me all about this strange man in Needley, and how you came to hear of him and believe in him," said Mrs. Thornton. "I was only able to get just the barest outline of it out there on the platform with the crowd around."

"Dat's easy," said the Flopper earnestly. "Sure, I'll tell you. I saw a piece about dis Patriarch in one of de Noo Yoik papers, so I writes to de postmaster of de town to find out if he was on de level — see?"

"Yes," said Mrs. Thornton. "And what did the postmaster say?"

The Flopper took Hiram Higgins' letter from his pocket and handed it to Mrs. Thornton.

"Youse can read it fer yerself, mum," he said, with an air of one delivering a final and irrefutable argument.

Mrs. Thornton read the letter carefully, almost anxiously.

"If only a part of this is true," she said wistfully, passing it to her husband, "it is perfectly wonderful."

Mr. Thornton read it — with a grin.

"I don't know, I am sure," he observed caustically, handing the letter to Miss Harvey, "how the medical profession would stand on this — would your school endorse it, nurse?"

Miss Harvey read it with her back to the others — then she glanced at Mrs. Thornton — and checked herself as she was about to speak. She folded the letter slowly and returned it to the Flopper without comment.

Robert Thornton, master of millions, hard-headed and practical for all his youth, leaned forward in his chair toward the Flopper.

"Look here," he said bluntly, "you don't mean to say that you believe this seriously, do you?"

"Oh, no!" said the Flopper softly. "Nothin' like dat! Of course I don't believe it! I'm only guyin' myself — see? I'm just goin' dere fer fun — an' spendin' me last red to get dere. Say" — his voice snapped — "wot do youse t'ink I am, anyway?"

"Surely, Robert," said Mrs. Thornton gently, "it is evident enough that he believes it."

Thornton did not look at her — he was still gazing at the Flopper, his brows knitted.

"How long have you been like this?" he demanded sharply.

"All me life," said the Flopper. "I was born dat way."

"And you expect to go down here and by some means, which I must confess is quite beyond my ability to grasp, be cured in a miraculous manner!" — Thornton smiled tolerantly.

"Sure, I do!" asserted the Flopper doggedly. "If he's done it fer de crowd dere, why can't he do it fer me? Didn't de postmaster say all yer gotter have is faith? Well, I got de faith — an' I got it hard enough to stake all I got on it. Dis time tomorrow — say, dis time tomorrow I wouldn't change places wid any man in de United States."

Thornton's tolerant smile deepened.

"I guess you're sincere enough," he said; "and I'm not trying to cut the ground of hope out from under your feet, as you put it out on the platform — but it seems to me that it is only the kindly thing to do to warn you that the more faith you put in a thing like this the worse you are making it for yourself — you are laying up a bitter disappointment in store that can only make your present misfortune the more unbearable."

The Flopper shook his head.

"If he's done it fer others, he can do it fer me," he repeated, with unshaken conviction. "An' dat goes — I can't lose."

Thornton tilted his chair back again, and stared at the Flopper with pitying incredulity.

There was silence for a moment; then Mrs. Thornton spoke.

"Robert," she said slowly, "I want to stop at Needley."

The front legs of Thornton's chair came down on the heavy carpet with a dull thud, and he whirled around in his seat to stare at his wife.

"You don't mean to say, Naida," he gasped, "that you've got faith in this thing, too!"

"No; not faith," she answered pathetically. "I hardly dare to *hope*. I have hoped so much in the last year, and —"

"But this is sheer nonsense!" Thornton broke in with irritable impatience. "I can understand this man here, in a way — he has the superstition, if you like to call it that, due to lack of education, if he'll pardon my saying so in his presence; but you, Naida, surely you can't take any stock in it!"

She smiled at him a little wanly.

"I have told you that I didn't even dare to hope," she said. "But I want to see — I want to see. I have tried sanatoriums and consulted specialists until it has all become a nightmare to me and I am no better — I sometimes think I never shall be any better."

"But," exploded Thornton, rising from his chair, "that's nothing to do with this — this is rank foolishness! Nurse, you —"

Miss Harvey, too, had risen, and was regarding Mrs. Thornton anxiously.

"It is better to humor her than to excite her," she said in a low voice.

Mrs. Thornton had dropped back on the couch and her face was turned away from the others, but she stretched out her hand to her husband.

"I am not asking very much, Robert, dear — am I?" she said. "Not very much. Won't you do this for me?"

Thornton bit his lips and scowled at the Flopper.

"Well, I'll be damned!" he muttered — and moving to the side of the car pushed a bell-button viciously. "Sam," he snapped, as his colored man appeared, "go and tell the conductor that I want my car put off on the siding at Needley."

"Yes, sah," said Sam.

Thornton sat down again heavily.

"Mabbe," announced the Flopper tactfully, "mabbe I'd better be gettin' back to me valise — we're most dere, ain't we?"

Mrs. Thornton turned toward him.

"No; please don't go, Mr. Coogan — it's too hard for you to get through the train. Sam will get your things as soon as he comes back. Do stay right where you are until we get to Needley."

"No; don't think of going, Mr. Coogan," said Thornton savagely.

The Flopper looked at Mrs. Thornton gratefully, and at Mr. Thornton thoughtfully.

"T'anks!" said the Flopper pleasantly — and wriggled himself into a more comfortable position in his chair.

Half an hour later, the train, that stopped only on signal to discharge eastbound passengers from Portland, drew up at Needley — and Hiram Higgins, on the platform, stared at a scene never before witnessed in the history of the town.

It was not one passenger, or two, or three, that alighted — they streamed in a bewildering fashion from every vestibule of every car. It is true that the majority got back into the train later, but that did not lessen the effect any on Mr. Higgins. Mr. Higgins' jaw dropped, and he grabbed at his chin whiskers for support.

"Merciful daylights!" he breathed heavily. "Now what in the land's sakes be it all about?" His eyes, following the hurrying passengers, fixed on the twisted shape of the Flopper, being helped to the platform from the private car.

"Three cheers for Coogan!" yelled some excitable passenger.

The cheers were given with a will.

"Good luck to you, Coogan!" shouted another — and the crowd took it up in chorus: "Good luck to you, Coogan!"

"*Coogan!*" — Mr. Higgins' face paled, and he took a firmer grip on his whiskers. "Now if you ain't gone an' put your fool foot in it, Hiram Higgins," he said miserably. "If that there's the fellow that you writ to, you've just laid out to make a plumb fool of the Patriarch, 'cause I reckon the Almighty knew His own mind when He made a critter like that, an' didn't calc'late to have His work upsot much this side of the grave — not even by the Patriarch."

IX

THE PILGRIMAGE

*F*aith is an inheritance common to the human race; and the human race in its daily life, in its daily dealings, man to man, could not go on without it — but faith is a matter of degree. Faith, in the abstract, the element of it, is inborn in every soul; and while dormant, until put to a crucial test along any given line, is boundless and unlimited — a sort of tacitly accepted, existing state, unquestioned. Faith in many is a sturdy, virile thing — to a certain point. It is the fire that proves.

Needley had faith in the Patriarch — a faith that never before had been questioned. But Needley had more than that — Needley held the Patriarch in affection, as a cherished thing, almost sacredly, almost as an idol. Faith the simple people of Needley had always had — to a certain point — but it faltered before this grotesque, inhuman, twisted shape that squatted in the road before the Congress Hotel like a hideous caricature of an abnormal toad. Their faith failed to bridge the span that gave the Patriarch power over such as this, and they saw their idol shattered in their own eyes, and held up to mockery before the eyes of these strangers who had so suddenly and tempestuously swarmed upon them.

Hiram Higgins, seeking out Doc Madison inside the hotel, was in a state bordering on distraction.

"I druve him over from the station 'cause he couldn't walk, him an' a man, an' two women, an' a wheel-chair," Mr. Higgins explained. "But what's to be done now? He wants me to drive him out to the Patriarch's. I got faith in the Patriarch, but I never said he could work miracles —

there ain't no one on earth could straighten that critter out. Don't stand to reason that the Patriarch's to be made a fool of."

"Certainly not," agreed Madison emphatically. "It's most unfortunate. I suppose all of us here in Needley" — he looked around at the assembled group of leading citizens — "feel the same way, too?"

"Of course we do," said Mr. Higgins helplessly. "Couldn't feel no ways else."

Madison laid his hand suddenly, impressively, upon Mr. Higgins' shoulder and looked meaningly into Mr. Higgins' eyes — and into the eyes of the selectmen, the overseers of the poor, the general-store proprietor, and the school committee.

"Don't drive him over, then," he said significantly. "Don't any of the rest of you do it either — and tell everybody else not to. Make him *crawl.* If he's determined to go, let him get there by himself if he can, make him crawl — he'll never be able to do it."

"That's so," said Mr. Higgins, brightening, while the others nodded; then, dubiously: "But s'pose he *does* get there — how be we goin' to stop him?"

"If he can get there by himself you can't stop him," said Madison seriously. "You can't do anything like that. To use force would be carrying things too far, and would only place the Patriarch in a worse light. If this fellow — what's his name? — Coogan? — can crawl there, let him — that's his own business. None of *us* are encouraging him, the Patriarch didn't ask him to come, and no one has a right to expect miracles — so it can't hurt the Patriarch seriously under those conditions. Besides, if this Coogan has got faith enough to crawl that mile, who knows what might happen — make him crawl."

Mr. Higgins, with a grim nod, headed a determined exodus from the hotel office — and Madison strolled out onto the veranda.

Needley was in a furor. The news spread like an oil-fed conflagration. The farmers left their work in the fields and hurried into the village; from the houses and cottages came the women and children to cluster around the Congress Hotel; from the station, scarcely of less interest to the inhabitants than the Flopper himself, straggled in those curious enough to have left the train, nearly a dozen of them — and amongst them Pale Face Harry coughed, as he trudged laboriously along.

Larger and larger grew the circle around the Flopper, filling and blocking the road, overflowing into front yards, and massing on the little lawn of the hotel clear up to the veranda — until fields and houses were deserted, and to the last inhabitant Needley was there.

Upon the ground squatted the Flopper, his eyes sweeping the ring of faces that was like a wall around him — the grinning faces of his fellow passengers from the train; the stony, concerned and rather sullen faces of the men of Needley; the anxious, excited faces of the women; the bewildered, curious and somewhat frightened faces of the children, who pushed and shoved their elders for better vantage ground.

The Flopper licked his lips, and renewed the appeal he had been making for nearly five minutes.

"Ain't no one goin' to drive me out to de Patriarch's?"

"Horses are all busy in the fields," said a voice, uncompromisingly.

"Yes," said the Flopper, with bitter irony, "drivin' each other around, while youse are here starin' at me an' won't help."

His eyes caught Doc Madison's from the veranda and held an instant to read a message and interpret the almost imperceptible, but significant, movement of Madison's head.

"Gee!" said the Flopper to himself, as his eyes swept the faces around him again. "Dis is a nice game de Doc's planted on me — he wants me to do de wiggle out dere fer de rubes! Ain't dey a peachy lot — look at de saucer eyes on de kids!"

Mrs. Thornton, in her wheel-chair on the inner edge of the circle, turned to her husband.

"It's very strange that no one seems willing to drive him," she said.

"Oh, not very," responded Thornton, with a short laugh. "I don't blame them — they don't want this healer of theirs made a monkey of."

"If no one will drive him, he shall have my wheel-chair," announced Mrs. Thornton impulsively. "I think it is a perfect shame — the poor man!"

"Nonsense!" said Thornton gruffly. "You'll do nothing of the kind."

"Yes, Robert, I will," declared Mrs. Thornton with determination. She leaned forward and called to the Flopper. "Mr. Coogan," she said anxiously, "if you can't find any other way of getting out there, I want you to take this chair of mine — you'll be able to manage with it, I am sure."

The Flopper looked at her with gratitude — but shook his head — mindful of Doc Madison.

"T'anks, mum," he said, "but I couldn't t'ink of it — you needs it more'n me."

"Please do," she insisted.

"T'anks, mum," said the Flopper again, "but I couldn't. You needs it, an' I can get along widout it. Dey're stallin' on me, but I can get dere by myself if anyone'll show me de way."

"I'll show you, mister," piped a shrill voice — and young Holmes on his crutch hopped into the circle. "I'll show you, mister — an' 'tain't fur, neither."

"Swipe me!" muttered the Flopper, as he surveyed the lad. "Dis is de limit fer fair!" Perturbed and uncertain what to do, he tried to catch Doc Madison's eye again, but a movement in the crowd had hidden Madison.

Someone in the crowd, the lingerie drummer, getting the grim humor of the situation, laughed — and the laugh came like a challenge, taunting the quick-tempered, turbulent soul of the Flopper.

"Come on, mister!" urged the boy excitedly. "'Tain't fur — I'll show you."

"God bless you, son," said the Flopper, while he flung an inward curse at the man who had laughed. "Son, God bless you fer yer good heart — go ahead — I'll stick to you."

The crowd opened, making a lane through which the boy stumped on his crutch, his face flushed and eager, and through which the Flopper followed, slowly, rocking from side to side as he helped himself along with the palm of his left hand flat in the dust of the road, trailing his wobbling leg behind him.

The crowd closed in behind and moved forward.

Mrs. Thornton's face was fever-flushed, her eyes bright; in her weak state she was on the verge of nervous hysteria.

"I want to go, Robert," she cried. "I must go."

"But, my dear," protested Thornton harshly, "this is simply the height of absurdity. For Heaven's sake be sensible, Naida. Just imagine what people would say if they saw us here with this outfit of idiots — they'd think we'd gone mad."

"I don't care what they'd think," she returned feverishly, her frail fingers plucking nervously at the arms of her chair. "I must go — I must — I must."

Thornton glanced at the nurse, then stared at his wife — Miss Harvey's meaning look was hardly necessary to drive home to him the fact that Mrs. Thornton was in no condition to be denied anything.

Red-faced, Thornton strode to the back of the chair and began to push it along.

"Of all the damned foolishness that ever I heard of," he gritted savagely, "this is the worst!" His face went redder still with mortification. "If this ever leaks out I'll never hear the last of it. Look at us — bringing up the rear of a gibbering mob of yokels! We're fit for a padded cell!"

In the crowd, Madison rubbed shoulders for a moment with Pale Face Harry.

"Who's the party with the wheel-chair behind?" he asked.

"Millionaire — Chicago — private car — Flopper's got the wife going hard — rode down with them," coughed Pale Face Harry behind his hand.

"I guess I'll get acquainted," said Madison. "Circulate, Harry, and cough your head off – don't hide your light under a bushel – circulate." And Madison fell back to scrape acquaintance with the man of millions.

Close-packed upon the road, the procession spread out for a hundred yards behind the Flopper – barefooted children; women in multi-colored gingham and calico; men in the uncouth dress of the fields, the uncouthness accentuated by the sprinkling of more pretentious clothing worn by those who had come from the train. And slowly, very slowly, this conglomerate human cosmorama moved on, undulating queerly with the variant movements of its component parts, snaillike, for the Flopper's pace was slow – as strange a spectacle, perhaps, as the human eye had ever witnessed, something of grimness, something of humor, something of awe, something of fear exuding from it – it seemed to contain within itself the range, and to express, the gamut of all human emotion.

On the procession went – so slowly as to be almost sinister in its movement. And a strange sound rose from it and seemed to float and hover over it like a weird, invisible, acoustic canopy. Three hundred voices, men's, women's and children's, rose and fell, rose and fell – at first in a medley of scoffings, laughter, sullen murmurs, earnest dispute and children's prattle – a strange composite sound indeed! But as the minutes passed and the mass moved on and stopped as the Flopper paused to rest, and moved on and stopped and moved on again, gradually this changed, very gradually, not abruptly, but as though the scoffings and the laughter were dying away almost imperceptibly in the distance. For as the Flopper stopped to rest, those near him gazed upon his face, distorted, full of muscular distress, sweat pouring from his forehead, pain and suffering written in every lineament – and drew back whispering into the crowd, giving place to others until all had seen. And so the strange sound from this strange congregation grew lower, until it was a sort of breathless, long-sustained and wavering note, a prescience, a premonition of something to come, a ghastly mockery or a tragedy to befall, until it was an awe-struck murmuring thing.

Some spoke to him now and in pity offered to get him a horse and wagon, offered even to carry him – but the Flopper shook his head.

"'Tain't goin' to be but a few minutes now," he panted in an exalted voice, "before I'm cured – I got de faith to know dat – I got de faith."

And the crippled lad upon the crutch beside him urged him on. The boy's face was strained and eager, full of mingled emotions – pride in the leading part he played, wonder and expectancy.

"Come on, mister, come on!" he kept saying, impatiently accommodating his own restricted pace to the Flopper's still slower one.

Through the wagon track, through the woods beneath the trees, the dead, slow, shuffling tread went on — and now even the murmuring sound was hushed. Men and women stared into each other's faces — children sought their elders' hands. What did it mean? Faith — yes, they had had faith — but never faith like this. They looked at the awful deformity over one another's heads, crawling inch by inch along before them — watched the stubborn, bitter struggle of pain and suffering of the wretched man who led them, spurred on by a faith cast in a heroic mold such as none there had ever dreamed of before — and they spoke no more. There was only the sound of movement now — and that curiously subdued. Men seemed to choose their footing, seeking to tread noiselessly, as though in some solemn presence that awed them and held them in an intangible, heart-quickening suspense.

Onward they went — following the lurching, wriggling, reeling, broken thing before them — following the Flopper, his right hand and arm curved piteously inward to his chin, his neck thrown sideways, his sagging leg seeming to hold only to his body by spasmodic jerks to catch up with the body itself, like the steel when detached from the magnet that bounds forward to re-attach itself again, his eyes starting from his head, his face bloodless with exertion and twisted as fearfully as were his limbs, but upon his lips a smile of resolution, of indomitable assurance.

Onward they went — a huddled mass of humanity, literate and illiterate, of all ages, of all conditions, and none laughed, none grinned, none smiled, none spoke — all that was past. They stopped, they moved again — as the Flopper stopped and moved. Occasionally a child cried out — occasionally there came a discordant, racking cough — that was all.

Tenser grew the very atmosphere they breathed — heavier upon them fell the sense of something almost supernatural, beyond the human and the finite. Skeptic and faint believer, sinner, Christian and scoffer, they were all alike now in the presence of a faith whose evidence was before them in harrowing vividness, in the torment and agony of a fellow creature who sought again through faith a restoration to the image of his kind. There was no creed, no school of ethical belief, no conflicting orthodoxy to quibble over, no ground on which atheist and theologian even might stand apart — there was only *faith* — a faith whose trappings none might take issue with, for it was naked faith and the trappings were stripped from it — it was faith in its very essence, boundless, utter, simple, limitless, staggering, appalling them.

Its consummation? That was another thing — a thing that in the presence of such faith as this brought human pity, sympathy and sorrow to its full, brought dread and terror. Faith such as this they had never conceived; faith such as this, if it was to prove a shattered thing, was for its exponent to drink the very dregs of misery and despair — and yet, rising above that possibility, flinging grim challenge at their doubts, stood this very faith, mighty in itself, perfect in its confidence, heroic in its agony, that all might gaze upon from a common standpoint and know — as faith.

No whispering breeze stirred the young leaves in the trees; in the stillness of the afternoon came only the heavy, pulsing throb of Nature's breathing. One hundred, two, three hundred, they moved along, slow, sinuous, troubled, their eyes straight before them or upon the ground at their feet — only the children looked with frightened, startled eyes into their parents' faces, and clung the closer.

Out upon the wagon track they debouched and spread in a long, thin line beneath the maples on either side of the Flopper — and waited.

X

THE MIRACLE

*T*here was utter silence now — the tread of shuffling feet was gone — no man moved — it seemed as though no man *breathed* — they stood as carven things, inanimate, men, women and children strained forward, their faces drawn, tense and rigid. In the very air, around them, everywhere, imprisoning them, clutching like an icy hand at the heart, something unseen, a dread, intangible presence weighed them down and lay heavy upon them. What was to come? What drear tragedy was to be enacted? What awful mockery was to fall upon this maimed and mutilated creature within whose deformed and pitiful body there too was a human soul?

From the cottage door across the lawn came two figures — a girl in simple, clinging white, her head bowed, the sun itself seeming to caress the dark brown wealth of hair upon her head, changing it to glinting strands of burnished copper; and beside her walked the Patriarch, his hand resting lightly upon her arm, a wondrous figure of a man, majestic, simple, grand, his silvered-hair bared to the sun, his face illumined.

"There he is, mister!" whispered young Holmes hoarsely. "There he is! Go on, mister, go on — see what he can do for you!"

There came a sound that was like a great, gasping intake of breath, as men and women watched. Out toward the Patriarch, alone now, the Flopper began to wriggle and writhe his way along. God in Heaven have pity! What was this sight they looked upon — this poor, distorted, mangled thing that groveled in the earth — that figure towering there in the sunlight with venerable white beard and hair, erect, symbolic of some strange, mystic power that awed them, his head turned slightly in a curious listening attitude, the sightless eyes closed, upon the face a great calm like a solemn benediction.

Fell a stillness that was as the stillness of death; came a hush until in men's ears was the quick, fierce pound and throb of their own hearts. On, on toward the Patriarch slithered and twisted that frightful deformity that they had followed over that long, torturing mile — on, on he went, and they watched scarce drawing breath, their faces white, their very limbs held as in a palsied, fearsome spell — and then, sudden, abrupt, terrifying, there rose a shriek, wild, hysterical, prolonged, in a woman's voice, the cadence wavering from guttural to shrill and ending in a high-pitched, broken scream.

The Flopper halted and turned himself about, while his left hand swept his livid face, brushing from it the spurting drops, sweeping back the damp, tangled hair from his eyes — faced them till they saw an agony on human countenance that struck, stabbing, to their souls — faced them while his eyes traversed the long, long line of ghastly white faces before him, out of which eyes everywhere, row on row of them, straining, fixed, fascinated, seemed to burn like living fires as they held him in their focus.

He had not gone far, perhaps ten yards — no more. By the group around the wheel-chair, almost in the center of the line, stood Madison, his chin in his hand in a meditative, thoughtful attitude, the single soul who watched the scene from under lowered lids; Thornton had involuntarily edged a little forward from behind the chair until he stood now at its side in a strange, abashed way as though his own personality were overruled, obliterated, his face with a white sternness upon it, his eyes, like all other eyes, agleam with an unnatural fire; Mrs. Thornton had pulled herself forward in the chair, one hand clutching at her breast, the frail fingers of the other woven in a grasp so tight around the arm of the chair that the flesh was bloodless; a little way off, a group of three, the two salesmen and the metropolitan newspaper man, seemed as though stricken into stone, stripped of all assurance, all complacence, awed, tense, palpitant, as the patched, bare-legged tatterdemalion of ten

from the fields, that stood beside them, was awed and tense and palpitant.

And away on either side stretched the line of white, rigid faces, the
never-ending, burning eyes — but the silence with that shriek was gone
now, for another woman and another, overwrought, needing but that
sudden shock to unnerve them utterly, shrieked in turn — and through
the line seemed to run a shudder, and it moved a little though no foot
stirred, moved with a strange, sinuous, rocking, swaying movement,
from the hips, backward and forward and to either side. Men raised
their eyes, stole frightened, questioning glances at their neighbors — and
fixed their eyes on the Flopper again — on the Flopper and that majestic
figure in the center of the lawn, so calm of mien, of attitude and pose.

Once again the Flopper's eyes swept the scene. A few feet in advance
of the crowd, as though drawn irresistibly forward, young Holmes hung
upon his crutch. The boy's soul seemed in his face — hope, a world of
it, as he gazed at the Patriarch, sickening fear as he looked at the Flopper;
his lips moving without sound, his body trembling with emotional
excitement. Still once again the Flopper's eyes swept the line of men
and women and children, fast reaching toward a common ungovernable
hysteria — and then he turned with an unbalanced, impotent, broken
movement, flung out his good arm toward the Patriarch in piteous
supplication, and, jerking himself forward, went on.

Slowly, very slowly at first, he resumed his way, crawling it seemed
by no more than a painful inch on inch, in mortal pain, in mortal agony
and struggle — then gradually his movements began to quicken, as
though growing upon him were a mad, elated haste that he could not
control — quicker and quicker he went, pitching and lurching wildly;
from a pace that was beyond him.

A strange, low, moaning sound rose from behind him, fluttering,
inarticulate, that voiceless utterance that seeks to find some vent for
human emotion when human emotion sweeps with mighty surge to
engulf the soul. It rose and died away and rose again — and died away
— and children began to whimper with a fear and terror that they did
not understand, and seeking solace in their elders' faces found added
cause for fear instead.

Nearer to that saintly figure who stood so calm, so quiet, the massive
white-locked head still turned a little in that curious listening attitude,
beside whom, close drawn now, was that white-clad girlish form, whose
eyes were lowered, whose sweet face seemed to hold a heaven of pity and
infinite compassion, upon whose lips there was a smile of divine
tenderness, drew that piteous mockery of the image of a man, whose
every movement appeared one of agony beyond human power to endure

— and the agony found echo in the watchers' souls, and a low, muffled groan as of men in pain and hurt, ran tremulously along the line.

Still nearer to the Patriarch drew the Flopper. More heart-rending was his every movement, for with his quickened pace he sought to move without the aid of the only member that was as other men's, his left hand and arm that, in pleading, yearning supplication, was stretched out before him to the Patriarch.

The extreme ends of the long line of watchers curled a little inward, almost imperceptibly, a half step taken without volition. The crippled boy, swaying upon his crutch, his lips parted, trembling in every limb, edged forward hesitantly, fearfully, now a foot, now another, now the bare space of a single inch. And now down the entire length of the line from end to end that wavering, rocking movement in swaying, pregnant unison grew stronger — men knew not what they did — it seemed the very air they breathed must smother them — and, in that dull, weird, lingering note, rose again the sound of moaning that seemed to beat in consonance with the distant mournful rhythm of the endless beat of surf on shore.

Women clutched at their breasts now; men's knuckles went white beneath the tight-drawn skin; the children drew behind their mothers' skirts and, terror-stricken, cried aloud. Surcharged, on the edge, the bare and ragged edge of frenzy now was every man and woman in the crowd. It was a sight, a spectacle that racked them in every fiber of their beings, that stirred them to pity, to hope, to fear, until the awful misery of this blighted and crawling thing was their own in its every twitch of agony — that struck them with a terror, the greater because it was indefinable, a prescience, a reaching out beyond human realm, the invoking of a supernal power — the thought of which very power, once loosed, chilled them with panic-dread.

Yet still they watched — it was beyond their power to turn their eyes — enthralled, a moaning, swaying, rocking mob, they watched. Madness was creeping upon them rampant. Like a mighty tide, the ocean weight behind it, hurling itself against flood-gates that could never stand, it mounted higher and higher; and already, as the water first seeps between the gates, grim forecast of what was to come, it showed itself now in that long, sobbing, convulsive inhalation, in that strange, sinuous, restless movement.

On went the Flopper. There was still a yard to go — two feet — *one.* Stopped in a sudden deathless hush was all sound. The Flopper flung himself forward upon his face at the Patriarch's feet. Stopped was all movement, haggard and tense every face, strained every eye. For a moment that seemed to span eternity, in a huddled heap, that crippled,

twisted thing lay there before them motionless, without sign of life —
the venerable face above it, still intent, still listening, turned slowly
downwards. Then there was a movement, a movement that blanched
the watching faces to a more pallid white — that dangling, wobbling leg
drew inward slowly, very slowly, and hip and knee, as though guided by
some mighty power, immutable, supreme, came deliberately into normal form.

A shriek, a cry, a wail, a sob, a prayer — it came now unrestrained —
hysteria was loosed in a mad ungovernable orgasm — men clutched at
each other and cowered, hiding their faces with their hands — women
dropped to their knees and, sobbing, screaming, prayed. Loud it rose,
the turmoil of human souls aghast and quailing before a manifestation
that seemed to fling them face to face, uncovered, naked, before the
awful power and majesty and might of Heaven itself.

They looked again — fearfully. The twisted thing was standing now,
standing but still deformed — with crooked neck, with curved, bent,
palsied arm. And nearer had drawn little Holmes, his head thrust
forward, shaking as with the ague as he gazed on the group before him,
oblivious to all else around him.

A twinge of frightful torture swept the Flopper's face — and with that
same slow, awful deliberation the misshapen arm straightened out. Men
cried aloud again and again — a woman fainted, another here, another
there — children wailed and ran, some shrieking, some whimpering, for
the woods.

Again the spasm crossed the Flopper's face, a shuddering, muscular
contortion — and from the shoulder rose his head.

Inward drew the ends of the line of paroxysm-stricken people — not
far, not near to that hallowed group for something held them back; but
inward gradually until the line, no longer straight, was half a circle,
crescent shaped. Louder came that harrowing medley of sounds, its
component parts voicing the uttermost depths of the soul of each
separate individual man and woman there — some moaned in terror;
some prayed, mumbling, still upon their knees; some laughed hoarsely,
wildly, their senses for the moment gone; and some were dumb; and
some shrieked their prayers in frenzy. Louder it grew — the end had
come — that deformed thing stood erect, a perfect man — he turned his
face toward them — he stretched out his arms — and they answered him
with their wails, their sobs, their moans, their cries — they answered him
in their terror, in their shaken senses, clutching at each other again —
answered him from their knees, their voices hoarse — answered him with
trembling lips and tongues that would not move.

And then suddenly, as though riven where they stood and kneeled and crouched, all movement ceased — and every heart stood still as ringing clear above all else, shocking all else to stunned, petrified silence, there came a cry — a cry in a young voice. It rang again and again, trembling with glad, new life, vibrant, a cry that seemed to thrill with chords of happiness and ecstasy immeasurable. Again it came, again, exultant, pulsing with a mighty joy — young Holmes had *flung his crutch from him,* and, with outstretched arms, was running toward the Patriarch across the lawn.

For an instant more that stunned, awed silence held. All eyes were riveted and fixed upon the scene — none looked at Madison — if any had they would have seen that his face had gone an ivory white.

XI

THE AFTERMATH

"*I* am cured, Robert! Robert! Robert! See, I too am cured! Oh, Robert, what wondrous joy!" — Mrs. Thornton had left her wheel-chair and was standing beside her husband, standing alone, unaided for the first time in many months.

"Naida!" — it was a hoarse cry from Thornton. Then his hand passed heavily across his face as though to force his brain to coherent action, to lift the spell of what seemed a wild phantasm in all around him. "Naida!" — he sought now to control his voice — "Naida, get back into your chair again."

She laughed — a little hysterically — but in the laugh too was the uplift of a soul enraptured.

"But I am cured, Robert. See, dear, can't you understand?" She shook his arm. "See — I am cured. I can walk just as I could before I was ill. Oh, Robert, Robert! See! See!" — she went from him, walking a little, running a little — and laughing in a low, rippling, glorious laugh that was like the music of silver chimes ringing out in glad acclaim.

He stared at her, both hands now to his temples; then he turned to look strangely at the empty chair — but it was not empty. Miss Harvey, the nurse, on her knees, had flung herself across it and, with buried head, was sobbing unrestrainedly.

And now upon the lawn was a scene indescribable. The long line was broken. Men and women ran hither and thither, for the most part aimlessly, as though in some strange state of coma where the mind refused its functions. They talked and cried and shouted at each other in frenzy without knowing what they said — some with tears raining down their faces, others with blank countenances, no sign of emotion upon them other than in their wild, dilated eyes. Here and there they rushed without volition, their throat-noises rising above them, floating through the still air in a sound that no ear had ever heard before, weird, terrifying, without license, beyond control. Like mad creatures rushing against each other in the dark they were, stupefied by a sight that was no mortal sight, a sight that blinded them mentally because it was no *human* sight.

Faith? Faith is a matter of degree, is it not?

Or is it at its full in power and efficacy at moments when hysteria in paroxysm is at its height? Who shall define faith? Who shall say what it is, and who shall place its limitations upon it?

Out in the center of the lawn young Holmes was in his mother's arms, the father pathetically trying to wrap both mother and child in his own. Around them, attracted in that strange uncertain way, the crowd constantly grew larger. Further out again, Helena was leading the Patriarch toward the cottage, the Flopper close behind her — the Patriarch walking with a slow tread, his head still turned a little in that listening attitude — and at a distance followed a straggling crowd. Then the cottage door was shut — and Helena, the Patriarch and the Flopper disappeared from view.

A dozen yards from the wheel-chair stood Madison, riveted to the spot, motionless save for a nervous twitching of the lips, his eyes, now upon the invalid who walked about, now on the little lad who had thrown away his crutch. Someone plucked at his sleeve, but Madison gave no heed — again his arm was pulled, and he turned to look into Pale Face Harry's face. The other's countenance was grey, the eyes full of a shrinking, terrified light.

"Doc, for God's sake, Doc, what's it mean?" whispered Pale Face Harry shakily, moistening his dry lips with his tongue. "Doc, this ain't no bunk — there's something in it."

The words seemed to rouse Madison — to leadership. He stared at Pale Face Harry for a moment, then a grim smile flickered across his face.

"Something in it!" he repeated with an ironic laugh — and suddenly grabbed Pale Face Harry's arm and shook him. "There's so much in it that I'm drunk with it, crazy with it — but I'm trying to make myself believe it isn't too good to be true. Get that? Get a grip on that, and hang on. Don't lose your nerve, Harry!"

"I guess I ain't much worse than you," mumbled Pale Face Harry. "You're whiter than a sheet."

"You're right," admitted Madison frankly. "I'm queer, but I'm coming around. Helena seems to be the only one who never lost her grip — she's got the Patriarch and the Flopper out of the way and under cover. Brace up, Harry — what I thought we'd get in the Roost that night is counterfeit money to what'll come from this." His eyes fastened on a figure that, separating itself from the group around young Holmes, now dashed frantically, hatless, and with disheveled hair to Mr. and Mrs. Thornton. "Who's that, Harry? He came down on the train with you — know him?"

"He's only some newspaper guy or other," answered Pale Face Harry mechanically, his eyes still roving wildly over the scene around him.

"Oh, is that *all!*" ejaculated Madison with a little gasp. "I've already exhausted my thanks to Santa Claus and here he comes with another package done up in dinky pink paper tied with baby ribbon — and the gold platter it's on goes with it!"

"What d'ye mean?" asked Pale Face Harry heavily.

The newspaper man, the instinct of his calling now rising paramount to all else, had left the Thorntons and was tearing for the wagon track on his way to the station and the telegraph office like one possessed.

"By tomorrow morning," said Madison softly, "the missionaries will be explaining this to the Eskimo at Oo-lou-lou, the near-invalids in California will be packing their trunks, likewise those in the languid shade of the Florida palms; they'll be listing it on the stock exchange in New York, and the breath of Eden will waft itself o'er plain and valley until —" he stopped suddenly, as Mrs. Thornton's voice reached him.

"I am going to *walk* back, Robert."

"Yes; but, Naida," Thornton protested, "you're not strong enough yet."

"Don't you understand?" she cried, half laughing, half sobbing. "There is no 'yet' — I am cured, dear — *all* cured. I'm well and strong. Try to understand, Robert — oh, I'm so happy, so — so thankful. I know it's miraculous, that it's almost impossible to believe — but try to understand."

"I am trying to," said Thornton numbly, watching her as she moved about. "And it seems as though I were in a dream — that this isn't real — that you're not real."

"It's not a dream," she said. "Oh, I'm so strong again. Why, Robert, it would be just as absurd for me to be wheeled back in that chair as for you to be — and besides I have no right to do that now. It would be a sacrilege, profaning the gratitude in my heart — I am cured and these poor people here must see that I am cured — Robert, we must leave that wheel-chair here that others, poor sufferers who will come now, will see and believe and be cured too. And, Robert, in some way, I do not know just how, we who are rich must do something to help people to get here."

"Naida," said Thornton, his voice low, shaken, "I feel as though I were in another world. I have seen what I can hardly make myself believe that I have seen. I can't explain — I am speaking, but my very voice seems strange to me. I feel as you do about helping others — how could I feel otherwise? What we could do I do not know as yet, either — but I will do anything. I was a scoffing fool — and you were cured before my eyes — a boy was cured — and that other, deformed as no creature was ever deformed before, was cured" — Thornton's lips quivered, and he hid his face in his hands.

"While the iron is hot — strike," murmured Madison. He gazed a moment longer at the group — Mrs. Thornton's hand was on her husband's shoulder now — then his eyes roved over the frenzied scenes still being enacted everywhere upon the lawn. "I wonder?" he muttered. The frown on his forehead cleared suddenly. "Of course!" said he to Pale Face Harry. "It's a cinch — it's as good as done!"

Pale Face Harry stared at him queerly.

"No, Harry," smiled Madison, "my pulse is quite normal now, thank you. Listen. This is where we call the first showdown on cold hands — and the dealer slips himself an ace." He drew a key from his pocket and put it in Pale Face Harry's hand. "That's the key of the small trunk in my room at the hotel — front room, right hand side of the hall. There's a checkbook in the tray — and I'll give you twenty minutes to get back here with it. You'll find me somewhere around here, but you needn't let the whole earth in on the presentation — see? Now beat it!"

As Pale Face Harry hurried away, Madison, seemingly as aimless, as hysterical as the hundreds about him, moved here and there, but unostentatiously he kept nearing the upper end of the lawn, and, finally, hidden by the woodshed at the further end of the cottage, he slipped quickly around to the rear. Here the garden stretched almost to the edge of the sandy beach — not a soul was in sight — and the beat of the surf deadened the sound from the front lawn to little more than a low, indistinct murmur.

Quickly now, Madison stepped to where one of the old-fashioned windows, that swung inward from the center like double doors, was open, and, reaching in his hand, tapped sharply twice in succession with his knuckles on the pane. The sill was not quite on a level with his shoulders and he could see inside — it was Helena's room, and the door to the hall was open. Again he knocked. Came then the sound of footsteps — and from the hall the Flopper's face peered cautiously around the jamb of the door.

"Tell Helena to come here," called Madison softly.

The Flopper turned his head, called obediently, and in a dazed sort of way came himself to the window. His face was haggard, and he shivered as he licked his lips.

"I pulled de stunt," said the Flopper in a croaking voice, "but de kid — Doc — did youse see de kid? I got de shakes — it's like de whole of hell an' de other place was loose, an' Helena's gone batty, an' — pipe her, dere she is."

Into the room came Helena, her face like chalk — all color gone from even her lips. She clutched at the window beside the Flopper for support.

"I'm frightened," she whispered. "We've gone too far — it's — it's — John Madison, I'm frightened."

Madison did not speak for a moment — Madison was a consummate leader. He looked, smiling reassuringly, from one to the other — and then leaned soothingly, confidentially, in over the sill.

"I know how you feel — felt just the same myself for a bit," said he quietly. "But now look here, you've got to pull yourselves together — there's nothing to be afraid of. It's natural enough. It's faith, Helena — and that's what we were banking on — only not quite so hard. That kid and Mrs. Thornton annexed the real brand, that's all — and when the genuine thing is on tap I cross my fingers and yell for faith — there's nothing to stop it. And that's the way it's got both of you too, eh? Well, that only makes our game the safer and the more certain, doesn't it? So, come on now, pull yourselves together."

"In de last act when I was gettin' me head into joint," mumbled the Flopper, "was when de kid yelled — I can hear it yet, an' —"

"Forget it!" Madison broke in a little sharply; then, tactfully, his voice full of unbounded admiration: "You're an artist, Flopper — a wonder. You pulled the greatest act that was ever on the boards, and you pulled it as no other man on earth could have pulled it. Flopper, you make me feel humble when I look at you."

"Swipe me!" said the Flopper, brightening. "D'ye mean it, Doc — honest?"

"Mean it!" ejaculated Madison. "You're the whole thing, Flopper — you win. Come on now, Helena, buck up — we've got another little act due in about fifteen minutes — don't let a lot of yowling rubes get your goat. Why, say, we've got the whole show on the stampede — and we've got to rush our luck."

"Sure!" said the Flopper. "Dat's de way to talk — leave it to de Doc every time —. I ain't feazed half de way I was."

"I'm all right," said Helena a little tremulously. "What is it we're to do?"

"Good!" said Madison, smiling at her approvingly. "That sounds better. Now listen — and listen hard. From this minute this cottage is the Shrine. Get that? — Shrine. You've got to keep the hush falling here, and keep it falling all the time — a sort of holy, hallowed silence, understand? Lay it on thick — make the crowd stand back — make the guy that comes in here feel as though he ought to come in on his knees and as if he'd be struck dead if he didn't. Get the slow music and the low lights working. And keep the Patriarch well back of the drop except when he's on for a turn. Get me? He's no side-show with a barker in front of the tent — don't forget that for a minute. The harder it is to see the Patriarch and the less he's seen, the bigger he plays up when he's on. He goes to no man under any conditions, and the only man or woman that gets to him is through faith and supplication, and a double order of it at that. Keep the solemn, breathless tap turned on all the time."

Helena looked at him with a strange little smile quivering on her lips.

"It's a good thing I've got a sense of humor," she said slowly, "or else I think I'd — I'd —"

"No, you wouldn't," said Madison cheerfully. "But time's flying. You're going to have visitors in a few minutes, and here's where the Patriarch gets tucked away out of sight behind the veil for a starter, leaving his presence hovering and throbbing all around in the air — you stay with him, Flopper, in a back room somewhere and hold his hand. Where is he now?"

"In his armchair in the sitting room," said Helena. "And he's still listening in that queer way he did out on the lawn. I think he knows in a little way what's happened."

"That's good," said Madison; "it'll make him happy. Well, lead him gently into retirement. I guess that's all — now hurry."

"Who is it that's coming?" interposed Helena quickly, as Madison started away from the window.

Madison grinned.

"Some friends of the Hopper's. Mr. and Mrs. Thankoffering — you'll like them immensely, Helena. The lady walks quite well now, and —"

"Walks!" exclaimed the Flopper, who evidently had not assimilated Madison's previous reference to Mrs. Thornton. "De lady dat I come wid in de private car — *walks?*"

"Of course," said Madison pleasantly.

"Cured? All cured?" gasped the Flopper.

"Of course," said Madison again — complacently.

"Say," said the Flopper, "say, I'm goin' dippy. Another one de same as de kid, Doc?"

"Same as the kid, Flopper — faith."

"Swipe me!" said the Flopper helplessly.

XII

"SAID THE SPIDER TO THE FLY"

*B*y the wheel-chair, Mrs. Thornton, her husband and Doc Madison were in earnest conversation — and around them was a mass of people. The crowd had divided into two, or, rather, was constantly coming and going between two points — young Holmes and Mrs. Thornton — and still the hysteria was upon men and women, still that wavering, moan-like sound floated over the lawn.

"I am stunned and stupefied," Madison was saying, and his hand trembled visibly in its outflung gesture. "I am not, I am afraid, a man of deep sensibilities, but I cannot help feeling that I have been permitted, been chosen even, to witness this sight, a sight that will stay with me till I die, for some great, ulterior purpose. It's as though this place were hallowed, set apart; that here, if only one has faith, that man's miracu- lous power is boundless — that I should help someway. I — I'm afraid I don't explain myself well."

"I know what you mean," Mrs. Thornton returned eagerly. "It is what I was saying to my husband — to make this place known, to help to bring suffering people here."

Madison nodded silently.

"And if you, who have no personal cause for gratitude, feel like that, how much more should we who — who — oh, there are no words to tell it — my heart is too full" — Mrs. Thornton smiled through tears. "Robert, you said you would do anything."

"Yes, dear," Thornton answered gravely. "But what? We cannot do things in a moment. If money —"

Madison shook his head.

"It's beyond money," he said. "Money is only a secondary consideration. It's the needs of the place that are paramount. It's not so much the bringing of people here — they will hear of what has taken place and will come of their own accord, they will flock here in numbers as time goes on. But then — what? What can be done with them in this little village? For a time perhaps they could be accommodated — but after that they must be turned away."

"Turned away!" exclaimed Mrs. Thornton, in a hurt cry. "Turned away from hope — to bitterness and misery again! No, no, they must not I Why" — she grasped her husband's arm agitatedly — "why couldn't we buy land and put little houses upon it where they could stay?"

Madison leaned suddenly toward her.

"I believe you've hit on the idea, Mrs. Thornton," he said excitedly. "Why not? It would be the finest thing that was ever done in the world. But why not go further — this should not be a private enterprise with the burden on the few." He turned abruptly to Mr. Thornton. "What a monument from grateful hearts, what a tribute to that saintly soul a huge sanatorium, built and properly endowed, would be! And it is feasible — purely from the voluntary contributions of those who come here and have money — free as the air to the poor who are sick — free to *all*, for that matter — no one asked to give — but the poorest would gladly lay down their mites."

"Yes — oh, yes!" cried Mrs. Thornton raptly.

"Yes," admitted Mr. Thornton thoughtfully; "that might be done."

"There is no doubt of it," asserted Madison enthusiastically. "It needs but the initiative on the part of someone, on our part, and the rest will take care of itself. But we must, of course, have the endorsement of the Patriarch — why not go to the cottage now, at once, and talk it over?"

"Can we see *him?*" asked Mrs. Thornton wistfully. "Oh, I would like to kneel at his feet and pour out my gratitude. But see how all these people go no nearer than that row of trees, as though love or fear or reverence kept them from going further, as though it were almost forbidden, holy ground, as though they were held back by an invisible barrier in spite of themselves."

"True," said Madison; "and I sense that very thing myself — all men must sense it after what has taken place, all must feel the presence of a power too majestic, too full of awe for the mind to grasp. This faith" — he threw out his hands in an impotent gesture — "we can only accept it unquestioningly, as a mighty thing, an actual, living, existent thing, even if we cannot fully understand. But I feel that with what we have in mind we have a right to go there now — and we should take that little lad who was cured as well — and his parents, they should come too."

"And shall we see *him?*" Mrs. Thornton asked again tensely.

"Why, I do not know," Madison replied; "but at least we shall see his niece, Miss Vail, and it is with her in any case that we would have to discuss the plan, for the Patriarch, you know, is deaf and dumb and blind."

"You know them, don't you?" Thornton inquired.

Madison smiled, a little strangely, a little deprecatingly.

"If one can speak of 'knowing' such as they — yes," he answered. "When I came two weeks ago, the Patriarch was not wholly blind, and he was very kind to me. I learned to love the gentle soul of the man, and in a way, skeptical though I was, I felt his power — but I never realized until this afternoon how stupendous, how immeasurable it was."

"Let us go to the cottage, then," said Thornton. "Naida, dear, let me help you; it is quite a little distance and —"

She put out her hands in a happy, intimate way to hold him off.

"You can't realize it, Robert, can you? That dear, practical business head of yours makes it even harder for you than it is for me — and I can hardly realize it myself. But I *am* cured, dear, and I'm well and strong, and I don't need any help — why, Robert, I am going to help you now, instead of always being a source of worry and anxiety to you. Come, let us go."

"If you will walk slowly," suggested Madison, "I'll speak to the little Holmes boy and his parents, and bring them with us."

He moved away as he spoke — in the direction of a racking cough, that rose above the confused, murmuring, whispering, shaken voices on every hand; and in a little knot of people he was, for a moment, pressed close against Pale Face Harry.

"All right," whispered Pale Face Harry, "it's in your pocket now — but, say, no more runs like that for me, I'm all in. I thought sure I was cured myself — I hadn't coughed for —"

"Never mind about that now," said Madison rapidly. "I want the crowd kept away from the doors of the bank vault if they show any tendency to get too close, though I don't think that'll happen — they're too numbed and scared yet. But you know the game. Keep the awe going and the 'holy ground' signs up. Anybody that steps across that stretch between the trees and the cottage on and after the present date of writing does it with bowed head and his shoes off — get the idea?"

Pale Face Harry grinned.

"That's easy," he said. "Anything'd steer 'em now — they're like sheep. Leave it to me to keep the soft pedal on."

With a nod, Madison turned away, the tense expression on his face assumed again — and presently he was talking to Mr. and Mrs. Holmes, and patting the boy's head in a clumsy, overwrought way.

"I — I don't dar'st to go," said Mrs. Holmes, clutching wildly at the boy, still sobbing, still beyond control of herself.

"But Mrs. Thornton is going," said Madison gently, "and I know your gratitude is no less than hers — it couldn't be less with this little lad restored to you. I am sure you want to show it — don't you?"

"I think we'd orter go, ma," said Mr. Holmes uneasily.

The boy put his hand in Madison's.

"I want to go, mister," he choked. "Take me, mister, won't you?"

"Yes, I think we'd orter go," repeated Mr. Holmes. "Come along, ma," he said, taking his wife's arm.

It was a strange group — the Thorntons, rich, refined, to whom luxury was necessity; the Holmes, poor, uncultured, coarsely dressed; and Madison, who walked with set face, head lowered a little, his pace slowing perceptibly, humbly it seemed, the nearer he came to the cottage door. Neither Thornton, nor Holmes, nor Holmes' wife spoke. Mrs. Thornton's arm was flung around the boy's shoulder, and he kept looking up into her tearful face — there was a bond between them that, young as he was, held him in its thrall. Out across the lawn, dotted here and there, in knots and groups and little crowds, men and women stopped where they stood and watched, making no effort to follow — and some, at the renewed evidence of the miraculous, once more so vividly before their eyes, dropped again to their knees.

They reached the door, and Madison drew back a little and with the others waited silently after he had knocked. Then the door opened slowly, and Helena, slim and girlish in her simple white dress, appeared upon the threshold. Her great dark eyes traveled slowly from one to another, and then her face lighted with a gentle smile.

"Miss Vail," said Madison diffidently, "this is Mrs. Thornton and her husband, and the little lad, with his parents, who owes so much to the Patriarch, and they have come to —"

"To try and say a little of what is in their hearts" — Mrs. Thornton stepped impulsively forward and held out her hands to Helena — and then, breaking down suddenly, she began to sob, and the two were in each other's arms, Mrs. Thornton's head buried on Helena's shoulder, Helena's face lowered, her brown hair mingling with the gold of the other's, her arms about the frail form that shook convulsively.

Doc Madison shot a covert glance at the three behind him — Thornton, and Holmes, and Mrs. Holmes. Holmes, with downcast eyes, was shuffling awkwardly from foot to foot; Mrs. Holmes, her woman's instinct touched, was watching the scene with face aglow, her eyes moist anew; Thornton was staring fascinated at Helena, a sort of breathless, wondering admiration in his eyes.

Madison involuntarily followed Thornton's look; then stole a glance back at Thornton again — Thornton was still gazing intently at Helena.

"Say," observed Madison to himself, "the longer you live the more you learn, don't you? That's the kind of stuff Helena wears from now on, the clinging white with the bare throat effect and all that. Why, say, like that she's what the poets call radiantly divine — eh, what?"

Mrs. Thornton raised her head, and her hands creeping to Helena's face brushed the brown hair tenderly back from the white forehead.

"Oh, how good and sweet and pure you are!" she murmured brokenly.

A quick, sudden flush, passing to all but Madison as one of demure and startled modesty, swept in a crimson tide to Helena's face.

"You — you must not say that," she faltered, shaking her head. "I — you must not say that."

Mrs. Thornton smiled at her — and slipped her arm affectionately around Helena's waist.

"I could not help it, dear," she whispered. "It came spontaneously. And it makes me so happy to find you like this, and it makes it so much more a joy in doing what we have come to talk to you about."

"What you have come to talk to me about?" — Helena, steadying herself, repeated the words almost composedly.

"Oh, yes," said Mrs. Thornton, an eagerness in her voice again. "But — may we come in? Is it —"

"All may come in here," Helena answered softly, "and" — her eyes met Thornton's fixed gaze and dropped quickly — "please come in," she ended abruptly.

XIII

REAL MONEY

*T*he two women passed inside the cottage, Mrs. Thornton holding out her hand again to the little lad; while Holmes and his wife followed hesitantly, awed. In the rear, Thornton grasped Madison's arm suddenly.

"I never saw such a beautiful face," he whispered tensely. "It's wonderful."

"Yes," assented Madison. "But everything here seems full of a rare, strange beauty, a hallowed something — it lifts one beyond material things. You *feel* it — a great, calm solemnity all about you."

He closed the door softly behind him.

Mrs. Thornton's eyes swept questioningly, anxiously and a little timidly about the plain, simple, quiet room; and then she spoke, her voice unconsciously hushed:

"He — he is not here?"

Helena shook her head, as she led Mrs. Thornton to a chair.

"Not now," she said in a low voice. "The strain of this afternoon has left him very weary and very tired — much has gone out of him in response to the faith he felt but could not see."

"But he knows?" said Mrs. Thornton eagerly, reaching for Helena's hand. "He knows?"

"Yes," Helena replied quietly, "he knows. He always knows." She nodded gravely to the others. "Please sit down," she said.

Madison quietly took the chair nearest the table; Thornton one a little in front of Madison and nearer his wife and Helena, who were close by the big, open fireplace; the two Holmes sat down on the edges of chairs a little behind Madison; while young Holmes knelt, his arms in Mrs. Thornton's lap, his head turned a little sideways, his chin cupped in one hand, as he stared breathlessly around him.

It was the boy who broke the momentary silence.

"Ain't that other fellow here, neither — the fellow that was worse'n me?" he whispered.

Helena leaned toward him.

"Yes; he is here," she answered, smiling sweetly. "He is with the Patriarch." She lifted her head to include the others in her words. "It is very wonderful, his gratitude. He will not leave the Patriarch — he says he will not leave him ever, that all he has to give for the debt he owes is the life that the Patriarch gave back to him, and he will listen to nothing but that he should devote that life to the Patriarch's service."

"I'd like to, too," said young Holmes, with a quick flush on his face. "Can I, miss — can I?"

"Perhaps," said Helena gently. "Who knows what there may be that you can do?"

"Dear boy," said Mrs. Thornton, stroking the lad's head. She looked quickly at Helena. "We, too, are grateful, more than there are words to tell, and we, too, would like to show our gratitude. We are rich and money —"

"Money!" the word came in shocked, hurt interruption from Helena, as a signal flashed from Madison's eyes. "The Patriarch does not do these things for money — it would be a bitter grief to him to be misjudged in that way, even in thought. It is the love in his heart for the suffering ones, and his power goes out to all who ask it freely, with no thought of recompense or gain, and his joy and happiness is the joy and happiness of others."

"And right off the bat too!" said Madison admiringly to himself. "Now, wouldn't that get you! Say, could you beat it — could you beat it!"

"Oh, I did not mean that," said Mrs. Thornton almost piteously. "Please, please do not think so, for I know so well that money in a personal sense could have no place here, that it would indeed be sacrilege. It is in quite another way — Robert, Mr. Madison, you explain what we would like to do."

It was Madison who explained.

"It is Mrs. Thornton's idea, Miss Vail," he said earnestly; "and it is one that I know will realize the Patriarch's dearest wish — to extend his sphere of helpfulness to others, to reach out to all who are stricken and have faith to come. I remember his writing that on the slate, which he used for conversation before his sight was completely taken from him. I remember the words as though they were before me now: 'I have dreamed often of a wider field, of reaching out to help the thousands beyond this little town — it would be wondrous joy.'"

"Yes?" said Helena in a suppressed voice.

"In a way," Madison went on gravely, "his dream is already realized. What has happened here this afternoon will in a few hours be known to the whole civilized world, and there will be no room for incredulity or doubt — on whatever ground people see fit to base their belief, they must still believe; and, believing, they will come here in ever increasing numbers — but this little village is totally inadequate to accommodate them. At first, yes, as I said to Mrs. Thornton; but afterwards — no. Mrs. Thornton's idea, Mr. Thornton's idea and my own, if I may say so, is to build and endow a great sanatorium that, in consonance with the Patriarch's ideals, shall be free to all — and we feel that the money for this purpose will come gladly and spontaneously, as it so appropriately should come, from those who find joy and peace and health again at the Patriarch's hands."

Helena half rose from her chair, as she stole a veiled glance at Madison.

"It would be wonderful," she said, with a little catch in her voice. "And he — it would be the one thing in the world for him. But — but it would take a great deal of money."

"Yes," said Madison slowly; "at least half a million."

Thornton turned toward Madison.

"As much as that?" he asked tentatively.

"I should say so," replied Madison thoughtfully. "You see, it's the endowment after all that is the most important. Say that the building and equipment cost only a hundred thousand, that would only leave an income, from the other four hundred thousand at six percent, of twenty-four thousand dollars — not enough in itself even, but it would be augmented of course by the contributions that would still go on."

Thornton nodded his head.

"That is so," he agreed; "but there is the time to consider — it would take a long time to raise that amount."

"No," said Madison. "A few months at the outside. Thornton" — he reached out and laid his hand impressively on the other's sleeve — we are not dealing with ordinary things here — we have witnessed this afternoon a sight that should teach us that. Here, in this very room, beside us now, your wife, that little boy, is evidence of power beyond anything we have ever known before. Have we not that same power to count on still? It would be an ingrate heart indeed that, owing all, returned nothing."

"Yes," murmured Mrs. Thornton. "Mr. Madison is right. I know it, I feel it — the money will come faster than we have any idea of."

Madison smiled at her quietly.

"It will come," he said. "People will give their money, their jewels, anything, and give joyfully — and until the amount in hand is large enough to warrant beginning operations, Miss Vail naturally will be its guardian."

"I?" said Helena hesitatingly. "I — I am only a girl, I would not know what to do."

"You would not have to do anything, Miss Vail," Madison informed her reassuringly. "When the time comes for advice, the making of plans and the carrying of them out, the brightest minds in this country will be offered freely and voluntarily, you will see."

"And meanwhile," inquired Thornton — he had been studying Helena's profile intently, "would you propose keeping the contributions here?"

"Of course!" said Madison. "And not only here, but openly displayed as an added incentive for others to give — if added incentive be needed. Here, for instance" — he rose as he spoke, went to the mantel over the fireplace and lifted down a quaint, japanned box, fashioned in the shape of a little chest, which he placed upon the table. "And here, too" — he crossed to the bookshelves in the alcove, and took down a very old, flexible-covered book. "Once," he said, "the Patriarch showed me this. It was a blank book originally, half of it is blank still; but in the front,

in the Patriarch's own writing, is an essay he wrote in the years gone by
on 'The Power of Faith' — what could be more fitting than that the
remaining pages should be filled with a record of the contributions to
that faith?" He laid the book on the table beside the little chest, and sat
down again. "There is no display, no ornamentation, no attempt at
anything of that kind — it is simplicity, those things serving which are
first at hand — as it seems to me it should be — those who give record
their names and gifts in this book — the little chest to hold the gifts is
open, free to the inspection of all."

"But is that wise?" demurred Thornton. "So large a sum of money as
must accumulate to be left openly about? Would it not be a temptation
to some to steal? Might it not even endanger Miss Vail and the Patriarch
himself — subject them, indeed, to attack?"

"I get your idea," said Madison to himself — while he gazed at
Thornton in pained surprise; "but there'll never be more than the day's
catch in the box at a time, though of course you don't know that. You
see, we'll empty it every night, and start it off fresh every morning, with
a trinket or two put back for bait. I'm glad you mentioned it though,
it's a little detail I mustn't forget to speak to the Flopper about." But
aloud he said, and there was a sort of shocked awe in his voice: "Steal
— *here!* In this sacred place! No man would dare — the most hardened
criminal would draw back. Why do even we who sit here speak as we
have been speaking with hushed and lowered voices? — that very sense
of a presence unseen around us, that hovers over us, is a mightier
safeguard than the strongest bolts and locks, than the steel-barred vaults
of any bank. It would seem indeed to profane our own faith even to
entertain such an idea — to me this place is a solemn shrine, and there
is only purity and faith and stillness here, the dwelling place of a power
as compassionate as it is mighty."

Madison stopped abruptly — and a silence fell. Each seemed busy
with their own thoughts. About them was quiet, stillness, peace —
twilight was falling, and a soft, mellow light was in the room.

"No one would dare" — the words came from Mrs. Thornton in
almost breathless corroboration, almost of their own accord it seemed,
as though heavy upon her lay the solemnity of her surroundings.

Madison's hand went to his pocket — slowly he drew out his checkbook and laid it upon the table.

"I am not a rich man" — his voice was very low, very earnest — "but
I feel that this is something deeper, grander, bigger than anything the
world perhaps has ever known before; something higher and above one's
own self; it seems as though here were the chrysalis that, once developed
to its perfect state, would sweep pain and sorrow from suffering human-

ity; it is as though a new, glad era had dawned for all mankind. I am glad to give and humbly proud to have a part in this." He took out his fountain pen, opened the checkbook, and began to write.

Thornton leaned forward a little, watching him.

Silence fell again — there was no sound save the almost inaudible scratching of Madison's pen. Upon Mrs. Thornton's face was a happy, radiant smile; Helena's face was impassive, but in the dark eyes lurked a puzzled light; the two Holmes sat awkwardly, still upon the edges of their chairs, gazing at their son across the room, incredulously, as though they still could not believe — and occasionally Mrs. Holmes wiped her eyes.

Madison's pen moved on: "Pay to the order of Miss Helena Vail the sum of ten thousand dollars." He carefully inscribed the amount in numerals in the lower left-hand corner. "Honest," he confided to himself, as he signed the check, "I feel so philanthropic I could almost make myself believe I had this money in the bank." He tore the check from its stub, and, standing up, handed it to Helena. "I am not a rich man, Miss Vail, as I said," he smiled gravely, "but I can give this, and I give it with great joy in my heart."

Helena took the check, glanced at it, gasped a little, lifted her eyes, an instant's mocking glint in them, and veiled them quickly with her long lashes.

"No" — Madison's hand, palm up, went out protestingly — "no, do not thank me — it is little enough." He sat down again, drew the Patriarch's blank book toward him, and, on the line beneath the one where the Patriarch had ended his essay with the words, "such is the power of faith," wrote his name and set down the amount of his contribution after it.

"Ten thousand dollars!" — it was Mrs. Thornton speaking, as she took the check from Helena. She turned quickly to her husband. "Robert, have you your checkbook here?"

Thornton shook his head.

"No, dear," he said. "I'm afraid I haven't."

"Well, it doesn't matter," said Mrs. Thornton brightly. "You can use one of Mr. Madison's checks and write the name of your own bank on it — you've often done that, you know."

"A suggestion," said Madison to himself, "for which I thank you, Mrs. Thornton — it sounds so much less crude coming from you than from me." But aloud he said courteously, "Take my pen, Mr. Thornton."

"Thank you," said Thornton, as Madison placed it in his hand.

Mrs. Thornton and her husband had their heads together now, and were whispering — Thornton with his eyes on Helena, who sat with lowered head, twirling Madison's check in her hands. Then Thornton drew the checkbook toward him, scratched out the printed name of the bank that it bore, wrote in another, and went on filling out the check.

"Eeny-meeny-miny-mo," said Madison to himself. "The suspense is awful. How much does he raise the ante? Next to the miracle, this is the first real thrill I've had — I feel like an elevator starting down quick."

As Madison had done, Thornton tore out the check and handed it to Helena. Helena stared at it, lifted her eyes to Thornton, flushed — and looked down at the check again.

"Fifty thousand," she murmured breathlessly.

"Splendid!" cried Madison enthusiastically, rising from his chair and pushing the newly established record of contributions toward Thornton. "Splendid! There's sixty thousand of the five hundred already. Splendid!"

Young Holmes ran toward his parents.

"I want to give too, dad," he whispered. "I want to give too."

"Reckon so," said Holmes, getting up heavily. "Reckon so — an' I was a-goin' to. I ain't got much though," he added timorously, as his hand went into his pocket.

There was a little exclamation from Helena, and she moved a step forward as though to interpose. Madison looked at her quickly — and quietly stepped around the table, placing himself between her and Holmes; and, facing Holmes, leaned over the table from the far side toward the other.

"It's not the amount, Holmes," he said kindly. "In the broad, true sense the amount counts for nothing — all cannot give the same."

"Yes," said Holmes. "Reckon that's the way I feel." He counted the bills in his hand, and dropped them into the little japanned box; then scrawled his name in the book beneath Thornton's, adding the amount — eight dollars.

Madison looked around the group benignantly.

"I think they should know out there what we have done," he said, pointing toward the lawn. "Let us go and tell them, not in any set speech, but just simply — each of us speaking to a few — the few will tell others. Shall we go?"

"Yes," said Mrs. Thornton. "Yes; let us tell them." She turned to Helena and kissed her. "Try and come often to see me, dear — we shall be here now for a little while at least. Is it asking too much? Robert will bring you back and forth from the village. And perhaps, if I may, I will come out here to see you — may I?"

"I shall be very glad to do as my wife suggests," said Thornton, holding out his hand. "You will come, Miss Vail?"

"You are very good, both of you," Helena answered simply. She raised her eyes to Thornton — her hand was still in his. "Yes, I will try to come."

"Oh, break away!" muttered Madison impatiently — but silently. He stepped to the door and opened it. "Will you lead the way, Mrs. Thornton?" he said calmly.

Thornton and his wife passed out; and the Holmes, with clumsy, earnest words upon their lips to Helena, followed. Madison hung back — then stepped quickly to Helena.

"Tear up that check of mine so small you can't find the pieces, Helena," he said hurriedly; "and send Thornton's right off to any old bank you like in New York. Endorse it, and write them a note saying you wish to open an account. Enclose your signature, and tell them to mail back the bank-book, a checkbook, deposit slips and all that. They'll know by the newspapers that Thornton's subscribed fifty thousand before they get the check, and they'll feel honored to be your depository. Do it tonight, understand?"

"Yes," said Helena, nodding her head. "I'll see to it all right." Then, a little perturbed: "But those poor Holmes and their eight dollars, Doc, I —"

"Now don't be greedy, Helena," said Madison cheerfully. "You mustn't expect everybody to hand out ten and fifty thousand, just because Thornton and I did — try and appreciate the little things of life too."

"Oh!" exclaimed Helena angrily. "Doc Madison, I'd like to —"

"Yes, all right, of course," interrupted Madison, grinning. "Good-bye, that's all — I'm off — see, they're waiting for me" — and leaving Helena with an outraged little flush upon her cheek, he hurried through the door after the others.

XIV

KNOTTING THE STRINGS

*I*t is a very old saying, and therefore of course indisputably true, that some have greatness thrust upon them. True of men, it is, in one instance at least, true of places — Needley, from an unheard of, modest, innocuous and unassuming little hamlet, leaped in a flash into the focus of the world's eyes. In huge headlines the papers in every city of every State carried it on their front pages. And while the first astounding dispatch from the metropolitan newspaper man was being copied by leading dailies everywhere, there came on top of it, clinching its veracity beyond possibility of doubt, the news that Robert Thornton, the well known Chicago multi-millionaire, had given fifty thousand dollars to the cause. A man, much less a multi-millionaire, does not give fifty thousand dollars for a bubble, so the managing editors of the leading dailies rushed for their star reporters — and the star reporters rushed for Needley — and the red-haired, sorrowful-faced man in the Needley station grew haggard, tottered on the verge of collapse, and, between the sheafs of flimsy that the reporters fought for the opportunity of pushing at him, wired desperately for a relief.

Needley awoke and came to life — as from the dead. There was bustle, activity, and suppressed and unsuppressed excitement on every hand — the Waldorf Hotel once more opened its doors — the Congress Hotel was already full.

The reporters interviewed everybody with but one exception — the Patriarch.

They interviewed Madison — and Madison talked to them gravely, quietly, a little self-deprecatingly, a little abashed at the thought of personal exploitage.

"I wouldn't be interviewed at all," he told them, "if it were not that mankind at large is entitled to every bit of evidence that can be obtained. Yes; I gave what I could afford, but it was Holmes, a poor man, who gave most of all — have you seen him? Myself? What does that matter? I am unknown, my personality, unlike Mr. Thornton's, can carry no weight. I am, I suppose, what you might call a rolling stone, a world wanderer. My parents left me a moderate fortune, and I have traveled pretty well and pretty constantly all over the world during the last twelve or fifteen years. How did I come to Needley? Well, you can call it luck, or something more than that, whichever way it appeals to you. I was feeling seedy, a little off-color, and I started down for a rest and lay-off in Maine. I happened to ask a man in Portland if he knew of a quiet place. He meant to be humorous, I imagine. He said Needley was the quietest place he knew of. I took him at his word."

"But how do you account for these miraculous cures?" they asked.

"You have seen them — the results," Madison replied. "You know the cures to be living, vital, irrefutable facts — don't you?"

"Yes," they agreed.

"Then," said Madison, "there can be but one answer — faith. There is no other — faith. Are we not, in view of what has happened, of what exists before our very eyes, forced to the belief that faith is the greatest thing, the most potential factor in the world?"

"And do you believe then that all who come here will be cured?"

Madison shook his head.

"Ah, no," he said; "far from it. Many will come with but the semblance of faith, and for those there can be no cure — that is evident on the face of it, is it not?"

They interviewed Thornton — and Thornton, too, talked to them, but the very presence of Mrs. Thornton was weightier far than words.

They interviewed the Holmes, and they interviewed Needley individually and collectively; and they interviewed Helena — but they did not interview the Patriarch. Here Helena barred their way — they were free to enter the cottage, to copy the names, the record of gifts inscribed in the book, already a long list for Needley had required no other incentive to give than the example that had been set — but that was all. Quietly, with demure simplicity, Helena, prompted by Madison, like a priestess who guards some holy, inner shrine, told them that sensational notoriety had no place there — and the notoriety for that very cause became the greater! Not that they were denied a sight of the Patriarch's venerable and saintly form — they were permitted to catch glimpses of him on the beach, on the lawn, walking with bowed head in meditation, a figure whose simple majesty inspired words and columns of glowing tribute — but from personal contact, Helena and the Flopper, always in attendance, warded them off; retreating always to the privacy of the cottage, to the inner rooms.

All this had taken four days; and now, on the fourth day, there came to Needley the vanguard of those who sought this new healing power — just a few of them, two or three, like far, outflung skirmishers evidencing the presence of the army corps to follow. With the reporters, as far as Madison was concerned, it was simple enough; he had but to let them go their way, to let them revel in the stories that were on every tongue, to let them view with their own eyes *facts*, while he, modestly and diffidently, full of quiet earnestness, effaced himself, never thrusting himself forward, talking to them only when they pressed him — but the handling of the sufferers who would flock to Needley in response to a newspaper publicity and endorsement that had been beyond his wildest dreams, was quite another matter. Madison viewed the first arrivals — brought in from the station on cot beds to the Waldorf Hotel — and retired to his room in the Congress Hotel to wrestle with the niceties and minutiæ of the problem.

"You see," said Madison to the tip of his cigar, as he tilted back his chair and extended his legs full length with his heels comfortably up on the table edge, "you see, I believe in faith all right — and that's no josh. But the trouble with faith is that it's about the scarcest article on earth — and I haven't got anymore Floppers to lead the way." Madison adroitly sent the cigar ash through the window with a tap of his forefinger on the body of the cigar — he frowned, and for a long time sat musingly silent. Then he spoke again; this time addressing the toes of his boots: "With the house sold out for the season, the box-office doing itself proud and the audience crazy over the first two acts, how about Act Three — h'm? — how about Act Three? Kind of a delicate proposition, the staging of Act Three — and it's time for the curtain to go up. I can hear 'em stamping out front now. I can't pull off anymore orgies like last Monday afternoon, even if I wanted to — but everybody's got to have a run for their money. Say, how about Act Three?"

Madison burned up quite a little tobacco in the interval before supper, and quite a little more afterward before the setting for his perplexing "Third Act" appeared to unfold itself satisfactorily before his mind — indeed, it was close onto half past ten when, by a roundabout way, he very cautiously and silently approached the Patriarch's cottage.

In the front of the cottage, the Shrine-room, as he christened it, and the Patriarch's sleeping room were both dark. Madison passed around to the beach side — here, Helena's room was dark too, but in the Flopper's window, the end room next to the kitchen and woodshed, there was a light. The night was warm, and, though the shade was drawn, the window was open. Madison whistled softly, and the Flopper stuck out his head.

"Hello, Flopper," said Madison; "come out here — I want to have a talk with you. Helena in bed?"

"No; she's out," replied the Flopper.

"Well, hurry up!" said Madison. "Come around in front by the trellis where we can see the other fellow first if anybody happens to be strolling about."

Madison withdrew from the window and walked around to the front of the cottage. Here, a few yards from the porch, by the trellis, already beginning to be leafy green, was a rustic bench on which he seated himself. The moon was not full, but there was light enough to enable him to see across the lawn through the interposing row of maples, and, hidden by the shadows himself, the seat strategetically met his requirements.

Presently, the Flopper came out of the front door and joined him.

"Say, Doc," announced the Flopper abruptly, "de Patriarch's been askin' fer youse yesterday an' today."

"Asking?" repeated Madison.

"Sure," said the Flopper. "He can scrawl if he is blind, can't he? He scrawls yer name on de slate. We can't tell him nothin', an' he's kinder got de fidgets like he t'inks youse had flown de coop."

"That's so," said Madison. "It is rather difficult to communicate with him, isn't it? I guess we'll have to get him some raised letters."

"What's them?" inquired the Flopper.

"I don't know exactly," Madison answered. "I never saw any, but I believe they have such things. Been asking for me, has he? Well, I'll fix it to see him tomorrow. Where did you say Helena had gone?"

"I said she was out," said the Flopper. "If you ask me where, I'd say de same place as last night an' de night before — down to dat private car wid his nibs. Say, dere's some class to dat guy all right, an' I guess Helena ain't got her eyes shut."

"Hey!" ejaculated Madison. "What do you mean?"

"Well, he's got de rocks, ain't he?" declared the Flopper. "Why shouldn't she be after him? Dat's wot we're here fer, ain't it, de whole bunch of us? — an' she ain't t'rowin' us, is she, if she sees a chanst to pick up somet'ing on her own?"

Madison turned quickly on the Flopper.

"You mean," he said sharply, "that there's something going on between Helena and Thornton — already?"

"Aw, stop kiddin'!" said the Flopper. "Already! Wot's 'already' got to do wid it? We ain't none of us church members, are we? Say, where'd you pick up Helena yerself — and how long did it take youse? I don't know whether dere's anyt'ing goin' on or not — mabbe she's only gettin' lonely — youse ain't hung around her much lately, Doc."

Madison laughed suddenly.

"You're talking through your hat, Flopper," he said shortly. "You don't know Helena."

"It's a wise guy dat knows skirts," said the Flopper profoundly; then, with something approaching a sigh: "Say, Doc, dere's a lalapazoozoo, a peach down here."

"Hullo!" exclaimed Madison, shooting a hurried and critical glance at the Flopper in the moonlight. "What's this, Flopper — what's this? What have you been up to? You're supposed to be attending strictly to business."

"An' you needn't t'ink I ain't," asserted the Flopper. "But I can't stop de town fallin' over itself to bring de whole farmyard, an' eggs, an' butter, an' flour, an' everyt'ing else out here every mornin', can I? She's blown in twice wid cream fer de Patriarch."

"What's her name?" inquired Madison quizzically.

"Mamie Rodgers," said the Flopper. "She says her old man keeps a store in de village."

"I know her," nodded Madison. "Pretty girl and all right, Flopper. But mind what you're doing, that's all. I don't want any complications to queer things around here – understand? But let's get down to the business that I came out about – the lay from now on. You can put Helena wise."

"Sure," said the Flopper earnestly.

"Well then, listen," said Madison. "The patients have begun to arrive – there were three of them in today. There's no more circus parades – everything's under the tent after this. I want you to wean the Patriarch entirely from that front room – that's to be free for anybody to enter so's they can drink in atmosphere – and see the contribution box. But they don't see the Patriarch. Get his armchair into his own room, make him comfortable there – get the idea? Now, there's no consultation hours – the Patriarch can't be seen just by asking for him – the only chance they get at the Patriarch is by an exercise of patience that'll work their faith up to a pitch that'll do them some good. The harder it is to get a thing, the more it's worth and the more you want it – that's the principle. See?"

"Sure," said the Flopper, licking his lips.

"Sometimes," Madison went on, "you're to keep the Patriarch under cover for two or three days, while they hang around working themselves into a frenzy. And when they do see him they have to scramble for it. You don't lead him out to them – ever. Make them waylay him when you take him for a walk – make them crawl and hop and show they've got faith, make them believe they've got faith themselves – we'll get some more cures, or near-cures anyway, that way, and we won't get them any other way, and we've got to have some sort of cures coming along fairly regularly. Do you get me, Flopper? If there's a party on a cot a hundred yards away and he begs you to bring the Patriarch to him, say him nay. Everybody has got to get into the reserved paddock by themselves – tell them that no man can be cured who has not got the faith to reach the Patriarch by himself – tell them to get up and *walk* to him – tell them what you did."

"Swipe me!" said the Flopper. "Say, Doc, youse are de one an' only. I gotcher – put it up to *dem* everytime."

"Exactly," said Madison. "It's their move every minute – make them feel that if they don't get what they're after it's their own fault – that it's their own lack of faith that's to blame. And the longer they have to wait to see the Patriarch, the more they become impressed that faith is necessary, and – oh, well, psychology is the greatest jollier of them all."

"Eh?" inquired the Flopper. "I ain't on dere, Doc."

"It's very simple," smiled Madison, "They'll want to convince themselves that they *have* got faith, that it's all bottled up and ready to have the cork drawn when called for, and they'll prove it to themselves by laying an offering upon the shrine as evidence of faith *before* the goods are delivered."

"I gotcher!" said the Flopper enthusiastically. "Why say, Doc, dat's de way I'd do meself — swipe me, if I wouldn't!"

"That's the way nearly everybody would do," said Madison, laughing. "There's at least a few similar kinks common to our noble race — we're busy most of the time trying to fool ourselves one way or another. Well, that's about all. I can't lay out a program for every minute of the day — you and Helena have got to use your heads and work along that general idea. You play up your gratitude strong. And, oh yes — keep the altar box well baited. Let Helena put some of her near-diamond rings and joujabs in until we collect some genuine ones — and then keep the genuine ones going — change every day for variety, you know. And take the silver money out every time you see any in — not that we scorn it in the great aggregate, far from it — it's just psychology again, Flopper. I went to church once and sat beside a duck with a white waistcoat and chop whiskers, who wore the dollar sign sticking out so thick all over him that you couldn't see anything else; and when it came time for collection he peeled a bill off a roll the size of a house, and waited for the collection plate to come along. But he got his eye on the plate a couple of pews ahead and it was full of coppers and chicken feed, and he did the palming act with the bill slicker than a faro dealer — and whispered to me to change a quarter for him."

"And did you?" asked the Flopper anxiously.

"Oh, wake up, Flopper!" grinned Madison; then, suddenly: "Hullo! Who's that?"

Across the lawn, coming through the row of maples from the direction of the wagon track, appeared two figures.

"Dat's who," said the Flopper, after gazing an instant. "It's Helena an' Thornton."

"So it is," agreed Madison. "Get behind the trellis here then — it wouldn't do for him to see me out here at this time of night."

They rose noiselessly from the bench, and slipped quickly behind the trellis. Toward them, walking slowly came the two figures, Helena leaning on Thornton's arm. Thornton was talking, but in too low a tone to be overheard. Then a silence appeared to fall between the two, and it was not until they reached the porch, close to Madison and the Flopper, that either spoke again.

Then Thornton held out his hand.

"Good-night, Miss Vail — and good-bye temporarily," he said. "I suppose I shall be gone four or five days; I'm going up on the morning train, you know. I wish you'd go as often as you can to see Naida in the car while I'm away — will you? Her condition worries me, though she insists that she is completely cured, and she will not listen to any advice. I have an idea that she has overtaxed herself — apart from her hip disease, her heart was in a very critical state. You'll go to her, won't you?"

"Yes," said Helena, "of course, I will."

Their voices dropped lower, and for a moment only a murmur reached Madison; and then, with another "Good-night, Miss Vail," Thornton started back across the lawn.

Madison could hear Helena fumbling with the door latch, and by the time she had succeeded in opening the door the retreating figure of Thornton was a safe distance away. Madison called in a whisper:

"Here, Helena! Wait a minute!"

There was a quick, startled little exclamation from the doorway, and Helena came out hurriedly from the porch.

"Who's there?" she cried in a low voice. "Oh" — as they stepped into view — "you, Doc, and the Flopper! What were you doing behind that trellis?"

"Keeping out of Thornton's road," said Madison. "So he's going away, eh? What for?"

"Business," replied Helena. "Has to go to some meeting in Chicago — he's leaving his wife and the private car here. What did you come at this hour for?"

"Lines for the next act," said Madison; "but the Flopper's got it all, and he'll put you on." He stepped toward Helena and slipped his arm around her waist. "Come on, it's early yet, let's go for a little walk. The Flopper'll excuse us, and I —"

"I thought you said," Helena interrupted, disengaging herself quietly, "that we had to play the game to the limit and take no chances."

"Well, so I did," admitted Madison, and his arm crept around her again; "but I guess we've earned a little holiday and —"

"'Nix on that,' I think was what you said," said Helena with a queer little laugh, drawing away again. "And I really think you were right, Doc — we ought to play the game without breaking the rules, and so — good-night" — and she turned and ran from him into the cottage.

Madison stared after her in a sort of helpless state of chagrin.

"Mabbe," said the Flopper, "mabbe she's lonely."

XV

A MIRACLE OVERDONE

*H*elena sat in the Patriarch's room, and her piquant little face was pursed up into a scowl so daintily grim as to be almost ludicrous. The Patriarch, in his armchair, had been scrawling words upon the slate all evening – and she had been wiping them off! He scrawled another now – and mechanically, without looking at it, by way of answer she pressed his arm to appease him.

She had been restless all day, and she was restless now. What had induced her to treat Madison the way she had the night before? Pique, probably. No; it wasn't pique. It was just getting back at him – and he deserved it. He hadn't seemed to mind it much, though – he had only laughed and teased her about it that morning when he had joined the Patriarch and herself in their walk along the beach.

With her chin in her hands, she began to study the Patriarch through half closed eyes – deaf and dumb and blind – and somehow it all seemed excruciatingly funny and she wanted to laugh hysterically. He seemed to sense the fact that she was looking at him, and, with quick, instant intuition, he smiled and reached out his hand toward her.

Unconsciously, involuntarily, she drew back – then, recovering herself the next instant, she took his hand. Now, why had she done that? What was the matter with her? Again she felt that sudden impulse to scream, or laugh, or shout, or make some noise – it seemed as though she were penned in, smothered somehow, imprisoned. What *was* the matter? Nerves? She had never known what nerves were in all her life! Couldn't she play the game and act her part without making a fool of herself? She had played a part all her life, hadn't she? Maybe it was quite a shock to her system to take a place amongst really good and simple folk!

She laughed a little shortly – then rose abruptly from her chair, and began to walk up and down the room. The trouble was that the soft pedal was getting unbearable. That air of awed hush and solemnity, morning, noon and night, without anything to relieve it, was just a trifle too drastic and sudden a change in life for her to accept calmly and swallow in one dose without feeling any effects from it! If she could be transported now for an hour, say, to the Roost, or Heligman's and the turkey trot, or the Rivoli, or any old place – except Needley, Maine!

"Gee!" said Helena to herself. "If I don't break loose and kick the traces over for a minute or two, I'll be clawing the bars of a dippy asylum before I'm through — and just listen to the sweet, girlish language I'm using — I'd like to bite something!"

She turned impulsively to the door, stepped out into the hall, and called the Flopper from his room.

"Flopper, you go in there and stay with the Patriarch for awhile," she ordered curtly. "I'm going down on the beach to yell."

"Yell?" inquired the Flopper, blinking helplessly.

"I'm going outside to yell — *yell*. You know what 'yell' means, don't you?" she snapped.

"Swipe me!" observed the Flopper, gazing at her anxiously. "Skirts is all de same — youse never know wot dey'll do next. Wot you wanter yell fer?"

"You mind your own business and do as you're told!" said Helena tartly. "Go in there and stay with the Patriarch."

"Sure," said the Flopper, grinning a little now. "Sure t'ing — but youse needn't get on yer ear about it. Cheer up, mabbe de Doc'll be out tonight, an' if he don't hear youse yellin' himself will I tell him youse are out on de beach t'rowin' a fit?"

"No," Helena answered sharply; "tell him nothing — I'm out." Then, quite as quickly, changing her mind: "Yes; tell him I'm down there — or come and get me yourself" — and she walked abruptly into her own room.

"Now wot do youse t'ink of dat?" demanded the Flopper of the universe. He blinked at the door she had closed in his face. "Say," he asserted, with sublime inconsistency, "if Mamie Rodgers was like all de rest of dem, I'd t'row up me dukes before de gong rang." The Flopper went into the Patriarch's room, and took the chair beside the other that Helena had vacated. "Swipe me, if I wouldn't!" he added fervently, by way of confirmation.

Helena, in her own room, opened one of her trunks, lifted out the tray, worked somewhat impatiently down through several layers of yellow, paper-covered literature, that would have made the classics on the Patriarch's bookshelves shrivel up and draw their skirts hurriedly around them in righteous horror could they but have known or been capable of such intensely human characteristics, and finally produced a daintily jeweled little cigarette case and match box. She slammed the tray back, slammed the cover of the trunk down, snatched up a wrap, flung it over her head and shoulders — and left the cottage.

She ran down to the beach at top speed, as if she couldn't get there fast enough.

"And now I'm just going to yell and go crazy as much as ever I like!"

panted Helena to the rollers.

Instead, she sat down with her back to a rock, and opened her cigarette case. She took out a cigarette, extracted a match from the match box, lighted the match — and flung both cigarette and match from her.

"I don't want to be crazy — I don't know what I want," said Helena petulantly. Her chin went into her hands, and she stared wide-eyed at the breaking surf. "I wonder what it all means?" she murmured, with a mirthless little laugh.

Her thoughts began to run riot. What *did* it all mean? What was this faith? There was, there *must* be something in it. There was the Holmes boy — suppose it *was* only some nervous disorder — well, something had risen superior to whatever it was and had *cured* him. There was Naida Thornton — true, she was ill again — her heart, Mr. Thornton had said — but she could still walk, a thing she had not been able to do for a long time until she came to Needley.

Helena laughed again — oh, it was a good game! The Doc had made no mistake about that — but then, when it came to planting anything the Doc rarely did make a mistake. Fancy fifty thousand dollars in one haul! *Fifty thousand in one haul!* The bank had sent her a passbook with that amount to her credit. And that was only the beginning — hardly anybody had come yet, and already there was several hundred dollars more in real money that she had handed over to Madison from the offering box.

Money! They'd have more money than they'd know what to do with before they got through — there was nothing the matter with the game — all there was to do was to play it to a finish. And there wasn't the slightest risk about it — everything was given voluntarily. Oh, the game was all right — but somehow she wasn't happy — not nearly so happy as she had been in New York, even in lean periods when she and the Doc had been pressed for money. But, anyway, then they had been together, and fought, and laughed, and loved, and quarreled through flush times and bad.

Maybe that was it! The Doc! Of course, she loved him — she had loved him ever since she had known him. There was no secret about that — she loved him fiercely, passionately, more than she loved anything else in the world, with all the love she was capable of — more than he loved her — he seemed to accept her, too often, so casually, so indifferently, so much as a matter of course. He was so confidently and complacently sure of her — and she was not at all sure of him. She was only sure that he was quite right in being sure — she couldn't help loving him if she tried.

She had hardly seen anything of him since that night in the Roost before he had left for Needley — and he hadn't seemed to care much whether she did or not. That talk about playing the game and taking no chances was all bosh — there had been plenty of chances where it wouldn't have hurt the game any. Perhaps the little jolt she had given him last night, turning the tables a little, would wake him up a bit. Perhaps, as the Flopper had said, he would come out tonight, and —

"Helena! Helena!"

Helena sat suddenly upright — the noise of the surf muffled the sound of the voice, but that was probably Doc now — she could hear footsteps running from the direction of the cottage. Deliberately, Helena leaned back again against the rock, took out a cigarette and with no attempt to shade the flame of the match, rather to use it as a challenging beacon, held it to the cigarette — but for the second time she flung both match and cigarette hurriedly away. It wasn't Madison at all — it was only the Flopper.

"Say!" gasped the Flopper, blowing hard. "Why can't youse answer when yer called? Wot you tryin' ter do — light a bonfire ter save yer voice? Say, youse wanter get a wiggle on — beat it — quick! Dey're after you."

"What?" cried Helena sharply, jumping to her feet. "After me? Who? What do you mean?"

"I dunno," said the Flopper with sudden imperturbability — and evidently quite pleased with the agitation he had caused. "He talks like his mouth was full, an' he's got a scare t'rown inter him so's his teeth have got de jiggles."

Helena caught the Flopper's arm and shook him angrily.

"What are you talking about — what is it?" she demanded fiercely.

"It's de porter from de private car," said the Flopper, wriggling away from her. "He drove out here. De lady's on de toboggan — sick. She's askin' fer youse an' —"

Helena waited for no more. She raced to the cottage and around to the front. A wagon was standing before the porch; the Negro porter on the seat.

"What is it, Sam?" she called anxiously, as she came up. "Is Mrs. Thornton seriously ill?"

"Yas — yas'um, miss," Sam answered excitedly. "I done feel in mah bones she's gwine to die. Miss Harvey she done tole me to get a team an' drive foh you-all like de debbil."

Without waste of words, Helena clambered in beside him.

"Then drive," she said shortly. "Drive as fast as you can."

At first, as they drove along, Helena plied Sam with questions — and then lapsed into silence. The man did not know very much — only that

Mrs. Thornton had been taken suddenly ill, and that the nurse had sent him on the errand that had brought him to the cottage. A turmoil of conflicting emotions filled Helena's mind, obtruding upon her anxiety, for she had grown to care a great deal for Naida Thornton — this was a complication that Doc Madison must know about — Thornton had left that morning and was already far away — the newspaper men, or some of them at least, were still in the town — and there were so many things else — they all came crowding upon her, as she clung to her seat in the jolting wagon. But Doc must know — that rose a paramount considera- tion. It seemed an age, an eternity before they stopped finally at the station.

She sprang out and turned to Sam.

"Sam," she directed hurriedly, "you go back to the Congress Hotel and get Mr. Madison. Mr. Madison is a friend of Mr. Thornton's, you know. Go about it quietly — you needn't let anyone know what you came for. You can tell Mr. Madison what the trouble is — and tell him that I sent you, and that I am here. Do you understand?"

"Yas'um, mum," said Sam impressively. "Just you done leab all that to me, missy."

Across the track on the siding, the private car was dimly lighted, the window curtains down. Helena crossed the track and mounted the steps. As she reached the platform, Miss Harvey, who had evidently heard her coming, opened the door and drew her quietly inside.

A glance at the nurse's face brought a sudden chill to Helena's heart. Miss Harvey, capable, controlled, grave, smiled at her a little sadly.

"I sent for you, Miss Vail," she said in a low tone, "because Mrs. Thornton has been asking for you incessantly ever since the attack came on three-quarters of an hour ago."

"You mean," said Helena, "that — that there is —"

"No hope," the nurse completed. "I am afraid there is none — it is her heart. The condition has been aggravated by her activity during the last few days since she has been able to walk — though I have done everything within my power to keep her quiet." Miss Harvey laid her hand on Helena's arm. "There is one thing, Miss Vail, I feel that I must say to you, in justice both to you and to myself, before you see her. Whatever my personal ideas may be of what has taken place here, my professional duty as a nurse demanded that I send for a doctor at once, and I want you to know that is what I did, though I have not been successful in getting one. There is no doctor here, so I telegraphed; but the doctor at Barton's Mills is away."

"Yes," said Helena mechanically.

"I just wanted you to understand," said Miss Harvey. "Will you come and see Mrs. Thornton now?"

"Does she know," whispered Helena, as she followed the nurse down the corridor of the car, "does she know that — how ill she is?"

"Yes," Miss Harvey answered simply. She stopped before a compartment door, opened it softly, and, stepping aside, motioned Helena to enter.

A little cry rose to Helena's lips that she choked back somehow, and a mist for a moment blinded her eyes — then she was kneeling beside the brass bed, and was holding in both her own the hand that was stretched out to her.

"Helena — dear — I am so glad you came," said Mrs. Thornton faintly. "I — I am not going to get better, and there are some things I want to say to you."

"Oh, but you are," returned Helena quickly, smiling bravely now. "You mustn't say that."

Mrs. Thornton shook her head.

"Dear," she said, "I know. And I know that what I have to say I must say quickly." Her voice seemed to grow suddenly stronger with a great earnestness. "Listen, dear. This must not make any difference to this wonderful work that has just begun here. I was cured of my hip disease — perfectly cured — no one can deny that — this is my own fault, I have overdone it — I would not listen to reason — to do what I have done in the last few days, when for a year and a half I had never moved a step, was more than my heart could stand. I should have been more quiet — but I was so glad, so happy — and I wanted to tell everybody — I wanted all the world to know, so that others could find the joy that I had found."

She paused — and Helena sought for words that, somehow, would not come.

The nurse was bending over the bed on the other side, and Mrs. Thornton turned her head toward Miss Harvey now. She smiled gently, as though to rob her words of any possible hurt.

"Nurse, I want — to be alone with Miss Vail for just a moment."

Miss Harvey, doubtful, hesitated.

"Only for a moment," pleaded Mrs. Thornton. "You can stay just outside the door."

Reluctantly, Miss Harvey complied, and left the room.

Mrs. Thornton pressed Helena's hand tightly.

"Listen, dear — this must not make any difference. It — it is the one thing that will make me happy now — to know that. I — I have written a little note to Robert about it, to be given to him. Oh, if I could only have lived to help — I should have tried so hard to be worthy to have a part in it. Not like you, dear, with your sweetness and nobleness, for

God seems to have singled you out for this — but just to have had a little part. How wonderful it would have been, bringing peace and health and gladness where only sorrow and misery was before, and — and —"

Mrs. Thornton's eyes closed, and she lay for a moment quiet.

A blackness seemed to settle upon Helena — and how cold it was! She shivered. Her dark eyes, wide, tearless now, stared, startled, dazed, at the white face on the pillow crowned with its mass of golden hair. Her sweetness! Her nobleness! Helena's lips half parted and her breath came in quick, fierce, little gasps — it seemed as though she had been struck a blow that she could not quite understand because somehow it had numbed her senses — only there was a hurt that curiously, strangely seemed to mock as it stabbed with pain.

"There is Robert" — Mrs. Thornton spoke again — "I am sure he will do as I have asked him to do about this, but — you can have a great deal of influence with him. It — it perhaps may seem a strange thing to say, but I pray that you two may be brought very close to each other. Robert needs a good, true woman so much in his life — and I — we — we — my illness — we have never had a home in its truest sense. Yes, it is strange for me perhaps to talk like this — but it is in my heart. I would like to think of you both engaged in this wonderful work together."

Again, through exhaustion, Mrs. Thornton stopped — and Helena, from gazing at the other's pallid countenance in a sort of involuntary, frightened fascination, dropped her head suddenly upon the bed-spread and hid her face.

Mrs. Thornton's hand found Helena's head and rested upon it.

"I would like to see Robert happy," she murmured, after a little silence. "Riches do not make happiness — they are so sad and empty a thing when the heart is empty. I know he would be happy with you — he has spoken so much of you lately — perhaps — perhaps —"

Mrs. Thornton's voice was very faint — the words reached Helena plainly enough as words, but they seemed to reach her consciousness in an unreal, unnatural, blunted way, comalike — pregnant of significance, yet with the significance itself elusive, evading her.

"A good woman," whispered Mrs. Thornton, "I have tried to be a good woman — but — but my life, our wealth, our position has made it so artificial. You have never known these things, dear — and so you are just as God made you — good woman, so pure, so wonderful in your freshness and your innocence. Robert's life has been so barren — so barren. I would like to know that — that it will not always be so. Oh, if it could only be that you and he should carry on this great, glad work together — and love should come into his life — and yours — and sunshine — promise me, dear, that —"

The voice died away. Helena, with head still buried, waited for Mrs. Thornton to speak again. It seemed she waited for a great length of time — and yet there was no such thing as time. It seemed as though she were transported to a place of great and intense blackness where it was miserably cold and chill, and she stood alone and lost, and strove to find her way — and there was no way — only blackness everywhere, immeasurable. She lifted her head suddenly, desperately, to shake the unreality from her — and her eyes fell upon the gentle face, peaceful, smiling, calm, and so *still* — and a startled, frightened cry rang from her lips.

There was the quick, hurried rush of someone coming into the room, and the nurse brushed by her and bent instantly over the bed — after that, quite soon after that it seemed, and yet it might have been quite a little while, she found herself outside in the corridor and the nurse was speaking to her.

"Sam is still out there," said Miss Harvey gently. "I told him to keep the team. You cannot help me, and I want you to go home, dear. And will you ask Sam to go for Mr. Madison at the hotel on the way back — I do not know who else I can call upon for advice."

"I've sent for him already," said Helena numbly.

"Have you, dear?" Miss Harvey said. "That was very thoughtful of you — I'm sure he'll be here presently then. And now, dear, it is much better that you should go."

There were no tears in Helena's eyes as she stepped down from the car vestibule to the tracks — only a drawn misery in her face. That was Doc over there, pacing up and down on the platform in the darkness — wasn't it weird the way his cigar glowed bright and then went out and then glowed bright again — like a gigantic firefly!

She was across the tracks before he saw her, then, hurrying forward, he helped her to the platform.

"Well?" he asked quickly.

Helena did not answer.

Madison took the cigar from his lips, leaned forward, and peered into Helena's face — then drew back with a low whistle.

"Dead?" he said.

Helena nodded.

"Miss Harvey wants to see you," she said.

"Say," said Madison slowly, "first crack out of the box this looks bad, don't it? If this gets around here without a muffler on it, it might make the railroad companies hang fire with those circulars for excursion rates to Needley — what?"

"I — I think I hate you!" Helena cried out suddenly, passionately.

"She's — she's dead — and that's all you think about!"

Madison stared at Helena for a moment calmly.

"Now, look here, Helena," said he quietly, "don't get excited. Of course I'm sorry — I'm not a brute and I've got feelings — but I can't afford to lose my head. Something's got to be done, and done quick. We don't want this headlined in every paper in the United States tomorrow morning — Thornton wouldn't want it either. You say Miss Harvey wants to see me? Well, that'll help some — she'll probably do as she's told, and —"

Madison paused abruptly, gazed abstractedly at the private car across the tracks on the siding, and pulled at his cigar.

Helena watched him in silence — a little bitterly. That quick, clever, cunning brain of his was at work again — scheming — scheming — always scheming — and Naida Thornton was dead.

"I'll tell you," said Madison, speaking again as abruptly as he had stopped. "It's simple enough. There's a westbound train due in an hour or so — we'll couple the private car onto that and send it right along to Chicago. What the authorities don't know won't hurt them. There's no reason for anybody except Thornton to know what's happened till she gets there — I'll wire him. The main thing is that the car won't be here in the morning, and that'll take a little of the intimate touch of Needley off. It might well have happened on her way home — journey too much for her — left too soon — see? Thornton'll see it in the right light because he's got fifty thousand dollars worth of faith in what's going on here — get that? He won't want to harm the 'cause.' There'll be some publicity of course, we can't help that — but it won't hurt much — and Thornton can gag a whole lot of it — he'd want to anyway for his own sake. Now then, kid, there's Sam over there — you pile into the wagon and go home, while I get busy — and don't you say a word about this, even to the Flopper."

And so Helena drove back to the Patriarch's cottage that night, a little silent figure in the back seat of the wagon — and her hands were locked tightly together in her lap — and to her, as she drove over the peaceful, moonlit road, and under the still, arched branches of the trees in the wood that hid the starlight, came again and again the words of one who had gone, who perhaps knew better now — "you are as God made you."

XVI

A FLY IN THE OINTMENT

*T*he days passed. And with the days, morning, noon and night, they came by almost every train, the sick and suffering, the lame, the paralytics and the maimed — a steady influx by twos and threes and fours — from north over the Canadian boundary line, from the far west, and from the southernmost tip of the Florida coast. No longer on the company's schedule was Needley a flag station — it was a regular stop, and its passenger traffic returns were benign and pleasing things in the auditor's office. And it was an accustomed sight now, many times a day — what had once been a strange, rare spectacle — that slow procession wending its way from the station to the town, some carried, some limping upon crutches, all snatching at hope of life and health and happiness again. Needley, perforce, had become a vast boarding house, as it were — there were few homes indeed that did not harbor their quota of those who sought the "cure."

But there were others too who came — who were not sick — who had not faith — who came to laugh and peer and peek. Pleasure yachts dropped their anchors in the cove around the headland from the Patriarch's cottage — and their dingeys brought women decked out *de rigeur* in middy blouses and sailor collars, and nattily attired gentlemen whose only claim to seamanship was the clothes, or rather, the costumes that they wore.

They came laughing, supercilious, tolerant, contemptuous, pitying the inanity of those they held less strongly-minded than themselves who should be taken in by so apparent, glaring and monstrous a fake. They came because it was the rage, the thing to do, quite the thing to do, quite a necessary part of the summer's itinerary. But that they, should they have been sick, would ever have dreamed of coming there was too perfectly ridiculous an idea for words. How strange a thing is the human animal!

They came in their rather cruel, merciless gaiety — and they left sobered and impressed; the ladies holding their embroidered parasols at a less jaunty angle; the men with lightened pockets, their names enrolled in the contribution book in that quiet, simple room, whose door was open, whose cash-box was unguarded, where none asked them to either enter or withdraw. They came and found no air of charlatanism such as they had looked for — only a peaceful, unostentatious, patient air of sincerity that left them remorseful and abashed. They came and went, a source of revenue not counted on or thought of before by Madison; but a source that swelled the coffers, brimming fuller day by day, to overflowing.

In three weeks from the night of Mrs. Thornton's death, which had had at least no visible effect on Needley, Needley was metamorphosed – with a spontaneity, so to speak, that astounded even Madison himself – into something that approximated very closely in reality the word-picture he had drawn of it that night in the Roost. Madison looked upon his work and saw that it was pleasing beyond his dreams. Money was pouring in – no single breath of suspicion came to disquiet him. Even the cures were working satisfactorily – even Pale Face Harry, who had become great friends with the farmer at whose house he boarded, and who now spent most of his time in the fields, was showing an improvement – Pale Face Harry coughed less. The Flopper was as happy as a lark – and Mamie Rodgers blushed now at mention of the name of Coogan. Helena, demure, adored by all who saw her, went daily about her housework in the cottage, and waited upon the Patriarch with gentle tenderness; while the Patriarch, docile, full of supreme trust and confidence in everyone, radiant in Helena's companionship, was as putty in their hands. And so Madison looked upon his work and saw no flaw – but with the days he grew ill at ease.

"It's too easy," he told himself. "I guess that's it – it's too easy. The whole show runs itself. Why, there's nothing to do but count the cash!"

And yet in his heart he knew that wasn't it – it was Helena. Helena was beginning to trouble him a little. She was playing the game all right – playing it to the limit – and making a hit at every performance. Her name was on every tongue, and men and women alike spoke of her sweetness, her goodness, her loveliness. Well, that was all right, Helena was a star no matter where you put her – but something was the matter. Helena wasn't the Helena of a month ago back in little old New York. He hadn't managed to get a dozen words with her since that night on the station platform, without taking chances and gaining admission to the cottage through the Flopper's window after dark – and then she had held him at arm's length.

"The matter with me?" she had said. "There isn't anything the matter with me – is there? I'm – I'm playing the game."

It certainly couldn't be grief over Mrs. Thornton's death – she had begun to act that way before Mrs. Thornton died – that night when she came home with Thornton, and he and the Flopper were behind the trellis. Thornton! Had Thornton anything to do with it, after all? No – Madison had laughed at it then, and he had much more reason to laugh at it now. Thornton was still in Chicago, and hadn't been back to Needley.

For three weeks this sort of thing occupied a considerably larger share of Madison's thoughts than he was wont to allow even the most vexing problems to disturb his usually imperturbable and complacent self — and then one afternoon, he smiled a little grimly, and, leaving the hotel, started along the road toward the Patriarch's cottage.

"What Helena needs is — a jolt!" said Madison to himself. "I guess her trouble is one of those everlasting feminine kinks that all women since Adam's wife have patted themselves on the back over, because they think it's a dark veil of mystery that is beyond the acumen of brute man to understand. That's what the novelists write pages about — wade right in up to the armpits in it — feminine psychology — great! And the women smile commiseratingly at the novelist — the idea of a man even pretending to understand them — kind of a blooming merry-go-round and everybody happy! Feminine psychology! I guess a little masculine kick-up is about the right dope! What the deuce have I been standing for it for? I don't have to — I don't have to go around making sheep's-eyes at her — what? She wants grabbing up and being rushed right off her feet *à la* Roost, and — hello, Mr. Marvin, how are you today!" — he had halted beside a middle-aged man who was sitting on the grass at the roadside.

"Better, Mr. Madison, better," returned the man, heartily. "Really very much better."

"Fine!" said Madison.

"We all saw the Patriarch today — God bless him!" said Marvin. "We've been waiting out there two days, you know — that woman with the bad back got up off her stretcher."

"Splendid!" exclaimed Madison enthusiastically. "And the glorious thing about it is that there's no reason why everybody can't be cured if they'll only come here in the right spirit."

"That's so!" agreed Marvin. "None are so blind as those who won't see — they're in utter blackness compared with the physical blindness of that grand and marvelous man. I'm going home myself in another week — better than ever I was in my life. It was stomach with me, you know — doctors said there wasn't any chance except to operate, and that an operation was too slim a chance to be worth risking it." He got up and laughed, carefree, joyous. "God-given place down here, isn't it? Clean — that's it. Clean air, clean-souled people, clean everything you see or do or hear. Say, it kind of opens your eyes to real living, doesn't it — it's the luxuries and the worries and the pace and the damn-fooleries that kill. Well, I'm going along back now to get some of Mrs. Perkins' cream — clean, rich cream — and homemade bread and butter — imagine me with an appetite and able to eat!"

He laughed again — and Madison joined him in the laugh, slapping him a cordial good-bye on the shoulder.

Madison started on once more — but now his progress was slow, frequently interrupted, for he stopped a score of times to chat and exchange a few words with those whom he passed on the road. There were cheery faces everywhere — even those of the sufferers who straggled out along the road coming back from the Patriarch's cottage. It was a cheery afternoon, warm and balmy and bright — everything was cheery. The farmers, their vocations for the moment changed, waved their whips at him and shouted friendly pleasantries as they drove by with those who were unable to make the trip from the Patriarch's unaided.

Madison began to experience a strange, exhilarating sense of uplift upon him, a sort of rather commendatory and gratified feeling with himself. Marvin had hit it pretty nearly right with his "clean-wholesome-ness" idea — it kind of made one feel good to be a part of it. Madison, for the time being, relegated Helena and his immediate mission to a secondary place in his thoughts.

Young girls, young men, middle-aged men, elderly women, all ages of both sexes he passed as he went along; some alone, some in couples, some in little groups, some on crutches, some in wheel-chairs, some walking without extraneous aid — he had turned into the woods now, and he could see them strewn out all along the wagon track under the cool, interlacing branches overhead.

Now he stepped aside to let a wagon pass him, and answered the farmer's call and the smile of the occupants in kind; now someone stopped to tell him again the story of the afternoon — there had been cures that day and the Patriarch had come amongst them. Some laughed, some sang a little, softly, to themselves — all smiled — all spoke in glad, hopeful words, clean words — there seemed no base thought in any mind, only that cleanness, that wholesomeness that had so appealed to Marvin — that somehow Madison found he was taking a delight in responding to, and, because it afforded him whimsical pleasure, chose to pretend that he was quite a genuine exponent of it himself.

He reached the end of the wagon track, and paused involuntarily on the edge of the Patriarch's lawn as he came out from the trees. Like low, lulling music came the distant, mellowed noise of waters, the breaking surf. And the cottage was a bower of green now, clothed in ivy and vine — upon the trellises the early roses were budding — fragrance of growing things blended with the salt, invigorating breeze from the ocean. And upon the lawn, flanked with its sturdy maples, all in leaf, that toned the

sunshine in soft-falling shadows, stood, or sat, or reclined on cots, the
supplicants who still tarried though the Patriarch had gone. And now
one came reverently out of the cottage door from that room that was
never closed; now another went in — and still another.

Madison smiled suddenly, broadly, with immense satisfaction and
contentment — and then his eyes fixed quite as suddenly on the single-
seated buggy that was coming toward him on the driveway across the
lawn. That was Mamie Rodgers driving — and that was Helena beside
her.

Madison recalled instantly the object of his visit — and instantly he
whistled a rather surprised little whistle under his breath. How alluringly
Helena's brown hair coiled in wavy wealth upon her head; there wasn't
any need of rouge for color in the oval face; the dark eyes were soft and
deep and glorious; and she sat there in a little white muslin frock as
dainty as a medallion from a master's brush.

"Say," said Madison to himself, "say, I never quite got it before. Say,
she's — she's lovely — and that's my Helena. It's no wonder Thornton
stared at her that day we touched him for the fifty, and" — suddenly —
"damn Thornton!"

But the buggy was beside him now, and he lifted his hat as Mamie
Rodgers pulled up the horse.

"Good afternoon, Miss Rodgers," he said. "Good afternoon, Miss
Vail — how is the Patriarch today?"

"He is very well, thank you," Helena answered — and being custodian
of the whip brushed a fly off the horse's flank.

"I was just coming out to pay you a little visit," remarked Madison,
trying to catch her eye.

"Oh, I'm *so* sorry!" said Helena sweetly, still busy with the fly. "Mamie
is going to take me for a drive — and afterwards we are going to her
house for tea."

"Oh!" said Madison, a little blankly.

Helena smiled at him, nodded, and touched the horse with the whip
— and then she leaned suddenly out toward him, as the buggy started
forward.

"Oh, Mr. Madison," she called, "I forgot to tell you! I had a letter
from Mr. Thornton today — and he's coming back tomorrow."

XVII

IN WHICH HELENA TAKES A RIDE

*T*he wind kissed Helena's face, bringing dainty color to her cheeks, tossing truant wisps of hair this way and that, as the car swept onward. But she sat strangely silent now beside Thornton at the steering wheel.

It seemed to her that she was living, not her own life, not life as she had known and looked upon it in the years before, but living, as it were, in a strange, suspended state that was neither real nor unreal, as in a dream that led her, now through cool, deep forests, beside clear, sparkling streams where all was a great peace and the soul was at rest, serene, untroubled, now into desolate places where misery had its birth and shame was, where there was fear, and the mind stood staggered and appalled and lost and knew not how to guide her that she might flee from it all.

At moments most unexpected, as now when motoring with Thornton in the car that he had brought back with him on, his return to Needley, when laughing at the Flopper's determined pursuit of Mamie Rodgers, when engaged in the homely, practical details of housekeeping about the cottage, there came flashing suddenly upon her the picture of Mrs. Thornton lying on the brass bed in the car compartment that night, every line of the pale, gentle face as vivid, as actual as though it were once more before her in reality, and in her ears rang again, stabbing her with their unmeant condemnation, those words of sweetness, love and purity that held her up to gaze upon herself in ghastly, terrifying mockery.

It stupefied her, bewildered her, frightened her. She seemed, for days and weeks now, to be drifting with a current that, eddying, swirling, swept her this way and that. How wonderful it was, this life she was now leading compared with the old life — so full of the better things, the better emotions, the better thoughts that she had never known before! How monstrous in its irony that she was leading it to *steal*, that she might play her part in a criminal scheme for a criminal end! And yet, somehow, it did not all seem sham, this part she played — and that very thought, too, frightened her. Why was it now that Madison's oft-attempted, and as oft-repulsed, kiss upon her lips was something from which she shrank and battled back, no longer from a sense of pique or to bring him to his knees, but because something new within her, intangible, that she did not understand, rose up against it! Why did she

do this — she, who had known the depths, who had known no other
guide or mentor than the turbulent, passionate love she had yielded
him and in her abandonment had once found contentment! Was her
love for him gone? Or, if it was not that — what was it?

What was it? A week, another, two more, a month had slipped away
since Thornton had returned, and there had been so much of genuine-
ness crowded into this sham part of hers that it seemed at times the part
itself was genuine. She had come to love that little room of hers, love
it for its dear simplicity, the white muslin curtains, the rag mat, the
patch-quilt on the bed; those daily duties of a woman, that she had never
done before, that she had at first looked at askance, brought now a sense
of keen, housewifely pride; the gentle patience of the Patriarch, his love
for her, his simple trust in her had found a quick and instant response
in her own heart, and daily her affection for him had grown; and there
was Thornton — this man beside her, whose companionship somehow
she seemed to crave for, who, in his grave, quiet manliness, seemed a
sort of inspiration to her, who seemed in a curious way to appease a
new hunger that had come to her for association, for contact with better
thoughts and better ideals.

What was it? Environment? Yes; there must be something in that. It
was having its effect even on Pale Face Harry and the Flopper. What
was it that Harry, a surprisingly lusty farmhand now, had said to her a
week or so ago: "Say, Helena, do you ever feel that while you was trying
to kid the crowd about this living on the square, you was kind of getting
kidded yourself? I dunno! I ain't coughed for a month — honest. But it
ain't only that. Say — I dunno! Do you ever feel that way?"

Yes; there must be something in environment. The old life had never
brought her thoughts such as these, thoughts that had been with her
now almost since the first day she had come to Needley — this disquiet,
this self-questioning, these sudden floods of condemnatory confusion;
and, mingling with them, a startled thrill, a strange, half-glad, half-pre-
monitory awakening, a vague pronouncement that innately it might be
true that she was not what she *really* was — but what all those around
her held her to be — what Mrs. Thornton had said she was — and —

Her fingers closed with a quick, fierce pressure on the arm-rest of her
seat — and she shifted her position with a sudden, involuntary movement.

Thornton, a road-map tacked on a piece of board and propped up at
his feet, raised his head, and, self-occupied himself, had apparently not
noticed her silence, for he spoke irrelevantly.

"I hope you won't mind if the road is a bit rougher than usual for a
few miles," he said; "but you know we decided we didn't like the looks

of the weather at teatime, and according to the map, which labels it
'rough but passable,' this is a short cut that will lop off about ten miles
and take us back to Needley through Barton's Mills."

"Of course, I don't mind," Helena answered. "How far are we from
Needley?"

"About thirty-five miles or so," Thornton replied. "Say, an hour and
a half with any kind of going at all. We ought to be back by nine."

Helena nodded brightly and leaned back in her seat. Rather than
objecting to the short cut that Thornton had begun to negotiate, the
road, now that she gave her attention to it, she found to be quite the
prettiest bit she had seen in the whole afternoon's run, where, in the
rough, sparsely settled north country, all was both pretty and a delight
— miles and miles without the sign of even a farmhouse, just the great
Maine forests, so majestic and grand in their solitude, bordering the
road that undulated with the country, now to a rise with its magnificent
sweep of scenery, now to the cool, fresh valleys full of the sweet
pine-scent of the woods. They had explored much of it together in the
little 'run-about,' nearly every day a short spin somewhere; today a little
more ambitious run — the whole afternoon, and tea, a picnic tea, an
hour or more back, in a charming glade beside a little brook.

"Oh, this is perfectly lovely!" she exclaimed; and then, with a breathless laugh, as a bump lifted her out of her seat: "It *is* rough — isn't it?"

Thornton laughed and slowed down.

"I don't fancy it's used much, except in the winter for logging. But
if the map says we can get through, I guess we're all right — there's about
an eight mile stretch of it."

It was growing dusk, and the shadows, fanciful and picturesque; were
deepening around them. Now it showed a solid mass of green ahead,
and, like a sylvan path, the road, converging in the distance, lost itself
in a wall of foliage; now it swerved rapidly, this way and that, in short
curves, as though, like one lost, it sought its way.

A half hour passed. Thornton stopped the car, got down and lighted
his lamps, then started on again. The going had seemed to be growing
steadily worse — the road, as Thornton had said, was little more indeed
than a logging trail through the heart of the woods; and now, deeper
in, with increasing frequency, the tires slipped and skidded on damp,
moist earth that at times approached very nearly to being oozy mud.

Silence for a long while had held between them. It was taking
Thornton all his time now to guide the car, that, negotiating fallen
branches strewn across the way, bad holes and ruts, was crawling at a
snail's pace.

"'Rough but passable'!" he laughed once, clambering back to his seat after clearing away a dead tree-trunk from in front of them. "But there's no use trying to go back, as we must be halfway through, and it can't be any worse ahead than it's been behind. I'd like to tell the fellow that made this map something!"

And then upon Helena, just why she could not tell, began to steal an uneasiness that frightened her a little. It had grown suddenly, intensely dark — quicker than the slow, creeping change of dusk blending softly into night. Sort of eerie, it seemed — and a wind springing up and rustling through the branches made strange noises all about. They seemed to be shut in by a wall of blackness on every hand, except ahead where, like great streaming eyes of fire, the powerful lamps shot out their rays making weird color effects in the forest — huge tree-trunks loomed a dead drab, like mute sentinels, grim and ominous, that barred their way; now, in the full glare, the foliage took on the softest fairy shade of green; now, tapering off, heavier in color, it merged into impenetrable black; and, with the jouncing of the car, the light rays jiggling up and down gave an unnatural semblance as of moving, animate things before them, a myriad of them, ever retreating, but ever marshaling their forces again as though threatening attack, as though to oppose the car's advance.

What was there to be afraid of? She tried to laugh at herself — it was perfectly ridiculous. A little bit of rough road — the forest that she loved around her — even if it was very dark. They would come out eventually somewhere on the trunk-road to Barton's Mills — that was all there was to it. Meanwhile, it was quite an experience, and she had every confidence in Thornton. She glanced at him now. It was too dark to get more than an indistinct outline of the clean-cut profile, but there was something inspiriting in the alert, self-possessed, competent poise of his body as he crouched well forward over the wheel, his eyes never lifting from the road ahead.

They appeared to be going a little faster now, too — undoubtedly the road was getting better. What was there to be afraid of? It didn't make it anymore pleasant for Thornton, who was probably reproaching himself rather bitterly for having been tempted by the "short cut," to have her sit and mope beside him!

She began to hum an air softly to herself — and then laughingly sang a bar or two aloud.

Thornton shot a quick, appreciative glance at her and nodded, joining in the laugh.

"By Jove!" he said approvingly. "That sounds good to me. I was afraid this beastly stretch, bumping and crawling along in the dark, was making you miserable."

"Miserable!" exclaimed Helena. "Why, the idea! What is there to be miserable about? We'll get through after a while — and the road's better now than it was anyhow, isn't it?"

"Better?"

"You're running faster."

"Oh — er — yes, of course," said Thornton quickly. "I wasn't thinking of what I said. I —"

He stopped suddenly, as Helena lifted her hand to her face.

"Why, it's beginning to rain," she said.

"Yes; I'm afraid so," he admitted. "I was hoping we would get out of here before it came."

"Oh!" said Helena.

"And the worst of it is," he added hurriedly, "there's no top to the car, and you've no wraps."

"Perhaps it won't be anything more than a shower," said Helena hopefully.

"Perhaps not," he agreed. "Anyway" — he stopped the car, and took off his coat — "put this on."

"No — please," protested Helena. "You'll need it yourself."

"Not at all," said Thornton cheerily. "And that light dress of yours would be soaked through in no time."

He held the coat for her, and she slipped it on — and his hand around her shoulder and neck, as he turned the collar up and buttoned it gently about her, seemed to linger as it touched her throat, and yet linger with the most curious diffidence — a sort of reverence. Helena suddenly wanted to laugh — and, quick in her intuition, as suddenly wanted to cry. It wasn't much — only a little touch. It didn't mean love, or passion, or feeling — only that, unconsciously in his respect, he held her up to gaze upon herself again in that mocking mirror where all was sham.

They started on — Thornton silent once more, busy with the car; Helena, her mind in riot, with no wish for words.

The rain came steadily in a drizzle. She could feel her dress growing damp around her knees — and she shivered a little. How strangely wonderful the rain-beads looked on their background of green leaves where the lamps played upon them — they seemed to catch and hold and reflect back the light in a quick, passing procession of clear, sparkling crystals. But it was raining more heavily now, wasn't it? The drops were no longer clinging to the leaves, they were spattering dull and lusterlessly to the ground. And Thornton seemed suddenly to be in trouble — he was bending down working at something. How jerkily the car was moving! And now it stopped.

Thornton swung out of his seat to the ground.

"It's all right!" he called out reassuringly. "I'll have it fixed in a minute."

It was muddy enough now, and the ruts, holding the rain, were regular wheel-traps. Apart from any other trouble, Thornton did not like the prospect — and, away from Helena now, his face was serious. He cranked the engine — no result. He tried it again with equal futility — then, going to the tool-box, he took out his electric flashlight, and, lifting the engine hood, began to peer into the machinery. Everything seemed all right. He tried the crank again — the engine, like some cold, dead thing, refused to respond.

"What's the matter?" Helena asked him from the car.

"I don't know," Thornton answered lightly. "I haven't found out yet — but don't you worry, it's nothing serious. I'll have it in a jiffy."

Helena's knowledge of motorcars and engine trouble was not extensive — she was conversant only with the "fool's mate" of motoring.

"Maybe there's no gasoline," she suggested helpfully.

"Nonsense!" returned Thornton, with a laugh. "I told Babson to see that the tank was full before he brought the car around — he wouldn't forget a thing like that."

Thornton, nevertheless, tested the gasoline tank.

"Well?" inquired Helena, breaking the silence that followed.

"There is no — gasoline," said Thornton heavily.

Neither spoke for a moment. There was no sound but the steady drip from the leaves. Then Helena forced a laugh.

"Isn't it ridiculous!" she said. "That is what one is always making fun of others for. I — I don't think it's going to stop raining — do you? And we're miles and miles from anywhere. What *do* people do when they're caught like this?"

Thornton did not answer at once. Bitterly reproachful with himself, he stood there coatless in the rain. If it had been a breakdown, an accident that was unavoidable, a little of the sting might have gone out of the situation — but *gasoline!* This — from rank, blatant, glaring, inexcusable idiocy. Not on his part perhaps — but that did not lessen his responsibility. They were miles, as she had said, from anywhere — four miles at least in either direction from the main road, and as many more probably after that from any farmhouse — he remembered that for half an hour before they had turned into the "short cut" they had seen no sign of habitation — and what lay in the other direction, ahead, would in all probability be the same — they were up in the timber regions, in the heart of them — she couldn't walk miles in the rain with the roads in a vile condition, and growing viler every minute as the rain sank in and the mud grew deeper. And then another thought — a thought that came now, sharp and quick, engulfing the mere discomfort of a miserable night spent there in the woods — the clatter of busy, gossiping tongues seemed already to be dinning their abominable noises in his ears. And that he, that he — yes, it seemed to sweep upon him in a sudden, overmastering surge, the realization that the delight and joy of her companionship through the month that was gone was love that leaped now into fierce, jealous flame, maddened at a breath that would smirch her in the eyes of others — that *he* should be the cause of it! "What *do* people do when they're caught like this?" — in their innocence there seemed an unfathomed depth of irony in her words, but as he unconsciously repeated them they cleared his brain and brought him suddenly to face the immediate practical problem that confronted them. What was to be done?

"Shall — shall I get out?" she called to him, a hint of reminder in her tones that she had spoken to him before and received no answer.

Thornton moved back to the side of the car.

"Miss Vail," he said contritely, "I — I don't know what to say to you for getting you into this. I —"

"I know," she interrupted quickly, leaning over the side of the car and placing her hand on his arm. "Don't try to say anything. It's not your fault — it's not either of our faults. Now tell me what you think the best thing is to do, and, you'll see, I'll make the best of it — there's no use being miserable about it."

"You're a game little woman!" he said earnestly, quite unnecessarily clasping the hand on his arm and wringing it to endorse his verdict. "And that makes it a lot easier, you know. Well then, we might as well face the whole truth at one fell swoop. We're up against it" — he laughed cheerfully — "hard. It's miles to anywhere — we don't know where 'anywhere' is — and of course you can't walk aimlessly around in the mud and rain."

"N — no," she said thoughtfully. "I suppose there's no sense in that."

"And of course you can't sit out here in the wet all night."

"That sounds comforting — propitious even," commented Helena.

"Quite!" agreed Thornton, laughing again. "Well, you wait here a moment, and I'll see if I can't knock up some sort of shelter — I used to be pretty good at that sort of thing."

"And I'll help," announced Helena, preparing to get out.

"By keeping at least your feet dry," he amended. "No — please. Just stay where you are, Miss Vail. You'll get as much protection here from the branches overhead as you will anywhere meanwhile, and you'll be more comfortable."

She watched him as he disappeared into the wood, and after that, like a flitting will-o'-the-wisp, watched his flashlight moving about amongst the trees. Then presently the cheery blaze of a fire from where he was at work sprang up, and she heard the crackle of resinous pine knots — then a great crashing about, the snapping of branches as he broke them from larger limbs — and a rapid fire of small talk from him as he worked.

Helena answered him more or less mechanically — her mind, roving from one consideration of their plight to another, had caught at a certain viewpoint and was groping with it. They were stalled more effectively than any accident to the car could have stalled them — they were there for the night, there seemed no escape from that. But there was nothing to be afraid of. She had no fears about passing the night alone with him here in the woods — why should she? *Why should she!* She laughed low, suddenly, bitterly. Why should she — even if he were other than the man he was, even if he were of the lowest type! Fear — of *that!* A yearning, so intense as for an instant to leave her weak, swept upon her — a yearning full of pain, of shame, of remorse, of hopelessness — oh, God, if only she might have had the *right* to fear! Then passion seized her in wild, turbulent unrestraint — hatred for this clean-limbed, pure-minded man, who flaunted all that his life stood for in her face — hatred for everybody in this life of hers, for all were good save her — hatred, miserable, unbridled hatred for herself.

And then it passed, the mood — and she tried to think more calmly, still answering him as he called from the woods. She had seen a great deal of Thornton lately — a great deal. He had been kind and thoughtful and considerate — nothing more. More! What more could there have been? Love! There was something of mockery in that, wasn't there? Everything she thought about lately, every way her mind turned seemed to hold something of mockery now. Of course, Mrs. Thornton's words expressing the wish that she and Thornton might come together had been often enough with her — mockingly again! — but Thornton could have known nothing of that — so, after all, what did that matter? She had snatched at every opportunity to motor with Thornton despite Doc's protests, protests that had grown sullen and angry of late — snatched at the opportunities eagerly, as she would snatch at a breath of air where all else stifled her — snatched at them because they took her out of herself temporarily, away from everything, where everything at times seemed to be driving her mad. Hate Thornton! No, of course, she didn't hate him — she had thought that a moment ago because — because her brain was — was — oh, she didn't know — so tired and weary, and she was cold now and quite wet. She didn't hate him, she even —

"All ready now — house to let furnished" — he was calling out, laughing as he came thrashing through the undergrowth — "excellent situation, high altitude, luxuriant pine grove surrounds the property, and – and" – he had halted beside the car and opened the door – "what else do they say?"

Helena caught his spirit – or, rather, forced herself to do so. It wasn't quite fair that one of them should do all the pretending.

"Flies," she laughed. "They always speak of flies in Maine."

"None!" said Thornton promptly. "There hasn't been one since the house was built. Now then, Miss Vail" – he held out his arms.

"Oh, but really, I can walk."

"And I can carry you," he said – and, from the step, gathered her into his arms.

And then, as she lay there passively at first, she seemed to sense again that curious diffidence, that gentleness, like the touch upon her throat of a little while ago, though now he held her in both his arms. How strong he was – and, oh, how miserably wet – her hand around his shoulder felt the thin shirt clinging soggily to his arm. Yes; she was glad he hadn't let her walk – it wasn't far, but she would have had to force her way continually through bushes that scattered showers from their dripping leaves, and underfoot she could hear his boots squash through the mud. And then suddenly it happened – the trees, just a yard or so from the fire, were thick together, tangled – she bent her head quickly, instinctively, to avoid a low-hanging branch as he for the same reason swerved a little – and their cheeks lay close-pressed against each other's, her hair sweeping his forehead, their lips mingling one another's breaths. He seemed to stumble – then his arms closed about her in a quick, fierce pressure, clasping her, straining her to him – relaxed as suddenly – and then he had set her down inside the shelter he had built.

Quick her breath was coming now, and across the fire for a moment she met his eyes. His face was grey, and his hands at his sides were clenched.

"I'll – I'll get the seat out of the car," he said hoarsely. "It will help to make things more comfortable." And turning abruptly, he started back for the road again.

Helena did not move. Mechanically her eyes took in the little hut, crude, but rainproof at least – branches heaped across two forked limbs for a roof; the trunk of a big tree for the rear wall; branches thrust upright into the ground for the sides – the whole a little triangular shaped affair. The fire blazed in front just within shelter at the entrance; and beside it was piled quite a little heap of fuel that he had gathered.

He came back bringing the leather upholstered seat, shook the rain from it, and dried it with the help of the fire and his handkerchief – then set it down inside the hut. His face was turned from her; and as he spoke, breaking an awkward silence, his voice was conscious, hurried.

"I'm not going to be gone a minute more than I can help, Miss Vail. It's mighty rough accommodation for you, but there's one consolation at least — you'll be perfectly safe."

Helena seated herself, and held her skirt to the fire.

"Gone!" she said, a little dully. "Where are you going?"

"Why, to get help of course," he told her.

"Help!" — she shook her head. "You don't know where to find any — you only know for a certainty that there isn't any within miles."

"I know there's a house back on the main road," he said. "I noticed it as we came along."

"That's seven or eight miles from here," she returned. "And it's raining harder than ever — mud up to your ankles — it would take you hours to reach it."

"Possibly two, or two and a half," he said lightly.

"Yes; and another two at least to get back. I won't hear of you doing any such thing — you are wet through now. It's far better to wait for daylight and then probably the storm will be over."

"But don't you see, Miss Vail" — his voice was suddenly grave, masterful — "don't you see that there is no other thing to do?"

"No," said Helena. "I don't see anything of the kind. I won't have you do anything like that for me — it's not to be thought of."

Thornton stooped, placed a knot upon the fire, straightened up — and faced her.

"It's awfully good of you to think of me," he said in a low tone; "but, really, it won't be half as bad as you are picturing it in your mind. And really" — he hesitated, fumbling for his words — "you see — that is — what other people might say — your — reputation —"

With a sudden cry, white-faced, Helena was on her feet, staring at him, her hands clutched at her bosom — a wild, demoniacal, mocking orgy in her soul. Her reputation! It seemed she wanted to scream out the words — *her reputation!*

Thornton's face flushed with a quick-sweeping flood of crimson.

"I'm a brute — a brute with a blundering tongue!" he cried miserably. "You had not thought of that — and I made you. I could have found another excuse for going if I had only had wit enough. I was a brute once before tonight, and —" He stopped, and for a moment stood there looking at her, stood in the firelight, his face white again even in the ruddy glow — and then he was gone.

Time passed without meaning to Helena. The steady patter of the rain was on the leaves, the sullen, constant drip of water to the ground, and now, occasionally, a rush of wind, a heavier downpour. She sat before the fire, staring into it, her elbows on her knees, her face held tightly in her hands, the brown hair, wet and wayward now, about her temples. Once she moved, once her eyes changed their direction — to fix upon her sleeve in a strange, questioning surprise.

"I let him go without his coat," she said.

XVIII

THE BOOMERANG

*I*t was early afternoon, as Madison, emerging from the wagon track, and walking slowly, started across the lawn toward the Patriarch's cottage. He was in a mood that he made no attempt to define — except that it wasn't a very pleasant mood. Before Thornton had returned to Needley it had been bad enough, after that, with his infernal car, it had been — hell.

Madison's fists clenched, and his grey eyes glinted angrily. His hands had been tied like a baby's — like a damned infant's! Helena was getting away from him further every day, and he couldn't stop it — without stopping the game! He couldn't tell Thornton that Helena belonged to him — had belonged to him! He couldn't even evidence an interest in what was going on. He had to put on a front, a suave, cordial, dignified front before Thornton — while he itched to smash the other's face to pulp! Hell — that's what it was — pure, unadulterated hell! He couldn't get near Helena alone with a ten-foot pole, morning, noon or night — she had taken good care of that. And he wanted Helena — he *wanted* her! It was an obsession with him now — at times driving him half crazy, — and it didn't help any that he saw her grow more glorious, more beautiful every day! Of course she knew she had him — had him where she knew he couldn't do a thing — where she could laugh at him — go the limit with Thornton if she liked. But, curse it, it wasn't only Thornton — that was what he could not understand — she had begun to keep away from him before ever Thornton had come back.

Madison was near the porch now, and, raising his eyes, noted a supplicant going into the shrine-room — a woman, richly dressed but in widow's weeds, who walked feebly. The game went on by itself, once started — there were half a hundred more about the lawn! Like a snowball rolling down hill, as he had put it at the Roost. The Roost! If he only had Helena back there for about a minute there'd be an end of this! She'd go a little too far one of these days — a little too far — it was pretty near far enough now — and then there'd be a showdown, game or no game, and somebody would get hurt in the smash, and —

He lifted his eyes again, as someone came hurrying through the cottage door. It was the Flopper. And then to his surprise, he found himself being pushed unceremoniously from the porch and pulled excitedly behind the trellis.

"What's the matter with you!" he demanded angrily. "Are you crazy!"

"T'ank de Lord youse have showed up!" gasped the Flopper. "Say, honest, I can't do nothin' wid him — he's got me near bughouse."

"Who?" — Madison scowled irritably.

"De Patriarch, of course. He's noivous, an' gettin' worse all de time. He won't eat an' he won't keep still. He wants Helena, an' he keeps writin' her name on de slate — he's got me going fer fair."

"Well, I'm not Helena!" growled Madison. "Why doesn't she go to him?"

"Now wouldn't dat sting youse!" ejaculated the Flopper. "How's she goin' to him when she ain't here?"

"Not here?" repeated Madison sharply. "Where is she?"

The Flopper looked down his nose.

"I dunno," said he.

Madison stared at him for a moment — then he reached out and caught the Flopper's arm in a sudden and far from gentle grip.

"Out with it!" he snapped.

"I dunno where she is," said the Flopper, with some reluctance. "She ain't back yet, dat's all."

"Back from where?" — Madison's grip tightened.

The Flopper blinked.

"Aw, wot's de use!" he blurted out, as though his mind, suddenly made up, brought him unbounded relief. "Youse'll find it out anyhow. Say, she went off wid Thornton in de buzz-wagon yesterday, an' I put de Patriarch to bed last night 'cause she wasn't back, an' dat's wot's de matter wid him, she ain't showed up since an' he's near off his chump, an' — fer God's sake let go my arm, Doc, youse're breakin' it!"

A sort of cold frenzy seemed to seize Madison. He was perfectly calm, he felt himself perfectly calm and composed. Off all night with Thornton — eh? Funny, wasn't it? She'd gone pretty far at last — gone the limit.

"Why didn't you send me word this morning?" — was that his own voice speaking? Well, he wouldn't have recognized it — but he was perfectly calm nevertheless.

"Fer God's sake let go my arm," whimpered the Flopper. "I – I ain't no squealer, dat's why."

Madison's arm fell away – to his side. He felt a whiteness creeping to his face and lips, felt his lips twitch, felt the fingers of his hands curl in and the nails begin to press into the palms.

"Mabbe," suggested the Flopper timidly, "mabbe dere was an accident."

Madison made no answer.

The Flopper shifted from foot to foot and licked his lips, stealing frightened glances at Madison's face.

"Wot – wot'll I do wid de Patriarch?" he stammered out miserably.

And then Madison smiled at him – not happily, but eloquently.

"Swipe me!" mumbled the Flopper, as he backed out from the trellis. "Dis love game's fierce – an' mabbe *I* don't know! 'Sposin' she'd been Mamie an' me the Doc – 'sposin' it had!" He gulped hastily. "Swipe me!" said the Flopper with emotion.

Madison, motionless, watched the Flopper disappear. He wasn't quite so calm now, not so cool and collected and composed. He must go somewhere and think this out – somewhere where it would be quiet and he wouldn't be disturbed.

A step sounded on the path – Madison looked through the trellis. A man, with yellow, unhealthy skin and sunken cheeks, his head bowed, was passing in through the porch. It caught Madison with fierce, exquisite irony. Why not go there himself if he wanted quiet – the shrine-room – the place of meditation! Well, he wanted to *meditate!* He laughed jarringly. The shrine-room – for him! Great! Immense! Magnificent! Why not? That's what he had created it for, wasn't it – to meditate in!

He stepped inside. The woman, whom he had seen enter a short while before, was sitting in a sort of rigid, strained attitude in the far corner; the man, who had just preceded him, had taken the chair by the fireplace – they were the only occupants of the room. There was no sound save his own footsteps – neither of the others looked at him. There was quiet, a profound stillness – and the softened light from the shuttered window fell mellow all about, fell like a benediction upon the simplicity of the few plain articles that the room contained – the round rag mats upon the white-scrubbed floor; the hickory chairs, severe, uncushioned; the table, with its little japanned box and book.

Madison's eyes fixed upon the japanned box, as he leaned now, arms folded, against the wall – a jewel, even in the subdued light, glowed crimson-warm where it nested on a crumpled bed of bank-notes – a ruby ring – the last contribution – it must have been the woman who had placed it there. Madison glanced at her involuntarily – but his thoughts were far away again in a moment.

Anger and a blind rage of jealousy were gripping him now. *Accident!* The thought only fanned his fury. Accident! Yes; it was likely – as an excuse! There would have been an accident all right – leave that to them! Thornton perhaps wasn't the stamp of man to seek an adventure of that kind deliberately – perhaps he wasn't – and perhaps he was – you never could tell – but what difference did that make! *Helena was that kind of a woman* – though he'd always thought her true to him since he'd known her – and Thornton, whatever kind of a man he was, wouldn't run away from her arms, would he?

The red glow from the ruby ring had vanished – the man had risen from his seat and was placing something in the box on top of the ring – Madison's mind subconsciously absorbed the fact that it was a little sheaf of yellow-backed bills. And now the man bent to the table and was writing in the book.

Yellow-backs and rubies! Rubies and yellowbacks! Madison's lips thinned and curled downward at the corners. Oh, it was coming all right, money, jewels, pelf, rolling in merrily every day, there wasn't any stopping it, but he was paying for it, and paying for it at a price he didn't like – Helena. Helena! She wanted Thornton, did she – with his money! Wanted to dangle a millionaire on her string – eh? She'd throw him over – would she! And she thought she had him where he couldn't lift a finger to stop it – just sit back and grin like a poor, sick fool!

The red crept up the knotted cords of Madison's neck, suffused the set jaws, and, as though suddenly liberated to run its course where it would, swept in a tide over cheeks and temples.

He couldn't do a thing – *couldn't he!* Well, he'd see the game in Gehenna before Thornton or any other man got her away from him. She belonged to him – to *him!* And he'd have her, hold her, own her – she was his – *his!* And he'd settle with Thornton too, by Heaven!

A laugh, low, unpleasant, purled to his lips – and he checked it with a sort of strange mechanical realization that he must not laugh aloud. His eyes swept the room – the man had returned to his seat, the woman had not moved, both were silent, motionless – that ghastly, hallowed, sanctimonious hush – that subdued, damnable light – meditation!

"For God's sake let me get out of here," he muttered, "or I'll go mad."

He turned – and stopped. Came a cry spontaneously from the man and the woman – they were on their feet – no, on their knees. The doorway at the further end of the room was framing a majestic figure, tall and stately – and a sun-gleam struggling suddenly through the lattice seemed to leap in a golden ray to caress in homage the snow-white hair, the silver beard that fell upon the breast, the saintly face of the Patriarch.

Then into the room advanced the Patriarch, and his hands were outstretched before him, and he moved them a little to and fro — and the gesture, the poise, the mien, as, touching nothing he seemed to feel his way through space itself, was as one invoking a blessing of peace ineffable.

Spellbound, Madison watched. Upon the face was a yearning that saddened it, and, saddening, glorified it; the head was slightly turned as though to listen — while slowly, with measured, certain tread, as though indeed he had no need for eyes, the Patriarch circled the table and passed on down the room. The man and the woman reached out and touched him reverently, and drew back reverently to let him pass, and, rising from their knees, followed him through the door and out onto the porch.

The room was empty. Madison stared at the doorway. Upon him fell a sudden awe — it was as though a vision, an ethereal presence, some strange embodiment of power, had been and gone — and yet still remained.

And now from without there came a sound like a distant murmur. It rose and swelled, and began to roll in its volume, and then, like the clarion sound of trumpets, voices burst into glad acclaim.

"The Patriarch! The Patriarch! The Patriarch!"

From the little hallway came the Flopper, running — and he stopped and gaped at Madison.

"I left him in his room fer a minute," he gasped. "He's — he's lookin' fer Helena."

And then Madison shook himself together — and smiled ironically. And at the smile the Flopper hurried on.

Madison stepped out onto the porch. Helena! Helena! Within him seemed to burn a rage of hell; but it seemed, too, most strangely that for the moment this rage was held in abeyance, that something temporarily supplanted it — this scene before him.

Onward across the lawn moved the Patriarch, and the Flopper had joined him now; but the Patriarch, unheeding, turning neither to the right nor to the left, his arms still extended before him, kept on. And the people cried aloud:

"He is coming — he is coming! The Patriarch! The Patriarch!"

Madison moved on — out upon the lawn himself.

From everywhere, from every scattered spot where they had been, men and women ran and limped and dragged themselves along, all converging on one point — the Patriarch.

Madison, in the midst of them now, hurried — for it was plainly evident that the Flopper's control over the Patriarch was gone. He reached the Patriarch and touched the other's arm — and at the touch the Patriarch halted instantly, his hand went out and lay upon Madison's sleeve in recognition, and he turned his face, and it was smiling and there was relief upon it — and confidence and trust, as, suffering himself to be guided, they started back toward the cottage.

And then upon Madison came again that sense of awe, but now intensified. From every hand tear-stained faces greeted him, white faces, faces full of sorrow and suffering through which struggled hope — hope — hope. They flung themselves before the Patriarch — yet never blocked the way. They cried, they wept, they prayed — and some were silent. It seemed that souls, naked, stripped, bare, held themselves up to his gaze. Men, prostrate on stretchers, tried to rise and stagger nearer — and fell. Friends, where there were friends to help, tugged and dragged desperately at cots — and from the cots in piteous, agonized appeal the helpless cried out to the Patriarch to come to them. All of human agony and fear and hope and despair and terror seemed loosed in a mad and swirling vortex. And ever the cries arose, and ever around them, giving way, closing in again, pressed the soul-rent throng.

And presently to Madison it seemed as though he had awakened from some terrifying dream, as, in the Patriarch's room again, he swept away a bead of sweat from his forehead, and stood and looked at the Patriarch and the Flopper.

The Flopper licked his lips, and pulled the Patriarch's chair forward — but his hands trembled violently.

"It's been gettin' me, Doc," he whispered, "an' I can't help it. It's been gettin' into me all de time. Say, I wisht it was over. Honest to God I do! Dis — dis makes me queer. Say, de Patriarch's got me, Doc — an' — an' — say — dere's been somethin' goin' on inside me dat's got me hard."

Madison did not answer — but he started suddenly — and as suddenly stepped to the window and looked out. Over the cries, the wailings, the confused medley of voices, growing lower now, subsiding, there had come the throb of a motorcar.

Madison's eyes narrowed — *that* was supreme again. A car was coming to a stop before the porch — Thornton was helping Helena to alight.

Madison turned and caught the Flopper's arm in a fierce, imperative grasp.

"You keep your mouth shut — do you hear?" he flung out, clipping off his words. "You haven't seen me today — understand!" And, dropping the Flopper's arm, he stepped quickly across the little hall to Helena's door, opened it, went in — and closed the door behind him.

And the Flopper, staring, licked his lips again.

"Swipe me!" he croaked hoarsely. "Pipe de eyes on de Doc! Dere'll be somethin' doin' now!"

XIX

THE SANCTUARY OF DARKNESS

*T*here was a grim, merciless smile on Madison's lips; and a whiteness in his face windowed the passion that seethed within him. He stood motionless, listening, in Helena's room. He heard the automobile going away again; then he heard Helena's light step in the hallway without — and the smile died as his lips thinned.

But she did not come in — instead, he heard her go into the Patriarch's room, heard her talking to the Patriarch, and bid the Flopper go to the kitchen and make her some tea. Then the Flopper's step sounded, passing down to the rear, of the cottage.

The minutes passed — then that light footfall again. The door of the room swung suddenly wide — and closed — there was a cry — and Helena, wide-eyed, the red of her cheeks fading away, leaned heavily back against the door.

Neither spoke. Madison, in the center of the room, did not move. The smile came back to his lips.

Helena's great brown eyes met the grey ones, read the ugly glint, dropped, raised again — and held the grey ones steadily.

Madison gave a short laugh — that was like a curse. His hands at his sides knotted into lumps.

Then Madison spoke.

"Why don't you say, 'you! — *you!*' — and scream it out and clutch at your bosom the way they do in story books!" he flung out raucously. "Why don't you do your little stunt — go on, you're on for the turn — you can put anything over me, I'm only a complacent, blind-eyed fool! Anything goes! Why don't you start your act?"

"You don't know what you are saying," she said in a low voice. "If there's anything you want to talk about, we'd better wait until you're cooler."

"Oh, hell!" he roared, his passion full to the surface now. "Cut out the bunk — cut it out! *Anything!* No, it isn't much of anything — for you

— out all night with Thornton. Do you think I'm going to stand for it! Do you think I'm going to sit and suck my thumb and *share* you, and —"

"You lie!" She was away from the door now, close before him, her breath coming fast, white to the lips, and in a frenzy her little fists pummeled upon him. "It's a lie — a lie — a lie! It's a lie — and you know it!"

He pushed her roughly from him.

"It is, eh?" — his words came in a sort of wild laugh. "And I know it — do I? Why should I know it? What do you think you are? Say, you'd think you were trying to kid yourself into believing you're the real thing — the real, sweet, shy, modest Miss Vail. Cut it out! You're name's Smith — maybe! And it's my money that's keeping you, and you belong to me — do you understand?"

She stood swaying a little, her hands still tightly clenched, breathing through half parted lips in short, quick, jerky inhalations like dry sobs.

"It's true," she faltered suddenly — and suddenly buried her face in her hands. And then she looked up again, and the brown eyes in their depths held an anger and a shame. "It's true — I was — was — what you say. But now" — her voice hurried on, an eagerness, a strange earnestness in it — "you must believe me — you must. I'll make you — I must make you."

"Oh, don't hurt yourself trying to do it!" jeered Madison. "We're talking plain now. I'm not taking into account how you feel about it — don't you fool yourself for a minute. The sanctity of my home hasn't been ruined — because it couldn't be! Get that? Thornton don't get you — not for *keeps!* But you and he don't make a monkey of me again. Do you understand — say, do you get that? You're *mine* — whether you like it or not — whether you'd rather have Thornton or not. But I'll fix you both for this — I'm no angel with a cherub's smile! I'll take it out of Thornton till the laugh he's got now fades to a fare-thee-well; and I'll put you where there aren't any strings tying me up the way there are here. Do you understand!" His voice rose suddenly, and for a moment he seemed to lose all control of himself as he reached for her and caught her shoulder. "I love you," he flashed out between his teeth. "I love you — that's what's the matter with me! And you know that — you know you've got me there — and you'd play the fool with me, would you!" He dropped his hands — and laughed a short, savage bark — and stepped back and stared at her.

"Will you listen?" — she was twisting her hands, her head was drooped, the long lashes veiled her eyes, her lips were quivering. "Will you listen?" she said again, fighting to steady her voice. "It was an accident."

"I saw the machine when you drove up — it was a wreck!" snapped

Madison sarcastically.

"We ran out of gasoline," she said quietly.

And then Madison laughed — fiercely — in his derision.

"Oh, keep on!" he rasped. "I told you I was only a blind fool that you could put anything over on! That accounts for it, of course — a breakdown isn't so easy to get away with. Gasoline!"

"We were miles from anywhere," she went on. "We had taken what we thought was a short cut. Mr. Thornton built a shelter for me in the woods, and went to — to —"

He caught up her hesitation like a flash.

"Fake the lines, Helena, if you haven't had enough rehearsals," he suggested ironically. "Anything goes — with me."

And now a tinge of color came to Helena's cheeks, and the brown eyes raised, and flashed, and dropped.

"He went to try and find help," she said. "He was out all night in the storm. I do not know how far he must have walked. I know the nearest house was five or six miles away — and there was no horse there — the man had driven to some town that morning. It was almost daylight before Mr. Thornton at last came back with a team. We were forty miles from here — we sent the team to the nearest town for gasoline and then motored back." She stopped — and then, with a catch in her voice: "He — he was very good to me."

"Good to me" — the words seemed to stab at Madison, seemed to ring in his ears and goad him with a fiercer jealousy — and her story of the night, what she had been saying, save those words, was as nothing, meant nothing, was swept from his consciousness — and only she, standing there before him, glorious, maddening in her beauty, remained. Soul, mind and body leaped into fiery passion — she was his, and his she always would be — those eyes, those lips, the white throat, those perfect arms to cling about his neck — and all of heaven and hell and earth were naught beside her.

"I love you!" — his face was white, his words fierce-breathed, almost incoherent — and he leaned toward her with a sudden, uncontrollable movement, his arms sweeping out to clasp her. "I love you, Helena — I love you. Do you understand — it's *you!* You — I love you!"

"You *love* me!" — she retreated from him, but her head was raised now, and her voice rang with a bitterness cold as the touch of death. "Love! What do you know of *love!* We talk plain, you say. Love — love for me! Passion, vice, lust, sin — and, oh, my God, degradation and misery and shame — love! Love! That is *your* love!"

He stood for a moment and stared at her again — and her face was as pallid ivory. And something seemed to daze him, and he brushed his hand across his eyes — the logic was faulty, torn and pitiful, and he groped after the flaw.

"It's — it's your love as well as mine," he said in a stumbling way — then his brain flashed quick into action. "My love — what other love have *you* known but that?" he cried. "It's *our* love — the love we have known together — and we're going back to it — see? I've had enough of this. You pack your trunks — and pack them quick! We're going to beat it out of here! We're going back to our — love. We're going back where I don't have to sit around like a puling fool and watch Thornton chuck you under the chin — we're going where he'll want a tombstone if he ever shows his face there. You thought the game would hold me to the last jackpot — did you? Well, I've got enough — and there's no game big enough to make me stand for this. That looks like love — doesn't it?" He burst again into a sudden, mirthless laugh — and once again swept his hand across his eyes. "We're going to beat it out of here now — tonight — tomorrow morning."

But now she had drawn further away from him — and there was a frightened look in her eyes, and her lips quivered pitifully.

"No — I can't — I can't," she cried out. "No, no — I can't — I can't go back to *that.*"

"That! That — is love," he said wildly. "The only love you know. What more do you want? There's loot enough now, and — ha, ha! — that little contribution of Thornton's, to give you all the money you want. Love, Helena — you and I — the old love — you and I together again, Helena. I tell you I love you — do you hear? I love you — and I'll have you — I love you! What do you know, what do you care about any other kind of love!"

She looked at him, misery and fear still in her eyes, and her slight figure seemed to droop, and her hands hung heavy, listless, at her sides.

"I care" — the words came in a strange mechanical way from her lips. "Oh, I care. I can't — I won't go back to that. And I know — I know now. I have learned what love is."

Quick over Madison's face surged the red in an unstemmed tide — volcanic within him his love that he knew now possessed his very soul, jealousy that, blinding, robbed him of his senses, roused him to frenzy.

"Oh, you've learned what love is, have you — *with him!*" he cried — and sprang for her and snatched her into his arms. "And you won't come, eh? Well, I've learned what love is too in the last month — and if I can't get it one way, I'll get it another" — he was raining mad kisses upon her face, her hair, her eyes — "I love you, I tell you — I love you!"

With a cry she tried to struggle from him — and then fought and struck at him, beating upon his face with her fists. Fiercer, closer he held her — around the little room, staggering this way and that, they circled. He kissed her, laughing hoarsely like a madman, laughing at the blows, beside himself, not knowing what he did — mad — mad — mad. He kissed her, kissed the white throat where the dress was torn now at the neck; imprisoned a little fist that struck at him and kissed the quivering knuckles; kissed the wealth of glorious, burnished-copper hair that, unloosened, fell about her, kissed it and buried his face in its rare fragrance. And then — and then his arms were empty — and he was staring at the calm, majestic figure of the Patriarch — and Helena was crouched upon the floor, and, sobbing, was clinging with arms entwined around the old man's knees.

And so for a little while Madison stood and stared — what had brought the Patriarch there — the Patriarch who could neither see nor hear nor speak — what had brought him from his own room across the hall! And Madison stared, and his hands crept to his temples and pressed upon them — weak he seemed as from some paroxysm of madness that had passed over him. The sunlight streaming through the window sheened the luxuriant mass of hair that falling over shoulders and to the waist seemed alone to cloak the little figure in its crouched position — the little figure that shook so convulsively with sobs — the little figure that clung so desperately at the feet of this godlike, regal man, whose beard was silver, whose hair was hoary white, upon whose face, marring none its strength or self-possession, was a troubled, anxious, questioning look.

Strange! Strange! Madison's hands fell to his sides. The Patriarch's eyes were turned full upon him, wavering not so much as by the fraction of an inch — full upon him. And then, as into some holy sanctuary, fending her from harm and danger, the Patriarch turned a little to interpose himself before Madison, and, raising Helena, held her in his arms, her head against his bosom — and one hand lay upon her head and stroked it tenderly. But upon Madison was still turned those sightless eyes, that noble face, serene, commanding even in its pertur-bation, even in its alert and searching look.

Madison stirred now — stirred uneasily — while the silence held. There was a solemnity in the silence that seemed to creep upon and pervade the room — a sense of a vast something that was the antithesis of turmoil, passion, strife, that seemed to radiate from the saintly figure whose lips were mute, whose ears heard no sound, whose eyes saw no sight. And upon Madison it fell potent, masterful, and passion fled, and in its place came a strange, groping response within him, a revulsion, a penitence — and he bowed his head.

And then Helena spoke — but her head was turned away from him, hidden on the Patriarch's breast.

"Once," she said, and her words were like broken whispers, for she was sobbing still, "once, long, long ago, when I was a little girl, I read the story of Mary Magdalen. I had almost forgotten it, it was so long ago, but it has come back to me, and — and it is a glad story — at the end."

She stopped — and Madison raised his head, and his face was strained as with some sudden wonder as he looked at her.

"It is a glad story," she said presently. "It — it is my story."

"You mean" — Madison's voice was hoarse — "you mean that you've turned — *straight!*"

"They love me here," she said. "They trust me and they think me good — as they are. All think me that — the little children and this dear man here — and for a little while, since I have been here, I have lived like that. They made me believe that it was true — *true*. And there was shame and agony — and hope. It seemed they could not all be wrong, and I have asked and prayed that I might make it true always — and — and forgiveness for what I was."

"You mean," he said again hoarsely, and he stepped toward her now, "you mean that you are — *straight!*"

She did not answer — only now she turned her face toward him and lifted up her head.

And for a long minute Madison gazed into the tear-splashed eyes, deep, brave in chastened wistfulness, gazed — and like a man stunned walked from the room, the cottage, and out across the lawn.

XX

TO THE VICTOR ARE THE SPOILS

*M*any were still about the lawn as he left the cottage — they were all about him, those sick, half frantic creatures — and still they made noises; still some of them cried and sobbed; still in their waning paroxysms they moved hither and thither. They appealed to some numbed, dormant sense in Madison, in a subconscious way, as things to be avoided. And so, almost mechanically, he took the little path that, striking off at right angles to the wagon track where it joined the Patriarch's lawn, came out again upon the main road at the further end of the village.

And, as he walked, like tidal waves on-rushing, emotions, utterly at variance one with another, hurled themselves upon him, and he was swept from his mental balance, tossed here and there, rolled gasping, strangling in the chaos and turmoil of the waters, as it were, and, rising, was hurled back again.

White as death itself was Madison's face; and at times his fingers with a twitching movement curled into clenched fists, at times his open palms sought his temples in a queer wriggling way and pressed upon them. Doubt, anger, fear, a rage unhallowed — in cycles — buffeted him until his brain reeled, and he was as a man distraught.

It began at the beginning, that cycle, and dragged him along — and left him like one swooning, tottering, upon the edge of a precipice. And then it began over again.

And it began always with a picture of the Roost that night — the vicious, unkempt, ragged figure of the Flopper — the sickly, thin, greedy face of Pale Face Harry, the drug fiend, winching a little as he plunged the needle into his flesh — the easy, unprincipled gaiety and eagerness of Helena for the new path of crime — crime — crime — the Roost exuded crime — filth — immorality — typified them, framed them well as they had sat there, the four of them, while that bruised-nosed bouncer had brought them drink on his rattling tin tray. And then his own self-satisfied, smug, complacent egotism at his own cleverness, his unbounded confidence in his own ability to pull off the game, and —

Well, he had pulled it off — he'd won it — won it — won it — everybody had fallen for it — the boobs had been plentiful — the harvest rich. What was the matter with him! He'd won — was winning every time the clock ticked. Somebody back there was probably throwing good hard coin at him this minute — the damned fool! Madison threw back his head to laugh in derision, for there was mocking, contemptuous laughter in his soul — but the laugh died still-born upon his lips.

It was fear now — fear — staggering, appalling him. He was facing something — *something* — his brain did not seem to define it — something that was cold and stern and immutable, that was omnipotent, that embodied awe — a condemnation unalterable, unchangeable, before which he shrank back with his soul afraid. Before him seemed to unfold itself the wagon track, the road to the Patriarch's cottage; and he was there again, and whispering lips were around him, and men and women and children were there, and in front of them, leading them, slithered that twisted, misshapen, formless thing — and now they were upon the lawn, and about him everywhere, everywhere, everywhere was a sea of white faces out of which the eyes burned like living coals. What power was this that, loosed, had stricken them to palsied, moaning things!

Madison shivered a little — and a sweat bead oozed out and glistened upon his forehead. Hark — what was that! Clarionlike, clear as the chimes of a silver bell, rang now that childish voice — rang out, and rang out again — and the crutch was gone — and the lame boy ran, ran — *ran!* And who was that, that stood before him now — that golden-haired woman beside an empty wheel-chair, whose face was radiant, who cried aloud that she was *cured!* And who were these others of later days, this motley crowd of old and young, that passed before him in proces-sion, that cried out the same words that golden-haired woman by the wheel-chair had cried — and cried out: "Faith! Faith! Faith!"

Madison swept the sweat bead from his forehead with a trembling hand. It was a lie — a lie — a lie! He had taught them to say that — but it was all bunk — and all were fools! He could laugh at them, jeer at them, mock at them, deride them — they were his playthings — and faith was his plaything — and he could laugh at them all!

And again he raised his head to laugh; and again the laugh was choked in his throat, still-born — *Helena was straight!* To his temples went his twitching hands. Anger raged upon him — and died in fear. Anger, for the instant maddening him, that he should lose her; rage in ungov-ernable fury that the game, his plans, the hoard accumulated, was bursting like a bubble before his eyes — died in fear. No, no; he had not meant to laugh or mock — no, no; not that, not that! What was this loosed titanic power that had done these things — that had brought this change in Helena; that had brought a change in the Flopper, transform-ing the miserable, pitiful, whining thief into a man reaching out for decent things; that had wrought at least a physical metamorphosis in Pale Face Harry — that had transfigured those three who, in their ugly, abandoned natures then, had hung like vultures on his words in the Roost that night! What was this power that he was trifling with, that brought him now this cold, dead fear before which he quailed! What was this *something* that in his temerity he had dared invoke — that rose now engulfing him, a puny maggot — that snatched him up and flung him headlong, shackled, before this nebulous, terrifying tribunal, where out of nothingness, out of a void, the calm, majestic features of the Patriarch took form and changed, and changed, and kept changing, and grew implacable, set with the stamp of doom. What was it — in God's name, what was it brought these sweat beads bursting to his forehead! Was he going mad — was he mad already!

And then the cycle again — doubt, anger, fear — until his brain, exhausted, seemed to refuse its functions; and it was as though, heavy, oppressing, a dense fog shut down upon his mind and enveloped it; and now he walked as a man in great haste, hurrying, and now his pace was slow, uncertain.

And so he went on, following the little path that bordered the woods on one hand and the fields on the other; went on until he neared the village – and then he stopped suddenly, and turned about. Someone had called his name.

From the field, a man climbed over the fence and came toward him. The man's face was tanned and rugged, his form erect, and the sleeves rolled back above the elbows displayed browned and muscular forearms. Madison stared at the man apathetically. This was the farm of course where Pale Face Harry boarded, and this was Pale Face Harry – but –

"Doc," said Pale Face Harry, and he shuffled his feet and looked down, "Doc, I got something I've been wanting to say to you for a week."

Madison still gazed at him apathetically – Pale Face Harry for the moment was as some unwarrantable apparition suddenly appearing before him.

Pale Face Harry raised his eyes, lowered them, kicked at a clod of earth with the toe of his boot – and raised his eyes again.

"Say," he blurted out, "I'm through, Doc. I'm – I'm going to quit."

Into Madison's stumbling brain leaped and took form but one idea – and he jumped forward, reaching savagely for Pale Face Harry's throat.

"You'd throw me, would you! You'd throw the game – would you!" he snarled, as his fingers locked.

Pale Face Harry, twisting, wriggled free – and retreated a step.

"No; I ain't!" he gasped – and then his sentences came tumbling out upon each other jerkily, as though he were trying to compress what he had to say into as few words as possible and as quickly as he could, while he watched Madison warily. "I ain't throwing nothing. I just want to quit myself. I keeps my mouth shut – see? I don't want none of the share what's coming. Say, I've got more'n a hundred times that out of it. Look at me, Doc! Say, I'm like a horse. That's the Patriarch and living honest. Say, in all me life I never knew what it was before till we comes here. If I took the dough what's coming I'd go back to the old hell, and I'd go down and out again. Say, it ain't worth it, there's nothing in it. I ain't throwing you, Doc – I just blows out of here with me trap closed. Say, look at me, Doc – don't you get what I mean?"

And then Madison burst into a peal of wild, strange laughter; and, as though no man stood before him, started on along the path – and Pale Face Harry sidled out of his way and stared after him.

"For – for God's sake, Doc," he called out, stammering, "what's the matter?"

But Madison made no answer. He heard Pale Face Harry call out

behind him; in a subconscious, mazed way, he sensed the other following him, gropingly, hesitantly, for a few yards, then hold back — and
finally stop.

The path swerved. Madison went on — blindly, mechanically, as
though, once set in motion, he must go on. Some ghastly, unnatural
thing was clogging his brain; not only in a mental way, but clogging it
until there was physical hurt and pain, an awful tightness — something
— if he could only reach it with his fingers and claw it away! There was
black madness here, and a pain insufferable — a damnable impotence,
robbing him of even the power, the faculty to think or reason, or to
make himself understand in any logical degree the meaning or the cause
of this thing that sent his brain swirling sick.

He halted. His lips were working; the muscles of his face quivered.
And suddenly, snatching his hat from his head, he flung himself on the
ground and plunged face and head, feverishly, tigerishly, into the little
brook that ran beside the path. Again and again he buried his face in
the cold, clear, refreshing water — and then, still on hands and knees,
he raised his head to listen. Softly, full of a great peace, full of a strange
sweetness that knew no discord, no strife, the notes of the chapel bell
floated across the fields. Evening had come; the day's work was done —
it was benediction time. It was the call of the faithful — the Angelus of
those who believed.

It came, the revulsion, to Madison in a choked sob — and he stood
up. The day's work was done — here. Here they would go in quiet
thankfulness each from the farm to his little cottage, each to his simple,
wholesome meal, each to the twilight hours of gentle communion as
they talked to one another from their doorways, each to his bed and his
rest, tranquil in the love of God and of man.

Madison flung back the dripping hair from his forehead. Strange,
the contrast that, unbidden, came insistently to him now: The liquid
notes of the bell wafted sweetly on the evening breeze; the howling,
jangling turmoil of the city slums, of his familiar haunts where, in mad
chaos, reigned the hawkers' cries, the thunder of the elevated trains, the
noisome traffic of the street, the raucous clang of trolley bells — the
sweet perfume of the, fields, the smell of trees, of earth, of all of God's
pure things untouched, unsoiled; the stench of Chatham Square, the
reek of whiskey spilled with the breath of obscene, filthy lips — the little
village that he could see beyond him, the tiny curls of blue smoke rising
like the incense from an altar over the roofs of houses whose doors had
no locks, whose windows were not barred, where plain, homely folk,
unsullied, lived at peace with God and the world; the closed areaways
of the Bowery, the creaking stairs, the dim hallways leading to dens of

vileness and iniquity where, safe by bolts from interruption, crime bred
its offsprings and vice was hatched. What did it mean!

And so he stood there for a little space; then presently he started
forward again; and presently he reached the village street, walked down
its length, greeted from every doorway with hearty, unaffected sincerity,
and after a little while he came to the hotel, and to his room — and there
he locked the door.

Helena was straight — the words were repeating themselves over and
over in his brain. He began to pace up and down the room. The words
seemed to take form and shape in fiery red letters, being scrawled by
invisible hands upon the walls — *Helena was straight.* Straight with
Thornton, straight with any man — straight with her Maker. He knew
that now — he had read it as a soul-truth in those brave, deep, tear-
dimmed eyes. And he had *lost* her! It seemed as though he had become
suddenly conscious that he was enduring some agony that was never to
know an end, that from now on must be with him always. He had lost
her — lost Helena.

From his pocket he drew out his keys and opened his trunks, and
took out the trays and spread them about. There were very many trays,
they nested one upon the other — and they were exceedingly ingenious
trays — false-bottomed everyone. And now he opened these false-bot-
toms, everyone of them, and stood and looked at them. The surest,
safest, biggest game he had ever played, the game that had known no
single hitch, the game that had brought no whispering breath of suspicion flung its tribute in his face. Money that he had never tried to count,
notes of all denominations, large and small, glutted the receptacles —
jewels in necklaces, in rings, in pendants, in brooches, in bracelets,
diamonds, rubies, emeralds, winked at him and scintillated and glowed
and were afire.

And he stood and looked upon them. What was it the Flopper had
said when they had brought the Patriarch back — he did not remember.
What was it that Pale Face Harry had said a little while ago — he did
not remember. These were jewels here and money — wealth — and he
had won the greatest game that was ever played — only he had lost her
— lost Helena. And he stood and looked upon them — and slowly there
crept to his face a white-lipped smile.

"I'm beat!" he whispered hoarsely. "Beat — by the game — I won."

XXI

FACE VALUE

*I*t was evening of the same day – and there came a knock at the outer door of the cottage porch.

The Flopper answered it, and came back to the Patriarch's room; where the Patriarch sat in his armchair; where the lamp, turned low, throwing the little room into half shadow, burned upon the table; where Helena, far away from her immediate surroundings, quite silent and still, her own chair close beside the other's, nestled with her head on the Patriarch's shoulder.

Helena looked up as the Flopper returned.

Upon the Flopper's face was a curious expression – not one that in the days gone by had been habitual – it seemed to mingle a diffidence, a kindly solicitude and a sort of anxious responsibility.

"It's Thornton askin' fer youse," announced the Flopper.

Helena rose from her chair, and started for the door – but the Flopper blocked the way. Helena halted and looked at him in astonishment.

The Flopper licked his lips.

"Say, Helena," he said earnestly, "if I was youse I wouldn't go – say, I'll tell him youse have got de pip an' gone ter bed."

"Not go?" echoed Helena. "What do you mean?"

The Flopper scratched at his chin uneasily.

"Oh, you know!" he said. "De Doc let youse down easy ter-day. Say, if youse had piped his lamps when you drives up in de buzz-wagon dis afternoon youse wouldn't be lookin' fer anymore trouble. Say, I'm tellin' youse straight, Helena. When I was out dere in de kitchen an' youse was in yer room wid him me heart was in me mouth all de time. Youse can take it from me, Helena, he let youse down easy."

Helena's brown eyes, a little wistfully, a little softly, held upon the Flopper.

"Yes?" she said quietly.

"Youse had better cut it out ter-night, Helena," the Flopper went on. "Y'oughter know de Doc by dis time – de guy dat starts anything wid de Doc gets his – dat's all! Remember de night he threw Cleggy down de stairs in de Roost? – an' he was only havin' fun! Say, you go out wid Thornton again ter-night an' de Doc finds it out – an' something'll happen. Say, Helena, fer God's sake, don't youse do it – de Doc was bad enough dis afternoon when he let youse down easy, but he's worse now, an' —"

"Worse?" Helena interrupted, smiling a little apathetically. "In what way is he worse? And how do you know? You haven't seen Doc, have you?"

"No," the Flopper answered, circling his lips with his tongue again. "No; I ain't seen de Doc since — but I seen Pale Face. Say, Helena" — the Flopper's words came stumbling out now, agitated, perturbed, not altogether coherent — "wot's de answer I dunno; I dunno wot's de matter here. Say" — he pointed suddenly to the Patriarch, whose face was turned toward them as he stroked thoughtfully at his silver beard — "he's got me fer fair — dere ain't no fake here — dis way ter live is de real t'ing — he ain't like you an' me — he's *more'n* dat — look at him now — youse'd t'ink he could see us, an' was listenin' ter wot we said. I dunno wot's de end — I dunno wot's de matter wid me. I was scared more'n ever out dere dis afternoon on de lawn, an' I thought mabbe God 'ud strike me dead — but 'tain't only dat I'm scared ter buck de game anymore, 'tain't only dat — I don't *wanter* anymore, an' it don't make no difference about de dough — I wanter live straight, same as him, same as de guys around here, same — same as Mamie. Say, Helena, say, do youse believe in love — in — in de *real* t'ing?"

Helena's apathy was gone now — a flush dyed her cheeks. She was not startled at what the Flopper had said — she had seen it coming, subconsciously, vaguely, mistily, for days now, only she had been immersed in herself — she was not startled, and yet, in a way, she was. The end! She too had been thinking about that — and she too did not know. What *was* the end?

"You were going to say something about Pale Face," she said, prompting the Flopper. "Something about Pale Face and Doc."

"Yes," said the Flopper, and again the tip of his tongue sought his lips nervously. "Dat's why I don't want youse ter go out wid Thornton ter-night. Pale Face has got it de same as me, an' he told de Doc dis afternoon, out in de path dere, after de Doc left de cottage here. Dere was a showdown — see? De Doc 'ud kill youse an' Thornton ter-night if he caught youse tergether. He's like a wild man. When Pale Face tells him he was goin' ter quit, de Doc makes a grab fer him by de t'roat like a tiger, only Pale Face gets away, an' den de Doc goes off widout a word, laughin' like he'd escaped out of a dippy-house. An' Pale Face was shakin' like he had a fit when he gets here. Say, Helena, don't youse go ter-night."

Helena made no answer for a moment. Thoughts, a world of them, confused her, crowded upon her, as they had ever since Madison had left her room a few hours ago — and the future was as some dread, bewildering maze through which she had tried to stumble and grope her way — and had lost herself ever deeper. How full of utter, miserable, bitter irony it was that this thing, unscrupulous and shameful, that they had created in their guilt should have brought the beauty and the glory and the yearning of a new life to her — and yet should chain her remorselessly to the old! True, she had broken with Madison, irrevocably, forever, she supposed, it could not be other than that, for the ugly bond between them was severed — but the game still went on! In repentance, on her bended knees, sobbing as a tired and worn-out child, she could ask for forgiveness; but the double life, the duplicity, by reason of the very nature in which they had fashioned this iniquitous monster, still went on, and like some hideous octopus reached out its waving, feeling tentacles to encircle her — the Patriarch there; the world-wide publicity, those poor creatures upon whose misery and whose suffering, upon whose frantic, frenzied snatching out at hope they had preyed and fed and gorged themselves; the life itself that she had taken up, in its minutiæ, in its care of this great-souled, great-hearted man so dear to her now, the life itself because it was what it was, changed though she herself might be, though her soul cried out against it in its new-found purity — all this still held her fast! The end — she could not see the end. What would Madison do — and there was Thornton. Thornton! She caught her breath a little. Yes; she had promised Thornton she would see him tonight — she knew well enough why he wanted to see her — last night had told her that — he loved her. Her face softened. Last night — it seemed a thousand years ago, and it seemed but as an instant passed — last night — she had learned what love was, and —

The Flopper stirred uneasily.

"Wot'll I tell him?" asked the Flopper. "He's waitin' out dere by de porch."

"Why — why nothing," said Helena, and she smiled a little tremulously at the Flopper. "Nothing. I'll — I'll go and see him."

"Say, Helena," protested the Flopper, "don't youse —"

But Helena stepped by him now.

"Don't leave the Patriarch," she cautioned, turning on the threshold. "I — I won't be late."

She passed down the little hall, through the still, quiet room beyond, empty now, through the porch, and out into the night — and then from out the shadows by the row of maples, Thornton came hurriedly toward her, holding out his hands.

"It's good of you to come, Miss Vail," he said, in his grave, quiet way. "You must be nearly dead with weariness after last night, and I am afraid I am not very thoughtful — only I —" he broke off suddenly. "Shall we sit here on the bench for a little while, or would you rather walk — I — I have something to say to you."

It was very dark — the storm of the night before still lingered in a wrack of flying clouds, scurrying one after the other, veiling the stars — and the moon was hidden — and hidden too was the sudden whiteness of Helena's face. She knew what he had to say, knew it before she had come to him — and yet she was there — and she had come resolutely enough — only now she was afraid.

"I would rather walk a little, I think," she said. "Here where — where I can be within call. My absence last night seems to have made the Patriarch very uneasy, you know, and — and — let us just walk up and down here beneath the maples in front of the cottage."

How heavy upon the air lay the fragrance of the flowers; how still the night was, save for the constant muffled boom of the breaking surf! — for a moment an almost ungovernable impulse swept upon her to make some excuse, anything, no matter how wild, a sudden faintness, anything, and run from him back into the cottage. And then she tried to think, think in a desperate sort of way of some subject of conversation that she might introduce that would stave off, postpone, defer the words that she knew were even now on his lips — nothing — she could think of nothing — only that she might have let the Flopper have his way, have let him tell Thornton that she had gone to bed with — the pip. The *pip!* She could have screamed out hysterically as the word flashed all unbidden upon her — it stood for a very great deal that word — her world of the years of yesterday. Could she never get away from that world; was it too late — already! Could she, even with all the earnestness, all the yearning that filled her soul, ever live it down, ever be what Naida Thornton had called her that night — a good woman! Could she —

Thornton was speaking now — how strange that she would have done anything, given anything to prevent his speaking — and done anything, given anything to make him speak! How strange and perplexed and dismayed her brain was! Love! Yes; she wanted love! God knew she wanted love such as his was — for he had shown her what love, free from abasing passion, in its purest sense, was. Like a glimpse of glory, hallowed, full of wondrous amazement, it came to her — and then her head was lowered, and the whiteness was upon her face again.

He had halted suddenly and detained her with his hand upon her arm — with that touch, so full of reverence, of fine deference, that had thrilled her before — that thrilled her now, awakening into fuller life these new emotions whose birth was in gladder, sweeter, purer aspirations.

"Miss Vail," he said, in a low voice, "there was a letter — a letter that

Naida left — did you know of it?"

They were close together, and it was very dark — but was it dark enough to hide the crimson that she felt sweeping in a flood to her face! What was in that letter? Had Mrs. Thornton written as she had talked, or only about the Patriarch and the work in Needley? She had forgotten for the moment about the letter — if there were more in it than that, if it were about Thornton and herself and what Mrs. Thornton had hoped for between them, and she admitted knowledge of it, what would he think, what *could* he think of her! But to deny it — no, not now. Once, and this came to her in a little thrill of gladness, she would not have hesitated; but now it — it was — it was not that world of yesterday.

"Yes," she said faintly; "she told me that she had left a letter for you."

"It was about the work here," said Thornton gently. "Her whole soul seemed wrapped up in that — and she asked me as her last wish to do what she would have done if she had lived; and she spoke of you very beautifully." Thornton paused for a moment — then he laid his hands on Helena's shoulders — and she felt them tremble a little. "Miss Vail — Helena," he said, and his voice was full of passionate earnestness now, "I cannot say these things well — only simply. I came back here to take an interest in the work, for I too have it at heart — but I have more than that now — there is *you* — your dear self. I love you, Helena — you have come into my life until you are everything and all to me. Helena, look up at me — will you marry me, dear? Tell me what I long to hear. Helena, Helena — I love you!"

But Helena did not answer — only very slowly she raised her head. And his hands on her shoulders tightened, and he was drawing her gently toward him. Then he bent his head until it was close to hers, and his breath was upon her cheek as it had been that other night — and the longing to know that it was hers, a caress, pure in its motive, hers, snatched out of all that had gone before that sought to rob her of the right to ever know it, fascinated her, held her spellbound, possessed her. Closer his lips came to hers, closer, until they touched her — and then, with a cry, she sprang back, and her hands were fiercely pressed against her cheeks, her throbbing temples. Was she mad! Mad! Was it for this that she had forced herself to give him the opportunity to speak tonight, when her motive was so different, when it had seemed the only *right* thing left for her to do!

And now, still holding her temples, she raised her eyes to Thornton — he had stepped back like a man stricken, his hands dropped to his sides.

"I — we are mad!" she whispered.

"Helena!" he said in a numbed way; and again; "Helena!" Then, with an effort to control his voice: "You — you do not care — you do not love me?"

"No," she said — and thereafter for a long time a silence held between them.

Then Thornton spoke.

"Some day perhaps, Helena," he said, "you could learn to love me — for I would teach you. Perhaps now you feel that your whole duty lies here in this work to which you have so unselfishly given your life; but I would not hinder that, only try to help as best I could. Perhaps I have been abrupt, have spoken too soon — it is only a few weeks since I saw you first, but it seems as though in those few weeks I had come to know you as if I had known you all my life and —"

But now she interrupted him, shaking her head in a sad little fashion.

"You do not know me," she said. "Sometimes I think I do not know myself. Think! You do not know where I came from to join the Patriarch here; you have no single shred of knowledge about me; you do not know a single particular of my life before you knew me."

"I do not need to know," he answered gravely. "You are as genuine as pure gold is genuine — it is in your voice, your smile, your eyes. It is a crude simile perhaps, but one never asks where the pure gold was dug — it stands for itself, for what it is, because it is what it is — pure gold — at its face value."

The words seemed to stab at Helena, condemning, accusing; and yet, too, in a strange, vague way, they seemed to bring her a hope, a promise for the days to come — at face value! If she could live hereafter — at face value!

"Listen," she said, and her voice was very low. "I do not know how to say what I must say to you. Last night I knew that — that you loved me. I had not thought of you like that, in that way, until then, or — or I should have tried never to have let this hurt come to you. But last night I knew, and since then I have known that sooner or later you would — would tell me of it." She stopped for an instant — her eyes full of tears now. "And so," she went on presently, "I have let you speak tonight because it was better, it was even necessary that I should do so at once — because this could not go on — because you must go away and —"

"Necessary?" he repeated. "I — I do not understand."

"No," she said helplessly; "you do not understand — and I — I cannot explain. Oh, I do not know what to say to you, only that you must take what I say, as you have taken me — at face value."

"I do not understand," he said again. "Helena, I do not understand. Are you in trouble — tell me?"

"No," she said.

"But I cannot go away like this!" he cried out suddenly. "I cannot go and leave you, Helena. You have come into my life and filled it; and I cannot let you pass out of it — like this — without an effort to hold what has come to mean everything to me now. You may not love me now, but some day —"

She shook her head, interrupting him once more.

"There can never be a 'some day,'" she said. "Oh, I do not want to hurt you — you, to whom I owe more than you will ever know — but — but there can never be anything between us, and — and we are only making it harder for ourselves now — aren't we?"

And then he leaned abruptly toward her.

"Is there — someone else?" he asked in a strained voice.

And to Helena the question came as though it had been an inspiration given him — for after that he would ask no more, seek no more to understand, for he was too big and strong and fine for that; and even if it was hopeless now this love that she had known for Madison, even if it could never be again, still that love was hers, and she could answer truthfully.

"Yes," she said beneath her breath.

For a moment Thornton neither moved nor spoke. Then he held out his hand.

"Miss Vail," he said simply, "will you tell this 'someone else' that another man beside himself is the better for having known you. Good-night. And may God bring you happiness through all your life."

But she did not speak — they were standing by the rustic bench and she sank down upon it, and, with her head hidden in one arm outflung across the back of the seat, was sobbing softly.

And he stood and watched her for a little space, his face grave and white; then taking the hand that lay listlessly in her lap, he raised it to his lips — and turned away.

And so he left her — and so, because of this, he knocked upon another door that night, and all unwittingly gave to that "someone else" himself the message that he had asked Helena to deliver.

Madison, pacing his room like a caged beast, his teeth working upon the cigar that he had never thought to light, paid no attention to the summons until it had been repeated twice; then, with a glance around the room, his eyes lingering for a critical instant upon the trunks, closed now, the trays restored to their hiding places, he stepped to the door, unlocked it, and flung it open. And at sight of Thornton, mechanically, as second nature to him, outwardly, like a mask, there came a smile upon his working lips, a suave, unconcerned composure to his face;

while inwardly, in his dazed, fogged brain where chaos raged, surged an impulse to fling himself upon the other, wreck a mad vengeance upon the man — and then swift upon the heels of this an impulse to refrain, for if Helena was straight why should he harm Thornton — and then the shuttle again — why should he not — hadn't Helena said that she had learned what love was last night — and last night she had been with Thornton. How his brain whirled! What had brought Thornton here, anyhow? If he stayed very long perhaps he would batter Thornton to jelly after all! Quick, almost instantaneous in their sequence came this wild jumble singing dizzily its crazy refrain through his mind — and then to his amazement he heard someone speaking pleasantly — and to his amazement it was himself.

"Come in, Thornton. Come in — and take a chair."

"Thanks," Thornton answered; and, entering the room, closed the door behind him. "No; I won't sit down — I shall only remain a moment."

The lamp was on the washstand, and, intuitively again, Madison shifted his position to bring his face into shadow — and leaned against the foot of the bed. He stared at Thornton, nodding — Thornton's face was white and exceedingly haggard — rather curious for Thornton to look that way!

"Madison," said Thornton abruptly, "I believe you to be a gentleman in the best sense of the word, and because of that, and because of the unusual circumstances that first brought us together and the mutual interests that have since been ours, I have come to you tonight to tell you, first, that I am going away from Needley and that I shall not return — and then to ask a service and repose a trust in you. You have said several times that you intended to remain here and take a personal and active part in the work?"

Madison removed the chewed cigar end from one corner of his mouth — and placed it in the other.

"Yes," said Madison.

"Then this is what I want to say," said Thornton seriously. "For my own sake, because it was my wife's wish, and for other reasons as well, my interest here, though I am going away, will be just as great as it has ever been; and so I want you to keep me thoroughly posted, and when the time comes that I can be of further material assistance to let me know. I impose only one condition — you are to say nothing to Miss Vail about it — you can make anything that I may do appear to come from yourself."

"Say nothing to Miss Vail!" repeated Madison vaguely — then a sort of ironic jest seemed to take possession of him: "But Miss Vail keeps all the funds."

"That is why I am asking you to represent me," said Thornton quietly. "I am afraid that she might have a natural diffidence about accepting anything more from me — I asked Miss Vail to marry me tonight, and she refused."

The cigar kind of slid down unnoticed from the corner of Madison's mouth — and he leaned forward, hanging with a hand behind him to the bedpost — and stared at Thornton.

"You — *what!*" he gasped.

"Yes; I know," Thornton answered — and moved abruptly toward the door. "Love makes one's temerity very great — doesn't it? I asked her to marry me — because I loved her." He came back from the door and held out his hand, "I've told you what I would tell no other man, Madison. You understand now why — and you'll do this for me?"

What answer Madison made he never knew himself — he only knew that he was staring at the door after Thornton had gone out, and that he wanted to laugh crazily. Marry Helena! Thornton had asked Helena to marry him because he loved her. God, there was humor here! His brain itself seemed to cackle at it — *marry* Helena!

And then suddenly there seemed no humor at all — only black, infamous shame and condemnation — and he straightened up from where he leaned against the bedpost, his face set and strained.

"Thornton had asked Helena to marry him because he *loved* her" — the words came slowly, haltingly, aloud — and then he covered his face with his hands. But he, he who loved her too — what had *he* done!

XXII

THE SHRINE

*F*or a little time Madison stood there in his room, motionless, staring unseeingly before him — and then, as one awakening from a dream that had brought dismay and a torment too realistic to be thrown from him on the instant, his brain still a little blunted, he took up his hat mechanically, went out from the room, descended by the back stairs to the rear door of the hotel, and took the road to the Patriarch's cottage.

And as he walked in the freshness of the night, the restless turmoil of his soul that since early afternoon had brought him near to the verge of madness itself, that had robbed him of sane virility, that a moment since in his room had suddenly begun to lift from him even as the leaden clouds in the vault above him now were scattering, breaking, and through the rifts a moon-glint and the starlight came, passed from him utterly — and a strange calm, a strange joy, a strange sadness was upon him — and his brain for the first time in many hours was rational, keen — and he was master of himself again — and yet master of himself no more!

He smiled a little at the seeming paradox — smiled a little wistfully. He was beaten — by the game — he had won. How strange it was that sense of more than resignation now — a sense that seemed like one of thankfulness — a sense that bade him fling wide his arms as though suddenly they had been loosed from bondage and he was free, free as the God-given air around him.

He could understand Helena, and the Flopper, and Pale Face Harry now. With them it had come slowly, in a gradual concatenation, a progression, as it were, that had worked upon them, molding them, changing them day by day — and he had been too blind to see, or, seeing, had measured the changes only by a standard as false as all his life had been false. With him it had come in a crash, unheralded, that had left him a naked, quivering, stricken thing to know madness, terror and despair, to taste of emotions that had sickened the soul itself.

On Madison walked — along the road, across the little bridge, into the wagon track where, under the arched branches, it was utter dark. There was no one upon the road — he passed no one — saw no one — he was alone.

He had lost Helena — but he understood her now — understood the depth of remorse that she was living through, the terror and the dread as she sought escape, the fear of him — yes, it would be fear now where once it had been love! He had lost Helena — that was the price he had paid — but he understood her now, and he was going to her to help her if he could, going to tell her that he, too, was changed — as she was changed.

His hands clenched suddenly. God, the misery, the hopelessness, the wreck and ruin that lay at his door! And amends — what amends could he make — it was too late for that! How clearly he saw now — when it was too late! Her life was a broken thing, robbed, stripped and despoiled for all the years to come. Their love had not been love — she had given it its name — "passion, vice, lust, sin, degradation and misery and shame." And then love had come to her, into her life, love as God had meant love to be, and she had learned what love was she had said — only that she might never know its fullness, only that it might bring her added bitterness and added sorrow! Thornton had asked her to marry him that night — and she had refused him — because the past, it must have been as a shuddering, hideous phantom that the past had risen before her, had left her no other thing to do but turn away. It seemed he could see her — see her bury her face in her hands and —

He stopped short in his walk. Was he changed so much as this! Did he care so much that it was her happiness — even with another — that counted most! Yes; it was true — he was changed indeed. And the change had brought him too, it seemed, to learn what love was — too late.

He went forward again — a little more slowly; now; a sadness upon him, but, through the sadness, an uplift from that new sense of freedom that was as a balm, soothing him in the most curious way. His had been a rude awakening — mind and body and soul had been torn asunder; but he knew now, as he recalled the hours just past when he had looked on fear, when the gamut of human passion had raged over him, when he had stood staggered and appalled before, yes, before his God, that he had come forth a new man. And how strange had been the ending, how strange and simple, and yet how significant, typifying the broad, clean outlook on life, bringing coherency to his tottering mind, had been those words of Thornton's — "because he loved her."

He had reached the end of the wagon track now, and he walked across the lawn, his steps noiseless on the velvet sward, and passed between the maples; and the moon gleam — for the flying clouds, rear-guard of the routed storm, were flung wide apart, dispersed — fell upon a coiled and huddled little figure all in white, that was quite still and motionless upon the rustic seat beside the porch.

She did not see him, did not hear him, until he stood before her and called her name.

"Helena!" he said unsteadily. "Helena!"

She raised her head and looked at him; and then she rose from the bench, and, still holding to it by one hand, drew back a little. There was no outcry, no startled action. Her dark eyes played questioningly upon him — and he could see that they were wet with tears, and that the face from out of which they looked was very white.

"Why have you come back here tonight?" she asked in a low tone; and then, suddenly, a fear, a terror in her voice, as the Flopper's warning flashed upon her: "Thornton — you have seen Thornton?"

"Yes," he said, surprised a little that she should know; "I saw Thornton a few minutes ago."

She came toward him now and clutched his arm.

"What have you done?" she cried tensely. "Answer me! You — you met him on your way here?"

It was a moment before Madison replied. He had schooled himself of course for more than this, yet the words hurt — that was why she had asked for Thornton — she was afraid that he had harmed the man.

"No," he said; "I did not meet him. I think you must have been longer here on that bench than you imagined — haven't you? He came to my room."

"Your room! What for? Tell me!"

Madison smiled with grave whimsicality.

"To call me a gentleman and repose a trust."

She stepped back again, uncertainly.

"I do not know what you are talking about," she said in a strained way. "And you are talking very strangely."

"Yes," he said. "Everything is strange tonight. It is like a new world, and — and I have not found my way — yet."

She drew back still further.

"Are you mad?" she whispered.

"No," he answered. "Not now — that Is past."

She looked at him for a little time; and, her hands joined before her, her fingers locked and interlocked nervously.

"And — and Thornton?" she asked, at last.

"It was a trust," said Madison slowly; "but it was betrayed before it was given. He did not know — the game. He did not know what was between — you and me."

"No," she said — and the word came almost inaudibly.

"And so," he said, "I will tell you, for it cannot matter now in any case. He told me that he had asked you to marry him tonight — and that you had refused."

Madison paused, and swept his hand across his forehead — his voice somehow had suddenly grown hoarse, beyond control.

"Yes," she said — and reached again for the back of the bench, supporting herself against it.

"He is going away," Madison continued; "and he is to send more money here for the 'cause' — when I ask for it — only you are not to know, because you might be diffident about taking it after refusing him."

She stared at him numbly — there was no sarcasm in his words; in his tones only a sort of dreary monotony. She shivered a little — how cold it seemed! She did not quite grasp his words — and yet she shrank from them. And then her very soul seemed to cry out against them, to pit itself against their meaning, as their meaning surged upon her. And unconsciously she drew herself up, and the whiteness of her face fled before a rush of color.

"Oh, the shame of it!" she burst out. "The bitter shame of it! You shall not touch the money — do you hear! You shall not touch it! I — I thought that you had understood this afternoon. I am glad then that you have come tonight — if I must say more to make you understand. This is the end! I do not care what happens — the little I can do now to atone for what I have done, I am going to do. The game is at an end — you shall not touch another cent — and everything that we have taken goes back to those whom we have worse than robbed it from! You hear — you understand! I will cry it out in the town street if there is no other way — but it shall stop — it shall stop tonight" — she was panting, breathless, the little figure erect, outraged, quivering — and then suddenly the shoulders seemed to droop, the lips to tremble, and she was on her knees upon the grass beside the bench, and sobbing as a child.

"Helena!" Madison said hoarsely. "Helena! Listen! That is what I came for tonight — to find a way out for you, for us all, if I can."

The passionate outburst passed — and she was on her feet again, facing him.

"You are clever — clever!" she cried fiercely. "But you shall not play with me — you shall not trick me — I meant every word I said!"

But now Madison made no answer. The moonlight bathed them both in its clear, white radiance; and touched the sward, shading it to softest green; and the trees limned out like fairy things against the night; and the calm light flooded the little cottage with its hidden walls where the ivy and the creepers grew, and lingered over the trellises to drink the fragrance of the flowers that peeped out from their leafy beds. And upon Madison's face crept slowly the anguish that was in his soul — until it was mirrored there — until unconsciously it answered her where words would have been useless things. Like some white-robed, sorrowing angel, she seemed, as she stood there before him — the brown eyes full of shadow, troubled; the sweet face tear-splashed; the little figure in its simple muslin frock, pitiful in its brave defiance. And pure — just God, how pure she looked! — the brow stainless white under the mass of dark, coiled hair; the perfect throat of ivory. And — and the misery that was in every feature of her face, in every line of her poise — and he had brought her that — *he* had brought her to that — and now when he loved her as he might have loved her once and known her love in return, when his heart cried out for her, when she was all in life he cared for, she was gone from him, out of his life, and between them was a barrier he could never pass — a barrier of his own raising.

And so he made no answer, for indeed he had not heard her; but she was coming toward him now, her hands outstretched in a wondering way, wistfully, pleadingly, as though to hold back a refutation that would change the dawning light upon her face to dismay and grief again.

"It – it is true," she faltered. "It has come to you too – this change, this new life that has come to me. It is true – I can see it in your face."

"Yes; it is true," he answered, in a low voice.

"Thank God!" she whispered – and hid her face in her hands – and presently he heard her sob again.

A tiny cloud edged the moon, and the light faded, and it grew dark, and the darkness hid her; then softly, timidly almost it seemed, the radiance came creeping through the branches overhead again – and then he spoke.

"Helena," he said, steadying his voice with an effort, "you spoke of atonement a little while ago; but there is no atonement that I can make to you – nothing that I can do to change what I would give my soul to change. I know what it meant to you to send Thornton away tonight, for I love you now as you love him – I know why you did it, and –"

She was staring at him a little wildly – her hands pressed against her cheeks.

"Love – Thornton," she repeated in a sort of wondering way, a long pause between the words.

"Yes," he said gently; "I know. Have you forgotten what you told me this afternoon? – that you had learned – last night – what love was."

She shook her head.

"I do not love Thornton," she said in a monotone. "And yet it is true that through him I learned what love was, what it *could* be – don't you understand?"

Understand! No; it seemed that he could never understand! She did not love Thornton! And then, as some fiery cordial, the words seemed to whip through his veins, quickening the beat of his heart into wild, tumultuous throbbing. Yes, yes, he could understand – it was true – true – she did not love Thornton.

"Helena!" he cried – and stretched out his arms to her. "I thought, oh, God, I thought that I had lost you – Helena!"

But she did not move.

"What does it matter to you whether I love Thornton or not?" she said dully. "Does it change anything where you and I are concerned – does it change what I told you this afternoon – that I would not go back to *that.*"

"To that! Ah, no!" – his voice rang dominant, vibrant, triumphant now. "Helena, don't you understand? We are to begin life again – in a new way, the true way, the only way. Don't you see – I love you!"

Still she did not move – but there was a great whiteness in her face, and in the whiteness a great light.

"You mean?" — her lips scarcely seemed to form the words.

"Yes!" he cried. "Yes; to make a home for you, to marry you if only you love me still, to live in God's own sight and hold you as a sacred gift — Helena! Helena!" — his arms went out to her again, and the yearning in his soul was in his voice — to crush her to him, to hold her in his arms, and hold her there where none should take her from him, to shield and guard her through the years to come, to live with her a life that seemed to break now in a vista of gladness, of glory, as the day-dawn breaks with its golden rays of God-given promise — the new life, perfect and pure and innocent — because he loved her. "Helena! Speak to me. Tell me that it is not too late — tell me that you love me too."

And then her eyes were raised to his, and they were wet — but there was love-light and a wondrous happiness shining through the tears.

"Helena!" he murmured brokenly — and swept her into his arms — and kissed the eyelids, lowered now, the hair, the white brow, the lips — kissed her, and held her there, her clinging arms about his neck, her face half hidden on his shoulder.

And so for a space they stood there — and there were no words to say, only the song in their hearts in deathless melody — but after a little time he held her from him, and lifted up her face that he might look his fill upon it.

"Helena," he said, "I cannot understand it all yet — it is as though it were born out of the sin and the darkness and the blackness of what is gone — as though here at this Shrine that we created in mockery and crime it was meant that you and I should save each other for each other. And yet this Shrine as we have made it is a thing of guilt, and it has brought us all, you and I, and Harry, and the Flopper to a new life."

She lay still for a moment in his arms — then her hand crept up and touched his forehead and smoothed back his hair.

"I do not quite know how to say it," she said a little timidly. "When you went away this afternoon, the Patriarch took me back into his room, and — and I knelt at his knees — and after a little while my mind seemed very calm and quiet — do you know what I mean? And I tried to think things out — and understand. And it seemed to come to me that there was a shrine everywhere if we would only look for it — that God has put a shrine in every heart, only we are so blind — that everyone can make their own surroundings beautiful and good and true, no matter where they are, or how poor, or how rich — and if they live like that they must be good and true themselves."

"Yes," he said slowly; then, after a moment: "And faith too is very much like that."

"Only some need a sign," she said.

There was silence again, while her hand crept over his face and back to his forehead to smooth his hair once more — and then very gently she slipped out of his arms.

"What are we to do about — about everything here?" she asked soberly. "We are forgetting that in our own happiness. How are we going to return the money that we have taken?"

"I don't know yet," he answered. "I haven't thought much about it — but we'll manage somehow."

She shook her head.

"I've thought a great deal about it since yesterday — and I'm not so sure it is to be 'managed somehow' — and the more I've thought the more tangled and complicated it has become."

"Well, we'll untangle it tomorrow," said Madison, with a smile, "and —"

"No" — she touched his sleeve. "Tonight. Let us do it now — tonight. I should be so happy then."

He smiled at her again, and drew her to him.

"But we ought to have Pale Face and the Flopper too, don't you think so?" he said.

"Of course," she said; "and so we will. The Flopper is here, and we can send him for Harry. It's early yet — not ten o'clock."

"All right," said Madison; "if you wish it. We'll go in then and get the Flopper."

And so they walked to the cottage door, and into the porch — but in the porch Madison held her for a moment, and lifted up her face again and looked into her eyes.

"My — wife," he whispered — and took her in his arms.

XXIII

THE WAY OUT

Strange scene indeed! Strange antithesis to that other night when these four were gathered in that crime-reeked, sordid room at the Roost — where Pale Face Harry, gaunt, emaciated, coughed, and, trembling, plunged a morphine needle in his arm; where the Flopper, a wretched tatterdemalion from the gutter, licked greedy lips and gloated in his rascality; where Helena, flushed-faced, inhaled her interminable cigarettes and dangled her legs from the table edge; where Madison, suave, flippant, so certain of his own infallibility, glorying in his crooked masterpiece, laid the tribute to genius at his own feet!

Strange scene! Strange antithesis indeed! It was quiet here — very still — only the distant, muffled boom of the pounding surf. And the shrine-room, for the first time since its creation, was locked against the night. It lay now in shadow from the single lamp upon the table — and the light, where it fell in a shortened circle, for the lamp itself had a little green paper shade, was soft, subdued and mellow.

Where he had been wont to sit in the days gone by, the Patriarch sat now in his armchair by the empty fireplace — in the shadow — his head turned in his strange, listening, attentive way toward the table — toward the four who were grouped around it. There had been no one to stay with him in his own room, and so Helena had brought him there — to play his silent part.

At the table, Pale Face Harry, bronzed and rugged, clear-eyed, a robust figure from his clean living, his months of the out-of-doors, traced the grain of the wood on the table mechanically with his finger nail, his face sober, perplexed; while the Flopper, clear-eyed too, his face almost a handsome one in its bright alertness, now that it had rounded out and the hard, premature lines were gone, mirrored Pale Face Harry's perturbed expression, his eyes fixed anxiously on Madison opposite him; and Helena, sitting beside Madison, was very quiet, her forehead wrinkled and pursed up into little furrows, the brown eyes with a hint of dismay and consternation lurking in their depths, one hand stretched out to lay quite unconsciously on Madison's sleeve — and from the sleeve to steal occasionally into Madison's hand.

Madison, his lips tight, pushed back his chair suddenly — they had been sitting there an hour.

"You were right, Helena," he said, with a nervous laugh. "The more you try to figure it out the worse it gets."

"Aw, say, Doc," pleaded the Flopper desperately, "don't youse give it up — youse have got de head — youse ain't never left us in a hole yet."

Madison looked at him, and smiled mirthlessly.

"My head!" he exclaimed bitterly. "I got you into this, all of you — but it will take more than my head to get you out. If I could stand for it myself, I'd do it — but I can't without dragging you in too — we're too intimately mixed up. If I said it was a deal of mine — they'd ask where Helena came from — they'd ask where you came from, Flopper.

We're beaten — beaten every way we turn. The game has got us — we haven't a move. We played it to the limit, the slickest swindle that was ever worked, and it worked till there's more money than I've tried to count. And then it changed us from thieves, from — from anything you like — and now that we want to quit, now that we want a chance to make good, it's got us in its grip and we can't get away." He flirted a bead of moisture from his forehead. "My God, I don't know what to do!" he muttered hoarsely. "It was easy enough to *talk* about stopping this thing, about returning the money — but I can't see the way out."

No one answered him — all were silent — as silent as the mute and venerable figure that sat, listening attentively it seemed, in the armchair by the fireplace.

Madison turned abruptly after a moment to Pale Face Harry.

"You, Harry," he said, laying a hand on the other's shoulder, "you're the only one of the four that can walk out of it — you don't show in the center of the stage — you go. You said the old folks would cry over you — twenty years is a long time to stay away from the old folks — I — I never knew mine. You go on back to the little farm out there in the West where you said you'd like to go, and — and give the old people a hand for the years they've got left."

Pale Face Harry shook his head.

"God knows I'd like to," he said, choking a little; "that's what I counted on. God knows I'd like to go out there and lead a decent life — but I don't go that way — I don't crawl out and leave you — what's coming to you is coming to me."

"That won't help us any, Harry," said Madison softly, and his hand tightened in an eloquent pressure on Pale Face Harry's shoulder. "You go — and God bless you!"

Again Pale Face Harry shook his head.

"No," he said. "I stick. If the game's got you, it's got me too — to the limit. There's no use talking about that."

The Flopper licked his lips miserably.

"Swipe me!" he mumbled. "Hell wasn't never like dis! Me an' Mamie we've got it fixed, an' her old man says he'll take me inter de store. Say, Doc, say — ain't dere a chanst ter live straight now we wants ter?"

But Madison did not hear the Flopper save in a vague, inconsequential way — he was looking at Helena. She had drooped forward a little over the table, her chin in her hands, her lips quivering — and a white misery in her face seemed to bring a chill, a numbness to his heart. His Hands clenched, and he began to pace up and down the room.

How buoyantly he had tackled the problem — buoyant in his own emancipation, buoyant in his love, in the future full of dreams, full of inspiration, full of the new life that Helena and he would live together! How confidently he had settled himself to undo in a moment the work of months, to outline a mere matter of detail, with never a thought that he was face to face with a problem that he could never solve — that brought him to the realization that the game, not he, was the master still, iron-handed, implacable — that though the mental chains were loosed it was but as if, in ironic justice, in grim punishment, only that he might look, clear-visioned, upon the ignominy of the physical shackles he himself had forged and fashioned so readily, whose breaking now was beyond his strength.

He had done his work well! In the first few moments, an hour ago, when he had begun to consider the problem, as seeming difficulties arose, he had turned coolly from one alternative to another. And then slowly a sickening sense of the truth had begun to dawn upon him — and like a man lost in a great forest, peril around him, he had plunged then desperately in this direction and in that, as a glimmering point of light here or there had seemed to promise an avenue of escape — only to find it vanish at almost the first step, the way closed as by some invisible, remorseless power. No, not invisible — it seemed to take the form of the Patriarch — for at every turn the majestic figure stood and would not let him pass.

Madison's face was grey now as he walked up and down the room — there was his own revulsion, his abhorrence at the part he had played, a frantic, honorable eagerness to be rid of it; there were these others too who looked to him, the Flopper and Pale Face Harry; and there was — Helena! He did not dare to look at the misery in her face again — he was unmanned enough now.

And then Helena spoke.

"It — it seems," she said, in a low broken way, "as if — as if God did not want to pardon us — as if our repentance had come too late, and that there was no Eleventh Hour for us." Then, in passionate pleading, facing Madison: "God cannot mean that — it is we who cannot see. There is some way out — there must be — there *must* be."

"It begins and ends with the Patriarch," said Madison monotonously. "We can't sacrifice him — can we! What's the use of going over it again? It all comes back to the same point — the Patriarch."

"Yes, yes; I know, I know," she said piteously. "But think, Doc — *think!* See now, we just send back all the money and jewels — we know to whom they belong."

"Well, what reason do we give?" Madison said heavily. "The Patriarch is alive and well. The immediate corollary is that from the moment we do that, tomorrow morning for instance, every gift, every offering here is suddenly refused. What reason do we give? If it were only the donors who were to be considered it might be done. It's human nature that ninety-nine out of every hundred of them" — his voice rose a little bitterly — "would probably be only too glad to get their money back — and the mere statement that you, as the Patriarch's grand-niece, his only relative, on mature thought did not consider the project as planned advisable might suffice. But this thing goes beyond that, beyond even the remaining few who are earnestly interested and would cause us trouble — it is world-wide in its publicity! Every newspaper in the land would snatch at it for a headline, and ask — why? And they would not be content with simply asking why — this thing is too big for that — too much before the people's eyes — too good 'copy.' They'd start in to find out — and the result is inevitable. Our safety so far has lain in the fact that there has been no suspicion aroused; but snooping around a bank vault at midnight with a mask on and a bull's-eye lantern fades to a whisper as a suspicion-arouser compared with anybody willingly cough-ing up a bunch of money once they've got their claws on it — and a yellow journal, let alone an army corps of them, on the scent of a possible sensation has all the detective bureaus in the country pinned to the ropes — they'd have us uncovered quicker than I like to think about it — and that means —"

He stopped, and with a hurried motion, carried his hands across his eyes — Helena, pure as one of God's own angels now, to come to that, to come to —

It was the Flopper who completed the sentence.

"Ten spaces up de river," said the Flopper, and shivered, and his tongue sought his lips; "or mabbe — mabbe twenty."

Pale Face Harry stirred uneasily.

"There's the other way," he said without looking up, his eyes on his finger nail that traced the grain of the wood again. "Get the money and the sparklers all done up and addressed to the ones they came from, send 'em off in a bunch to Thornton — and we fly the coop before he gets them, disappear, fade away — and take our chances of getting caught."

"An' den it's all off wid me an' Mamie" — the Flopper's face grew hard. "Nix on dat! Dat don't go!"

"We cannot do that, Harry," said Helena, in a tired voice. "There is — the Patriarch."

"Yes," said Madison, beginning his stride up and down the room again. "After all, whether we could give back the money without being caught, or whether we couldn't, is not the vital thing; there is — the Patriarch."

Helena's eyes were on the silent figure in the shadows by the fireplace.

"If — if it were not for him," she said, "I think that perhaps — perhaps I might be brave enough to confess it all, and — and not try to escape from the punishment that I deserve. But he would know — he cannot see, nor hear, nor speak, but he would know — as he seems so strangely, so wonderfully, so supernaturally to know and understand everything. And, oh, he means so much to me, to us all, for it is he, more than anyone else, who has saved us from — from what we were. And he loves us. It would shatter his faith, ruin all that his life has meant to him, and — and we cannot bring him grief and sorrow like that. Oh, what can we do! What *can* we do! We cannot stop — and we cannot go on! We cannot stay here even if we returned the money successfully, and we cannot stay here if we kept it as it is; for things would still have to go on as they are, even if we didn't mean to steal anymore, no matter what we might say or do, for it's beyond our control now, and to stay means that we should still have to live and lead our double lives, still have to practice hypocrisy and deceit, and — and I cannot — we cannot do that anymore. And the only way to get away from it all is to run away — and we can't do that, either! There is — the Patriarch. We cannot leave him — to break his heart — with none he loves to care for him. We can't do that. He is a very old, old man, and — and I think he has been happy with us, and — and we must make him happy always as long as he lives. We cannot go away and leave him. We can't do that." Then, in a heartbroken, despairing cry: "We can't do — *anything!*"

No one answered her. She had begged Madison to go over it all again — and she had summed it up herself. There was — the Patriarch.

There was utter silence in the room now, save only for that low, solemn boom of distant surf — for Madison had stopped his nervous pacing up and down, and stood now by the Patriarch's armchair gazing into the fireplace.

The minutes passed, and the silence in that dim, shadowed room grew tense — and tenser still — until the very shadows themselves, as the lamp flickered now and then, seemed to creep and shift and readjust themselves in stealth. No sound — no movement — utter stillness — only, from without, the mourning of the surf, like a dirge now.

And then, with a sudden sob, Helena flung out her arms across the table toward the Patriarch.

"Oh, if he could only speak!" she cried pitifully. "If he could only speak — he would show us the way out."

The words seemed to come to Madison as an added pang. He turned his eyes instinctively from the fireplace to the Patriarch beside him — and then, a moment, as a man stricken, he stood there — and then reaching quickly for the lamp from the table he held it up, and leaned forward toward the figure in the chair.

Helena, startled at the act, rose almost unconsciously to her feet, her hands holding tightly to the table edge — looking at Madison, looking at the silent form where Pale Face Harry, where the Flopper looked.

"What is it?" she asked tensely, under her breath.

Madison's lips moved — silently. His face was white, ashen — there was no color in it. Then his lips moved once more.

"The way out," he said; and again, in a low, awed way: *"The way out.* We can make restitution now — we can give it all back — he *has* shown us the way out."

Helena's lips were quivering, tears were dimming the brown eyes, trembling on the lashes, as she stepped now to Madison's side.

"It is God who has shown us the way out," she whispered brokenly — and dropping down before the chair, her little form shaken with sobs, she hid her face on the Patriarch's knees.

And serene and peaceful as a child in sleep, a smile like a benediction on the saintly face, the Patriarch sat in his armchair by the fireplace where he had been wont to sit in years gone by — and so he had passed on.

The Patriarch was dead.

XXIV

VALE!

*T*he years have passed — but in their passing have brought few changes to the little village nestling in the Maine pines that border on the sea. Not many changes — it is as though Time had touched it loath to touch at all; as though some spirit lingering there, sweet and fresh and vernal, had bade Time stay its hand.

Not many changes — the same familiar faces gather around the stove in the hotel office; and, neither as a memory, nor yet as of one who has gone, but as if he were amongst them, living still, they speak of the Patriarch as of yore.

And with this little circle of kindly, simple folk Time has dealt gently too, for there is only one who is no more — Cale Rodgers, the proprietor of the general store.

But the general store on the village street still flourishes, and in Cale Rodgers' place is one whose speech is still a marvelous thing in staid old New England ears — it is an Irish brogue perhaps, for his name is Michael Coogan. There are little Coogans too, and Mamie is a happy wife. And to the Coogans come sometimes letters from a far-western farm to say that things are well and that prosperity has come to one who signs himself — facetiously it always seems to Mamie who reads the letters to her husband — as Pale Face Harry.

And so the years have passed, and it is summertime again. The fields are green; the trees in leaf; the flowers in bloom. And there are visitors who have come again to the scenes of yesterday — a man and woman — and between them a sturdy little lad of eight. They stop at the end of the wagon track and look out across the lawn.

It is still and peaceful, tranquil — and to them conies the soft, low murmur of the surf. Slowly they walk across the lawn, and pass beneath the splendid maples — and pause again.

The cottage is like some poet's fancy, hidden shyly in its creepers and its vines; and seems to speak and breathe in its simple beauty of the gentle soul who once had lived there — and loved his fellow-men. It is as it always was, open, free for all to pass within who wish to enter; for loving hands have cared for it, and grateful purses, opened to its needs, have kept it as — a Shrine.

But they do not enter now, for Madison points to where the sunlight, as it glints through the trees at the far end of the cottage, falls on a slender shaft of marble.

"Let us go there, Helena," he said softly.

And so they walked that way, past the trellises laden with flowers, past the end of the cottage; and presently they stopped again where, beneath the maples' shade, rises the pure white stone — and beyond it is the sweep of the eternal sea.

Madison, his hair streaking just a little grey at the temples now, removed his hat — and his face softened, saddened, as he read the simple inscription:

THE PATRIARCH

The boy glanced at his father a little wonderingly — and then spelt out the words. He shook his head.

"I don't know what that means," he said. "What does that word mean?"

Madison patted his head.

"You tell him, Helena," he said — and came and stood beside her.

And so Helena told the boy in simple language as much of the Patriarch's story as she thought he could understand — and when she had finished the boy's face was aglow.

"And!" he said breathlessly, "and — and did he ever do a really, truly-truly miracle?"

There was silence for an instant — then a tender smile came trembling to Helena's lips, and into the brown eyes crept the love-light, as she reached out to Madison and her hand found his and held it very tightly.

And Madison bent and kissed her; and drew the little lad between them and laid his hand on the boy's head, and answered for Helena.

"Yes, my son," he said; "and some day when you are a man you will understand how great a miracle it was."

THE END